DEAD WEIGHT

A DCI Neil Paget Mystery

Frank Smith

severn House

This first world edition published 2016
in Great Britain and the USA by
SEVERN HOUSE PUBLISHERS LTD of
19 Cedar Road, Sutton, Surrey, England, SM2 5DA

Trade paperback edition first published 2018
In Great Britain and the USA by
SEVERN HOUSE PUBLISHERS LTD
Eardley House, 4 Uxbridge Street, London W8 7SY

British Library Cataloguing in Publication Data
A CIP catalogue record for this title is available from the British Library.

ISBN-13: 978-0-7278-8674-3 (cased)
ISBN-13: 978-1-84751-778-4 (trade paper)
ISBN-13: 978-1-78010-846-9 (e-book)

PART I

ONE

Wednesday, 28 March

The train was well past Oxford before Stephen Lorrimer began to relax. The weather outside was blustery, some of the gusts so strong that he could feel the carriage sway from time to time. Unusual weather even for March, but then 'unusual' was fast becoming the norm these days, with exceptionally high tides along the east coast and torrential rains and flash floods at Christmas. Nothing was predictable any more.

It felt good to be going home for the Easter break; good to get away from the rancour and turmoil of the House. The past few months had been rough, and things weren't going to get any better. The economy was better than it had been this time last year, but the average wage earner couldn't see it. What he or she saw was a steady erosion of their pay packet and rising personal debt. And, despite the best efforts of government, and the billions of pounds poured into the bottomless pit known as the NHS, waiting times for surgical procedures remained stubbornly high, and emergency rooms were . . .

Lorrimer exhaled noisily and shook his head, annoyed with himself for allowing his mind to dwell on such things. *Leave it! Let it go, for God's sake*, he told himself savagely. *What's the point of a break if you're going to bring the work home with you? Forget it, at least for the next few weeks.*

Which was all very well, but there was one thought he couldn't dismiss so easily. Nor did he want to, because he would have to do some serious thinking between now and when the House returned in April. Not that there was really any doubt about his answer.

He had worked hard; he'd been a good and faithful servant for fourteen years now, much of it in opposition, of course, but he'd served on God knows how many committees and studies in that time. He had friends on all sides of the House, and he'd been told by the prime minister himself that he was a 'good man'. Yet, good man or not, in all that time there had never been so much as a sniff at a cabinet post, shadow or otherwise. Until last Thursday, when he was asked, quite casually, about his thoughts on agricultural reform. That in itself was nothing to get excited about, except it wasn't every day that someone from the PM's office invited you for a quiet drink and a chat outside the listening walls of Westminster, then began by asking questions about your thoughts on some of the recently proposed policy changes regarding farm subsidies. And how did he think they would be perceived, not just by British farmers, but by Brussels and the EU generally . . . and France in particular? Then, suddenly, as if someone had thrown a switch, they were talking about the environment and the effects of climate change and declining fish stocks, and he'd found himself choosing his words very carefully. Oh, he'd had similar conversations on all those subjects with colleagues many times before; it was part of the daily fabric of life in the hallowed halls of Westminster. But never with Jason Cutter, sometimes referred to – behind his back, of course – as the PM's personal pit bull. Lorrimer recalled how the hairs on the back of his neck had started to prickle as it slowly dawned on him that this was no idle conversation. This was an interview, and every answer mattered. Just thinking about it now was enough to start the adrenalin flowing.

He leaned his head back against the seat and closed his eyes. Nothing had been promised, nor even hinted at, but it all made sense. The Secretary of State for Environment, Food and Rural Affairs had been ailing now for months. A pity, really, because he was a good man, relatively young and efficient at his job, but cancer was no respecter of age or ability, and the whisper was that it was terminal. A shame, yes, but – being a practical man – Lorrimer consoled himself with the thought that it was an ill wind and so on, so why not sit back and enjoy the moment? God knows he'd earned it.

He could hardly wait to tell Julia. She'd be so pleased.

The carriage swayed, buffeted by the wind. He opened his eyes. Rain streaked the window, blurring the images of the passing countryside, while half a mile away a shaft of sunlight pierced the clouds to illuminate a farmhouse and the surrounding fields. A flock of birds rose to battle against the wind, wheeling and diving in unison, and Lorrimer wondered idly what had prompted them to leave the shelter of the trees.

On the other hand, perhaps he should wait to tell Julia. After all, nothing had been *promised*. But Cutter didn't waste time on idle chatter. In fact, in all those fourteen years, Lorrimer could count on one hand the number of one-on-one conversations he'd had with Jason Cutter, none of which had lasted more than a couple of minutes. So, a half-hour chat over drinks had to mean *something*. Besides, he felt he would burst if he didn't tell someone.

Lorrimer stretched and settled himself more comfortably in his seat. 'Sorry, Terry,' he said when his foot caught those of the man seated opposite him.

'My fault,' the young man mumbled, pulling in his own long legs. His head remained bent in concentration, and his thumbs continued to fly across the tiny keyboard of his latest technological acquisition. Terry Baxter was the newest and youngest intern in the office. The boy – Baxter was twenty-six years old and a graduate of the LSE, but Lorrimer still thought of him as a boy – had barely lifted his eyes from the device since they'd boarded the train at Paddington.

Watching him now, Lorrimer was reminded of the latest message on his own dated but trusty BlackBerry. He slid it from his pocket and cupped it in his hand as if he thought someone might be watching as he read the message for perhaps the tenth time that day. There were only two short lines of text, but they were enough to cast a shadow over his earlier thoughts. He stared out of the window, but the scenes inside his head were far from those of the passing countryside.

Julia Lorrimer was waiting with the car outside Foregate Street station when he and Baxter left the train in Worcester. Baxter had spoken to her on the telephone, but he'd never met her until now. She was taller, slimmer and far better-looking than he'd imagined, and she knew how to dress to take advantage of her figure. Lorrimer himself was a solid, well-set-up man, but he was pushing fifty, and Terry had imagined that his wife would be . . . well, pretty ordinary. But there was nothing ordinary about Julia Lorrimer. For a woman in her early forties, as he knew she must be, Lorrimer's wife looked quite a bit younger and sexier than he'd imagined. Lucky old Lorrimer, he thought, as Julia gave her husband a perfunctory kiss before turning to him. 'And you must be Terry,' she said, thrusting out a hand in greeting. 'Delighted to meet you in person at last. Stephen told me you would be coming down to meet us and see for yourself the sort of things we have to deal with in a constituency office. How long can you stay, Terry?'

'Till the weekend, if that's all right, Mrs Lorrimer?' Baxter said. 'I'm going on to see friends in Penzance on Sunday. They have a cottage there, and they've invited me to join them for a week.'

'How very nice for you,' Julia said perfunctorily, 'and of course it's all right. I'll be more than happy to show you round. I may even put you to work. And please call me Julia.' She turned to her husband, who was putting the cases in the car. 'And speaking of work, Stephen, Sebastian came down from Leeds the other day. He's taking time out from his studies, so I've put him to work in the office. Sebastian is my son,' she explained for Baxter's benefit. 'He's taking politics and parliamentary studies at Leeds University, much the same as I imagine you did at the LSE, from what Stephen tells me, but he needs a break from his studies every now and again.'

Lorrimer had never spoken of a son old enough to attend university, and Terry knew that his boss had only been married to Julia for some six or seven years, so Sebastian had to be Julia's son from a previous marriage. 'Uni can be rough,' he agreed. 'Is this his first year?'

Julia looked surprised by the question. 'Didn't Stephen tell you?' she asked, flicking a glance at her husband. 'It's Sebastian's *third* year.'

Then what was he doing in Leeds? Baxter wondered, but wisely refrained from putting the question into words. The third year was usually spent in placement in positions similar to his own to gain experience.

Julia smiled as if sensing the unspoken question. 'He was at Bristol for two years,' she elaborated, 'but he wasn't happy there. He said the pace was far too rushed, too intense. He was doing his best, but I could see he was pushing himself too hard, so I suggested he take time out to see some of the world before starting in again. Which he did, and now he's at Leeds and doing very well.

'Traffic's getting pretty thick out there,' Lorrimer observed as he closed the rear door of the Range Rover, 'so perhaps we should get going. Would you like me to drive, Julia?'

She shook her head, 'Thank you, Stephen, but I'm sure you're tired. I'll drive.'

Perhaps it was his imagination, Terry thought as he climbed into the back seat, but it seemed to him that the temperature had dropped noticeably at the mention of Sebastian. Stephen Lorrimer had never mentioned that his wife had an older son, and he wondered why. He made a mental note to be careful about what he said until he could get a better picture of the way things were on Lorrimer's home ground.

Lorrimer settled into his seat and buckled up. He very much wanted to tell Julia about his chat with Cutter, but, with Terry sitting behind them, he decided it would be better to wait until he and Julia were alone. No need to set off another round of rumours and speculation, although, considering the speed with which rumours and gossip flew around the halls of Westminster, it was quite possible that Terry had known about his meeting with Cutter before he did. Still, best to stick to safer topics. 'So how are things at home?' he asked neutrally.

Julia shrugged, concentrating on her driving as she threaded her way through the late-afternoon traffic. 'Nothing's changed since I spoke to you yesterday,' she said. 'It's been fairly quiet so far this week. But I imagine you know as much as I do if Sylvia has been keeping you up to date.'

'Oh, yes.' Lorrimer smiled. 'Sylvia keeps us well informed, doesn't she, Terry? She must send us three or four emails each day.'

'More like six or seven,' Terry corrected from the back seat, 'and we hit eleven emails from her one day last week.'

'Good God!' Julia's brow wrinkled into a puzzled frown. 'I had no idea she was sending that many. Whatever does she say?'

'I think Terry can answer that better than I can,' Lorrimer said. 'It's Terry's job to deal with them and filter the wheat from the chaff before he passes them on to me.'

'Most of it is the day-to-day stuff that goes on down here,' the young man said. 'Letters to the editor in the local papers that might be of interest, along with her own editorial comments.' He chuckled. 'She has some pretty interesting views, does Sylvia. I'm quite looking forward to meeting her.'

'You may be surprised when you do,' Julia cautioned. 'She's very young – seventeen – and fascinated by politics, but I'm not sure she thinks some of these things through before offering an opinion.'

Stephen Lorrimer yawned. 'I think that's enough about work,' he said firmly. 'How is Michael? Sylvia said he found his way around the office without any trouble at all the other day. She thinks he sees more than we thought he could. She said he even helped her stack some files.'

Belatedly, he realized that he shouldn't have mentioned Michael being in the office, so he wasn't exactly surprised when Julia said, 'I don't know how many times I've told that girl he's not allowed in the office! It's no place for a small child.' She tried to keep her voice low and controlled, but it was clear she was angry.

'I think she was just trying to let me know in her own way that Michael is improving,' he said soothingly, 'and it didn't sound as if he had done any harm.'

'Even so . . .' Julia began, then stopped to flick a glance at the reflected image of Terry Baxter in the rear-view mirror. He had his eyes closed, but she was sure he was listening. 'It's a distraction for people coming in,' she continued in a milder tone, 'and it's not as if he doesn't have plenty of places to play in the rest of the house.'

'Five-year-olds like to explore,' Lorrimer said, with perhaps more emphasis than he'd intended, but he felt the need to come to Sylvia's defence. 'Don't be too hard on the girl.'

'It's not . . .' Julia began sharply, then softened her tone and began again. 'It's just that when people come to our office with grievances or problems, I want them to see they have our full attention. All I'm saying, Stephen, is that children running around the office can be distracting, and it's unprofessional.' She reached over and patted his knee. 'Don't worry,' she said soothingly. 'I know Sylvia didn't mean any harm by it, so I won't go on at the girl.'

But it wasn't about Sylvia, was it, thought Lorrimer. It was about Michael and the fact that he was blind and made unintelligible, guttural sounds when he tried to form words. Those sounds irritated Julia. Unconsciously, he made a face. *Irritated* was hardly the word. Julia couldn't *stand* them, any more than she could stand the tap-tap-tapping of Michael's cane as he made his way around the house.

Julia was thirty-seven years old when she became pregnant. It wasn't planned; it wasn't supposed to happen, but when it did, Lorrimer was over the moon. Forty-two, and he was finally going to be a father. So excited was he at the prospect of having a child of his own that he'd been oblivious to Julia's muted reaction to the news. He knew it must have come as a bit of a shock to her, but once she'd had time to think about it, he told himself, she would be just as happy about it as he was.

So he was stunned when Julia began to talk of having an abortion. She said she'd spent the best part of twenty years of her life raising her son, Sebastian, on her own, and now that she was free to pursue her own goals, she had no desire to start over again.

Sebastian was the result of a youthful roll in the hay while she was still in her teens. Shut out by her family, she had worked hard and long to bring the boy up on her own, determined to give him a better start in life than she'd had herself. Now, she said, it was her turn.

But he'd persisted, arguing that this time it would be different for her: she wouldn't be on her own as she had been when Sebastian was born, nor would she have to worry about money – they'd hire a nanny, and Julia could continue on as office manager.

He'd finally won her over, but it had turned out to be a hollow victory.

Things *might* have worked out if Michael had been a 'normal' child. But the boy was blind. And, as if that were not enough, they were told by the surgeon that Michael had no vocal cords to speak of. 'They're completely malformed,' the man explained, 'so while the boy will be able to make sounds, they could range anywhere from a harsh whisper to something like a growl, he will never be able to form words or speak properly.'

After suffering through a long and debilitating pregnancy, the shock had been too much for Julia, and she'd spent a month in the psychiatric ward before she'd even seen her son . . . and she'd rejected him out of hand.

Lorrimer stared out of the window. The road ahead was dry, but every so often a few drops of rain would spatter the windscreen, and the sky looked dark and threatening ahead.

Michael had been a good baby, sleeping through most of the night and taking his food easily. Bottle-fed, of course; Julia was incapable of nursing him.

They'd engaged a nanny – in fact, they'd engaged a series of nannies, none of whom seemed to be able to get close to Michael, until last year when the agency in Birmingham sent them Justine Delgado. 'She's twenty-eight years old,' the woman at the agency told Lorrimer. 'She is a registered nurse, trained to deal with children with special needs, including those who are visually impaired. The salary she is asking is higher than that of the nannies you have had before, but I think you will find she is worth it. She comes highly recommended, and she has excellent references.'

They agreed on a three-month trial period, but Justine Delgado had been there less than a month when both Stephen and Julia declared themselves satisfied. Stephen was happy because he could see the way Michael and Justine had taken to each other, and Julia was happy to be relieved of any responsibility for the boy.

Justine and Michael had bonded almost from the very first day. In fact, thought Lorrimer, it was a pleasure to see the two of them together. To all intents and purposes, Justine could have been Michael's mother . . . and therein lay the problem, because Julia no longer felt any responsibility for her son. She would, if it were absolutely necessary, see to Michael's basic needs when Justine wasn't there, but more in the way one might give a helping hand to a stranger or to the child of a friend, and it was clear that Michael felt no connection to his birth mother. Why would he when Justine was taking care of all his needs? Lorrimer, on the other hand, adored his son, and looked forward to spending as much time as possible with him every time he was home. Michael had grown into a handsome boy. Now five years old, he was looking more like his father every day. Like his father,

Michael would never be tall, although he had the same sturdy build. But it was the way the boy greeted him every time he came home that tugged at Lorrimer's heart and brought tears to his eyes. Whether in his own room or at his studies at the end of the hall, the boy would recognize his father's footsteps on the hallway's wooden floor and come running. To anyone else, Michael's guttural whoops of delight would have been disconcerting, but Lorrimer didn't mind them in the least.

They drove in silence for a while, but the question he had wanted to ask from the moment they'd left the station couldn't be contained any longer. 'And Justine?' he asked as casually as he could. 'Are the two of them still getting along all right?'

In other words, is she still doing the job I *should be doing?* Julia thought. She could feel the muscles tightening in her face. 'They're fine,' she said stiffly.

'Justine Delgado is Michael's nanny,' Lorrimer explained for Terry's benefit. 'She's from the Philippines. She's been very good with Michael.'

'Really?' said Terry. 'I spent a couple of months in the Philippines in my gap year. Which part does she come from?'

'Manila,' Lorrimer said cryptically, anxious to leave the subject.

But Terry was interested now. 'That's where I spent most of my time when I was there,' he said. 'It's a fascinating place. I look forward to meeting Miss Delgado. Do you know if she speaks Tagalog? I learned a few key phrases while I was there, and I wouldn't mind trying them out again. And speaking of Manila . . .'

Lorrimer tried to turn the conversation to other things, but Manila had struck a chord with Terry, and he was keen to share his experiences, and perhaps show off a little.

Julia tuned him out. Justine! Wonder-woman Justine, who was so bloody good with Michael. And she *was* good with him, so why did she resent her so much? The question, as always, was rhetorical, because she knew the answer. Guilt! Plain and simple, because she, Julia Lorrimer, who prided herself on being able to handle almost any situation calmly and logically, could hardly bear to be in the same room as her own small son!

Stone-faced, she drove the rest of the way in silence.

TWO

Tuesday, 3 April

Detective Chief Inspector Paget was feeling particularly happy as he drove to work on the Tuesday following the Easter weekend. For the first time in months, he and Grace had managed to arrange three whole days off together, and they had spent them in Beddgelert, North Wales. The weather was cold and blustery, but that hadn't stopped them from walking the hills each morning, following the path through the Aberglaslyn Pass, stopping every now and again as much to admire the magnificent views as to catch their breath before continuing on. The air was clean and fresh – *extremely* fresh first thing in the morning – but exhilarating, and it had felt good to be alive. A well-earned rest out of the wind at the halfway point; a mug of hot coffee from the thermos, and a relatively leisurely walk via the old copper mine to the town. A pub lunch and a pint by the fire, albeit an electric one with quite realistic flames, but the principle was the same.

Later, they'd wandered hand in hand beside the river, popping in and out of shops along the way until it was time for tea. Grace had to practically drag Neil away from the woodcraft shop, fascinated as he was with everything from carved wooden wind chimes to birds and doorstops and fearsome dragons.

'Yes, they are amazingly well done, Neil,' Grace had agreed, 'but I really don't think we need a dragon on the mantelpiece, especially one that looks like that. Perhaps the wind chimes . . .'

Paget smiled to himself. Grace was right; they didn't need a dragon on the mantelpiece, and he probably wouldn't have bought it anyway, but the wind chimes were hanging outside their door when he'd left this morning.

They'd stayed in a B&B run by a retired couple from Manchester, who had owned a small but apparently lucrative painting and decorating business, and the B&B was their way of staying active in retirement. The house itself was as solid as the rock on which it was built, and their room was comfortable, once he and Grace had stuffed strips of newspaper into the gaps around the wooden window frames to stop the moaning of the wind. The bed was extra large, the mattress deep and soft, and they'd had no trouble whatsoever keeping warm.

Pleasant as they were, the memories were beginning to fade as he drove into Charter Lane and parked the car. A brisk wind tugged at his coat as he mounted the steps and went inside, almost colliding with a woman coming out. He stood aside and held the door to let her pass, but she stopped. 'Chief Inspector Paget?' she said hesitantly. 'It *is* Chief Inspector Paget, isn't it? Julia Lorrimer,' she continued. 'We met at my husband's open house at Christmas?'

Recognition clicked in. 'Of course, Mrs Lorrimer,' he said, wondering what the local MP's wife was doing there at such an early hour. He was about to ask, but she spoke first.

'I'm *so* glad I've run into you,' she said breathlessly. 'I'm sure the young man I spoke to just now is quite capable, but I didn't get the feeling that he was as concerned as I am about the disappearance of our son's nanny. It's been two full days now, and she's never done anything like this before. She has a phone. She would have called. She would *never* go off and leave Michael alone like that without—'

'I think you'd better come back inside and tell me what this is about from the beginning,' said Paget. This wasn't the way he'd expected to start his day, but Julia Lorrimer didn't strike him as a woman who would panic easily. Yet here she was, at ten minutes to eight in the morning, clearly agitated about an employee who had been missing for two days. The fact that the woman was the wife of his member of parliament shouldn't make any difference to the way the report was treated, but this was the real world, and MPs and MPs' wives could make life difficult if they chose. He led the way to an interview room. 'Just take a seat while I get a copy of the report,' he told her. 'Do you recall the name of the officer you spoke to?'

'Constable Mercer, I believe he said his name was. A young man with gingery-coloured hair.'

'Right. I'll be back in a minute. Would you like a cup of tea or coffee?'

Julia Lorrimer shook her head. 'No, thank you,' she said. 'But thank you for taking the trouble. I really am worried about Justine.'

Justine Delgado, Paget learned as he skimmed through missing person report on his way back to the interview room, was twenty-nine years old. Employed in May of the previous year, dedicated to her job, she had never done anything like this before.

'It's so unlike her,' Mrs Lorrimer burst out as he sat down to face her across the table. 'As I told the constable, Justine goes off to mass every Sunday morning. She usually goes to the nine o'clock, but because it was Easter Sunday she thought it best to go to the early service at eight. She had asked if it would be all right if she spent the rest of the day with a friend – another girl from the Philippines by the name of Maria Navarro, a nurse at the hospital – so I said yes, of course it would. We were having Stephen's brother and his wife and family over for dinner on Sunday, but I had that in hand, so it was no problem. Justine is devoted to Michael, and she's rarely away from the house for more than a few hours at a time, so I could hardly refuse her.' Julia looked down at her hands. 'And that's the last I saw of her,' she ended softly. 'I've tried and tried calling her on her mobile, but it must be switched off.'

Paget glanced at the paper in his hand. 'And this friend, Maria Navarro, claims there were no plans to meet that day? She was working at the hospital in A and E?'

'That's what she told me when I spoke to her yesterday. In fact, she said she'd been at work all day on Sunday.'

'Did she offer any suggestions as to where Justine might have gone?'

Julia shook her head. 'She seemed to be as puzzled as we were.'

'Could there have been some mistake? Did Justine mention her friend by name? Could she have been talking about another friend?'

'No, I'm sure there was no mistake, Chief Inspector. She was talking about Maria Navarro.'

'So Justine *lied* about where she was going that day?'

Julia flinched at the word. 'I suppose it does look that way,' she said slowly, 'but I find it very hard to believe. There has to be some other explanation. And if she did lie, she must have had a very good reason.'

'I see you've been into her room – checked to see what she took with her.'

'As best I could,' Julia said, 'Everything is there as far as I can tell, apart from what she was wearing when she left the house, of course, and I gave that information to the constable, as you will see.' She indicated the open folder on the table.

'Blue-grey three-quarter-length jacket with detachable hood,' Paget read out. 'Navy blue skirt, black tights, black leather shoes, low heels . . .' He shot a quizzical look at Mrs Lorrimer. 'This is remarkably detailed,' he observed. 'Was there any particular reason you noticed what Miss Delgado was wearing that day?'

The woman smiled. 'Justine was wearing what she always wears when she goes to church,' she told him. 'She doesn't have a lot of clothes. What she does have are of good quality, so they last, but her wardrobe is quite limited.'

'Do you remember if she was carrying anything – a handbag, perhaps?'

'Oh, yes, of course. Sorry, I forgot to mention that. She was carrying her umbrella – one of those little fold-up ones – and a shoulder bag: a black, half-moon-shaped bag made to look like soft leather – you know the sort of thing. It's really much too big for her. She's quite short, you know.'

Paget glanced at the report. 'And you saw her as she was leaving the house at approximately twenty minutes to eight on Sunday morning?'

'That's right. I was in the kitchen when she came in to tell me that she was off, and Michael was still sleeping. Oh, yes, and she said she might be a bit late back, so would we mind seeing Michael off to bed, and she was sorry she would be missing the children's Easter egg hunt. It's something we'd planned to do after dinner for the children,' she explained. 'We usually go to Stephen's brother's place in the country at Easter, but this year we invited them to have dinner with us. Richard and his wife, Eloise, have two girls, Loren and Chelsea, and the Easter egg hunt is a sort of tradition in their house. We didn't want to disappoint the girls when they came to our place, so we decided to do it too. And Michael was able to join in as well. 'He's blind, you see – well, not *completely* blind – but the girls are very good with him, and they lead him to some of the eggs.'

'He's how old?

'Five. He'll be six in September.'

'Presumably, you have asked him if his nanny had said anything to him about where she might be going at the weekend?'

Julia gave a dismissive shake of the head. 'We have tried,' she said, 'but you have to understand that Michael is not only blind; he can't speak. Justine has taught him to respond electronically by typing answers to questions, but I'm sure he knows no more than we do, and he's extremely upset because she's not there.'

'Does Miss Delgado have any medical problems that you know of? Anything that might affect her memory or her ability to communicate?'

'No. Justine is very healthy. She takes very good care of herself.'

'Is there any doubt about her legal status in this country?'

'Absolutely not!' Julia Lorrimer all but bristled at the suggestion. 'Justine came to us through a reputable agency. As a matter of fact . . .' She paused to rummage around in her handbag before taking out a passport and handing it to Paget. 'Justine asked me to keep it in our safe for her, and I thought it might help if I brought it with me. The young man I saw before you came in wanted to keep it, but I told him Justine gave it to me for safe-keeping, and I couldn't let him do that. So he photocopied it instead.'

Paget opened it. Genuine, as far as he could tell. Justine Francesca Delgado. Strong features. Dark hair, dark eyes, plumpish face. 'Has there been any trouble recently?' he asked as he handed the passport back. 'Any arguments or concerns about her work? Has she seemed worried or upset?'

Julia Lorrimer was shaking her head, 'As I said, Justine is devoted to Michael, and we've been very pleased with her work. She's become part of the family.' She raised her hands in a gesture of helplessness. 'I'm sorry, Chief Inspector, but I don't know what else I can tell you.'

'Was there a particular time you would normally expect her to be in by?'

'You mean like a curfew? No. As I said, Justine is like a member of the family. She has her own key and she can come and go as she pleases.'

'But you didn't report her missing until this morning,' Paget pointed out. 'Why was that, Mrs Lorrimer?'

'Actually, we did ring the police yesterday when we were calling round, trying to find out where Justine might be. We asked if there had been any accidents involving a young woman, but they said there'd been nothing reported. We rang the police in Ludlow, and the hospital there as well as here – in fact, we rang several hospitals farther afield simply because we didn't know what else to do. We even rang Father Leonard to ask if Justine had been at mass that morning, but he didn't remember seeing her.'

Julia Lorrimer shrugged guiltily. 'I realize now that we should have come in yesterday, but we couldn't bring ourselves to believe that Justine was actually *missing* in the truest sense of the word. And then, of course, we'd spent a good part of the night – that is, Sunday night – and the early hours of Monday morning at the hospital with Michael, and we were dead tired, so we probably weren't thinking as clearly as we should have been. Michael suffers from croup,' she explained, 'and sometimes it gets out of hand and we have to take him over to the hospital to get him settled down. Normally, Justine would have taken him – it's happened several times before – so we left a note telling her not to worry, and Stephen and I took him over to the hospital ourselves. It was all that running around with the girls during the Easter egg hunt that brought it on, I expect, but Michael is all right now.'

'Were you not concerned that Justine still hadn't returned by the time you got home from the hospital?' asked Paget.

Mrs Lorrimer shook her head. 'We thought she had returned and gone to bed. Stephen had said in the note that he would keep Michael with him in his room for the rest of the night when we got back, so that she wouldn't worry.'

'Where did you leave the note?'

'On the kitchen table, and we left the light on.'

'Was it still there when you got back?'

Mrs Lorrimer thought for a moment. 'To tell you the truth, I'm not sure,' she said. 'But then we were all very tired and just wanted to get to bed.' Frowning worriedly, she looked directly at Paget. 'I know it must sound silly now,' she said, 'but I suppose the reason we kept putting off reporting Justine missing was because we didn't want to embarrass her if she turned up with a perfectly logical explanation for her absence.'

How many times had Missing Persons heard similar excuses? Paget wondered. But at least Mrs Lorrimer had been able to give them more information than most. 'Does Justine have a car?' he asked.

'No, she walks everywhere.'

'What about relatives or friends other than the nurse?'

'Her closest relative is her grandfather, but he's in Manila, of course. Justine told me that she was raised by her grandparents after her parents were killed when she was eight years old, but her grandmother died some years ago, so there's just her grandfather now. Justine calls him regularly every two weeks. I did wonder about calling him to see if she had said anything to him about going somewhere on Sunday, but I didn't want to alarm him. As for friends, I don't know of any others, and the Navarro girl didn't seem to know of any when I asked her.'

'No boyfriends, then?'

'Not that I'm aware of, and I think I would know if there were.'

'You say she calls her grandfather every two weeks. Always on the same day?'

'That's right. Sunday mornings, usually around midday. There's a time difference of something like seven or eight hours, I believe, so it would be Sunday evening in Manila.'

'Using her mobile phone?'

'No. Justine has her own mobile phone, but we provide the phone in her room, and she uses that for her overseas calls to her grandfather, which sometimes last for half an hour or more; it's cheaper on the landline, so she pays for each call when the bill comes in.'

'Was last Sunday the day Justine would have normally called her grandfather?'

Julia thought for a moment. 'Yes, it was,' she said. 'I suppose she *could* have called him on her mobile from wherever she was, but that would be expensive, and I don't know why she would do that. His name and number are in there, by the way.' She pointed to the folder.

Paget made a note in the margin and closed the folder. 'I know this may sound repetitious,' he said as he got to his feet, 'but just to be absolutely clear, Mrs Lorrimer, were you the only person to see Miss Delgado leave the house?'

She hesitated for a couple of seconds, then shook her head. 'As I said, I was in the kitchen when Justine popped her head in to say she was off, so I didn't actually see her leave the house, but Sebastian said he saw her from his bedroom window when he was getting dressed on Sunday.'

'And Sebastian is . . . ?'

'My older son,' Julia Lorrimer said as she got to her feet. 'He's twenty-four.' A wry smile touched her lips in response to the expression on Paget's face. 'Yes, I know,' she said,' it does sound odd, doesn't it? Nearly twenty years difference in the ages of my two sons.'

There was no reasonable response to that, so Paget simply said, 'Leave it with me, Mrs Lorrimer,' as he ushered her out. 'I will have someone come to the house as soon as possible. They will need to look at Miss Delgado's room and talk to anyone she may have spoken to recently.'

Julia nodded perfunctorily, pausing for a moment to adjust the silk scarf that had been disturbed when she'd shouldered her handbag. 'Thank you so *very* much, Chief Inspector,' she said. 'If there is any other way I can help . . . ?'

'We will let you know,' said Paget. He watched her as she walked down the corridor to the front door. Attractive woman. Very elegant; beautifully turned out and made-up for such an early call at a police station. Nice perfume, too. Most perfumes made his nose twitch, but this one was very pleasant, very subtle. He liked it. Probably Grace would, too, but he doubted if he could afford to buy it for her. But then Stephen Lorrimer was a wealthy man. Inherited most of his money from his father and grandfather, or so Paget had heard.

He opened the folder again. There, near the bottom of the

page, was Justine's mobile telephone number. He took out his own phone and thumbed in the number. Julia Lorrimer had said she'd tried to reach the girl by phone, but it wouldn't hurt to try again. Sometimes finding a person reported as missing was as simple as making a phone call.

Ringing, then: *The person you are calling is unavailable. Please leave a message* . . . He closed the phone. He hadn't really expected an answer, but it was worth a try.

THREE

'Nice view across the river,' DS John Tregalles observed as they drove down Lorrimer Drive, a steep, winding private road that led them to an irregularly shaped piece of hardstanding that served as a car park for visitors to the house on the hill above it.

Perched as it was on the hillside overlooking the river, Simla House looked completely out of place. Built in the 1890s of local stone and wood by an ancestor of Stephen Lorrimer, Lieutenant Colonel Arthur Desmond Lorrimer of the King's Light Infantry (Shropshire Regiment), who had spent half a lifetime in India, the house had the stamp of India on it. In fact, it was a replica of the building in which the lieutenant colonel had spent the last five years of his time in Simla, after which the house was named. The name, now weathered and dulled by time, could still be seen on the stone gateposts on either side of the entrance to Lorrimer Drive off Edge Hill Road.

Wooden steps led from the parking area up a terraced slope to an ornamental iron gate set in a tall and extremely dense cedar hedge. The house itself was built in the shape of a spread-eagled V, with steps leading up to the front door at the centre of the V. With its flat, sloping roof, and verandas that stretched the full length of the wings on either side of the entrance, DS Molly Forsythe thought it looked more like a 1950s motel than a house, and the outside wooden stairs leading to the first floor at the end of each wing only served to strengthen the image.

Tregalles's description was even less flattering. 'Looks like a couple of cricket clubhouses stuck together,' he said. 'You almost expect to see people lined up in deckchairs, drinking tea, while they wait for play to start again.'

Tregalles led the way up the steps to the gate and pushed it open. Molly followed him through, and they climbed the remaining steps together to face two identical front doors. A brass plate on the door on the left simply said *Private*, while the door on the right bore a similar brass plate that said *Constituency Office – Please Enter.*

Julia Lorrimer must have been watching for them, because it was she who opened the door when Tregalles rang the bell next to the door marked *Private*. '*Two* detective sergeants!' she exclaimed as she ushered them inside and they introduced themselves. 'I felt sure that Chief Inspector Paget was taking the disappearance of Justine seriously, but this is more than I had hoped for. However,' she continued briskly, 'I know you want to get on, so perhaps I should explain that these are our living quarters, and the constituency office is on the other side of this wall, and access is through that door.' She waved a hand in the general direction of a door further down the hall. 'Now,' she continued as she started up the stairs, 'I'll take you up to Justine's room and let you get on with whatever it is you have to do.'

Julia Lorrimer paused at the top of the stairs. 'Our bedrooms – that is, Stephen's and mine, and Sebastian's – are in the north wing,' she said, pointing to the right, 'while Justine and Michael have the south wing to themselves.' She turned to the left and set off down a dimly lit corridor with doors on either side. The only source of light came from long, narrow windows set in deep alcoves between the bedrooms.

'As you can see, there are five bedrooms here in the south wing,' said Julia in the manner of a tour guide, 'two on either side and one at the end, which we had converted into a classroom for Michael. There used to be seven, but two bedrooms were lost when Stephen's father got rid of the old plumbing and had the bedrooms enlarged to include toilets and showers. We have exactly the same thing in the north wing. I know,' she continued with mock weariness, as if sensing Tregalles's thoughts, 'it's a ridiculous house. Lord knows what Stephen's great, great, great . . . whatever he was, grandfather was thinking about when he built this place back in the eighteen hundreds. Perhaps it made sense back then, but, as I've told Stephen many times, the place is more like a barracks than a house, and we could build at least two decent houses on the property if we tore it down. But I might as well talk to the wall.'

Julia stopped beside one of the doors and turned to face them. 'This is Justine's room,' she said, lowering her voice as if afraid of disturbing someone inside. 'Michael's bedroom is across the hall, but he's with Sylvia in the classroom at the moment. We call it the classroom, but it serves as a playroom as well. It's where Michael and Justine spend most of their time during the day. Sylvia Lamb is one of our constituency office workers, and she's helping us out by seeing to Michael while Justine is . . . away.'

Julia opened the door with a key and stepped inside. 'As you can see, it's quite a good size,' she said as if she were letting the room. 'Stephen insisted on having it painted last year. I think we could have chosen something a little more colourful than ivory, but Stephen said we had to make the most of the light, since we're facing east. I wanted to take the old picture rail down while we had the chance, but Stephen thinks it gives the room character, so it was left, and I see Justine has made use of it.' She indicated a number of colourful prints hanging from the picture rail. Instead of picture wire, Justine had used thin white cord, and Molly thought it looked quite attractive.

'We couldn't do much with the old fireplace,' Julia continued, 'so we had to make the best of it and have the gas fire on the hearth. It looks a little odd, but it gives off a nice heat. As for the furniture, the bookcase belongs to Justine, but the rest of it is ours.'

'There are no kitchen facilities up here?' Molly ventured.

'There's a kitchen in the classroom,' Julia said, perhaps more sharply than she'd intended. 'Justine prefers to have her meals with Michael when they're working, but they eat with us down-stairs when it's convenient. And, as you can see, Justine has her own electric kettle so she can make herself a cup of tea before bed if she feels like it.'

Julia Lorrimer pressed the palms of her hands together as if she were about to pray, and looked at each of them in turn. 'If there is anything you need, I'll be in the office downstairs,' she said, 'although I do have to go out later. There's an in-house call button on the telephone in here; the office number is two-three.'

'We would like to talk to anyone who has been in contact with Justine recently, when we're finished here,' Tregalles said. 'Perhaps we could start with Mr Lorrimer?'

'Of course,' Julia said briskly. 'He has someone with him at the moment, but I expect he will be free in half an hour or so. It's a bit of a rabbit warren down there, so I think it would be best if you tell Sylvia when you're ready. She can text Stephen to see if it's convenient, then take you down. Just knock on the classroom door when you're finished here, and Sylvia will come out. I don't want Michael upset more than he is already, so I'll just pop along and let her know you're here.' Julia raised an eyebrow in a silent invitation for questions.

'There is just one thing,' Tregalles said. 'I don't know if DCI Paget told you, but in a missing person case such as this, we like to make absolutely sure that the person missing is not still in the house, possibly ill or incapacitated in some way, so we will need to look in every room. It shouldn't take long.'

'Really? No, Chief Inspector Paget did not mention that this morning,' Julia said, 'and, to be honest, considering the information I gave him, I think it's a waste of time. However, if that is what needs to be done, then, of course, you must do it. Now, if there is nothing else . . . ?'

Tregalles shook his head. 'Just the key,' he said, holding out his hand. 'We'll lock up and let you have the key back before we leave. Otherwise, I believe that will be all for now.' He glanced at Molly, who shook her head. She had the feeling that she would have to raise her hand if she had a question.

'Right, then, I'll leave you to it.' Julia Lorrimer turned to leave, then paused. 'I don't want you talking to Michael,' she said firmly. 'He's upset because he and Justine are very close, and he doesn't understand why she isn't here. It would be useless anyway,' she continued. 'As Chief Inspector Paget may have told you, Michael is not only blind, but he is also unable to speak. Any two-way conversation with him has to be done electronically. Now, I really must go.'

Julia Lorrimer had mentioned renovations, but Molly was still surprised to see how bright and modern everything was in the nanny's room. The old fireplace, with its heavy marble mantel, was a reminder of the age of Simla House, but the rest of the room wouldn't have been out of place in any modern apartment building. And everything was scrupulously clean. Light-coloured walls. Thick, dark rug on the floor, faded and worn in spots, but the deep pile would feel good under the toes when getting out of bed on a cold morning. Contemporary furniture and a flat-screen TV mounted on the wall beside the fireplace. The large window, fairly new by the look of it, brought a lot of light into the room, and the view across the river valley was far nicer than the view she had from any of her windows, Molly thought enviously. Certainly, the boy's nanny had no reason to leave because of poor accommodation.

The pictures hanging from the picture rail were all of colourful scenes cut from travel magazines and framed. The mattes were made of cartridge paper, probably by Justine herself, then mounted in cheap plastic frames. Neatly done, thought Molly. Perhaps she could do something similar in her flat . . . until she remembered she didn't have a picture rail.

There were touches of colour everywhere. A multi-coloured woollen shawl was draped artistically above the headboard of the bed, and a number of small, brightly coloured ornaments had been carefully arranged on the dresser. A large blue earthenware vase full of flowers stood by the window where they would catch the morning sun. A whimsical touch, perhaps, since the flowers were artificial.

A piece of unfinished knitting lay on the bed, and a well-thumbed pattern book lay open beside it. The picture in the book was of a cardigan knitted in grey, but the colour Justine had chosen was light yellow. Even half finished, it felt heavy, and Molly wondered if, coming from a warmer climate, Justine was feeling the cold. But while it wasn't exactly proof, the very fact that the knitting was there, unfinished, suggested that Justine Delgado had intended to return when she left the house on Sunday morning. Molly set the knitting aside and pulled the bedspread down. It was surprisingly heavy – an heirloom bedspread, if she wasn't mistaken. Very nice, she supposed, if you liked that sort of thing, but off-white and with fringes? No, thanks. Too old-fashioned for her taste, and far too heavy. Molly preferred her duvet.

The blanket and the sheets were clean, but the bed had been hastily made. Molly smiled. She could relate to that; it was much like the way she left her own bed when she was running late. She pulled the bedspread up and was about to turn away when she remembered the unfinished knitting and put it back on the bed.

'Not a lot of clothes in the wardrobe,' Tregalles observed. 'What was it Mrs Lorrimer said Justine was wearing when she left?'

'A blue-grey three-quarter-length coat with detachable hood,' quoted Molly from the briefing notes. 'Navy skirt, black tights and black shoes. Oh, yes, and a black handbag and a fold-up umbrella. Why? Have you found something?'

'Just a plastic mac, and I can't remember if it rained or not on Sunday.'

'It did, but not till the evening,' Molly reminded him. 'And then it poured.' She paused to look at the books in a varnished wooden bookcase that Justine had probably assembled herself. There were books on child care, child psychology and speech therapy, and a very large manual containing step-by-step programmes to be followed by those teaching life skills to the visually impaired. There were also magazines, almost all of which dealt with the same or similar subjects. Heavy stuff, indeed, thought Molly, but, probing further, she found some lighter reading on the bottom shelf. Historical romances – four of them – all from the local library and due back in nine days. It seemed that Justine was prepared to spend money on books pertaining to her work, but not on fiction.

There was a small radio on the top shelf. Molly turned it on. It was tuned to a local station. She turned it off again and turned her attention to the night table beside the bed, and picked up a photograph in a silver frame. It was of a grey-haired man sitting on a bench in what looked like a park. He was smiling into the camera; the sun was shining, and there were deep lines in his face. Probably Justine's grandfather, thought Molly. He'd been mentioned at the briefing this morning.

She set the picture down and opened the night-table drawer. There was something bulky inside, loosely wrapped in a white cloth. Curious, Molly unfolded the cloth to reveal a crucifix. About eight inches long, it was made of heavy, dark wood, and the figure of Christ was cast in what looked like solid silver. Beautifully made, the crucifix looked old. But what was it doing in the drawer? The metal fitting on the back was designed to hang on a wall. Molly looked closely at the wall above the bed, moving the shawl aside to reveal a small hole some eighteen inches above the headboard; it seemed like a natural place to hang the crucifix. She examined the back of the crucifix, looking for a reason for it to be taken down, but the metal hanger appeared to be sturdy enough. Molly rewrapped the crucifix and placed it back in the drawer, then turned her attention to the dresser and its contents.

The two top drawers appeared to be what passed for Justine's filing system – if the jumble of bills, bank and credit card statements and miscellaneous papers could be called a system. Molly looked at the dates, none more than a year old, which would be roughly when she had come to work at Simla House. The name on a recent bill from a dentist caught Molly's eye: Mathieson, who just happened to be Molly's own dentist. She looked at the amount and whistled softly. This girl had had some serious dental work done in the last six months.

At the bottom of the pile, she found a copy of the contract between the Lorrimers and an agency in Birmingham, setting out the responsibilities of employer and employee. She skimmed through it, but there were far too many pages and too much small print. She set it aside and picked up a bank book.

Molly had heard any number of stories about foreign nannies and au pairs being exploited and underpaid, but that wasn't the case here. According to her bank statements, Justine was paid on the first of every month, but roughly half of the amount was transferred out again a few days later.

'Sending money home to support the family, or, in this case, her grandfather, I expect,' Tregalles said when Molly showed him the book. 'That's why these girls leave home in the first place. They can earn more money abroad than they can at home.' He poked through the rest of the papers, then shook his head. 'Bag the lot,' he told her. 'You can go through them properly back at the office. And let's not forget her toothbrush and samples from her hairbrush for her DNA, in case we need them later. I hope we don't,' he added quickly when he saw the look on Molly's face, 'but best to be prepared.'

The next drawer down was a catch-all: cosmetics, creams, lotions and lipsticks, together with sunglasses, a wrapped bar of Pears' soap, a box of tissues, eye drops and a first-aid kit. The sort of things one might expect to see in a bathroom, except in this case the bathroom was very small, consisting of a washbasin, toilet and shower, but no cabinet or shelf. Obviously, there had been limitations to what could be done when renovating.

Molly opened a box containing a muddle of cheap jewellery: necklaces, brooches, bracelets and earrings, together with a sewing kit, safety pins, a silver hair comb and clips, and several foreign coins. Moving on, she dug through underclothes, a swim-suit and bathing cap, sweaters, more wool and knitting needles, and a music box that proved to be broken. All very ordinary, all very normal. Nothing to give them a clue as to why Justine had gone missing. She came to the bottom drawer. Towels, and tampons in a paper bag. The paper caught and tore when she pushed the drawer in. She pulled it out again and was pressing the bag down when a plastic packet slid out.

'Nothing,' Tregalles declared as he shoved a suitcase back under the bed. 'I think we're wasting our time here. Have you found anything of interest, Molly?'

'Yasmin,' Molly said quietly. 'It looks as if Justine is on the pill. Didn't Mrs Lorrimer tell Mr Paget that Justine didn't have a boyfriend?'

'Which could mean that Mrs Lorrimer may not know everything about her son's nanny,' Tregalles said. 'And maybe Justine is simply playing it safe in case.' He stood up and stretched. 'Can't have been much of a life for her, cooped up here with a disabled kid, even if she did like her work. All work and no play, as they say. Anyway, have you found anything else of interest?'

'Not really,' Molly said slowly. 'It's more a case of what I *haven't* found.'

'Like what?'

'Letters, correspondence of any kind. In fact, nothing – at least nothing on paper to suggest that she is keeping in touch with anyone, and I find that hard to believe of a young woman far from home. No laptop, no handheld device, and I find that very strange. Here is a well-educated young woman who has all kinds of reference books to do with her job, yet she doesn't have access to the internet where so much information is available. I know she sends money home, but she is well paid, so she could certainly afford a laptop. They're not all that expensive.'

'Perhaps it's in the classroom down the hall,' Tregalles

suggested. 'Mrs Lorrimer did say that her son uses a computer to communicate, so, if she does have a laptop, perhaps it's in there. Let's take a look.'

'Oh, it's you,' the girl who opened the door whispered. 'I wasn't expecting you quite so soon.' She stepped back, but instead of standing aside to let them in, she placed a finger against her lips and stepped into the corridor and closed the door behind her.

Sylvia Lamb looked to be little more than a schoolgirl. Long blonde hair framed a small face which would have been pretty if it hadn't been for the red eyes and tear-streaked cheeks. Thin as a rake, she was wearing a blue-and-white striped T-shirt beneath a loose-fitting white cardigan, tight-fitting jeans and Nike high-top trainers that looked more than a bit incongruous against her spindly legs. Sylvia Lamb looked as if she'd been crying her heart out, but when Molly asked if there was anything wrong, the girl shook her head. 'It's these new contact lenses,' she said. 'I've only had them a few days, and I'm still trying to get used to them.' She dabbed at her cheeks with a handful of tissues.

'Trying a bit too hard, by the look of it,' Tregalles said, not unkindly. 'It might be a good idea to give your eyes a bit of a rest. Do you still have your glasses?'

The girl responded with a grudging nod. 'I do,' she said, 'but they make me look like an owl, which is why I bought these.'

'Better to look like an owl than damage your eyes,' Tregalles told her. 'You'll get used to them faster if you put them in for short periods of time.'

Sylvia Lamb sighed. 'You sound just like my dad,' she said, dabbing at her wet cheeks. 'But you're probably right. I'll take them out when we get downstairs. Which reminds me: Mr Lorrimer sent me a text message a few minutes ago to say he'll be tied up for' – she glanced at her watch – 'about another fifteen minutes. So . . . ?' She looked uncertainly from Tregalles to Molly and back again.

'In that case, perhaps we can ask you a few questions while we wait,' said Tregalles, 'and we can take a look around the classroom as well.' He made a move towards the door, but the girl stepped in front of him and shook her head.

'No, please don't go in there,' she begged. 'I've spent half the

morning getting Michael to settle down. He's very upset about
Justine not being here. She's never been away for this long before,
so he knows something is wrong. He's listening to one of his
favourite talking books right now, so he'll be all right for a short
while. But if you go in there, he'll *really* know something is
wrong, and I'm not sure I'm up to dealing with that. So, if you
could leave it until after you've seen Mr Lorrimer, Mrs Lorrimer
will have gone out by then, and I can take Michael down to the
kitchen and make him some toast. He loves toast and blackcur-
rant jam.'

Tregalles hesitated. He didn't want to push the girl, but they
needed to take a look at the room. He shot a questioning glance
at Molly, who responded by saying, 'Michael is what . . . five
years old?'

'That's right.'

'And I understand he is visually impaired and has trouble
talking, but does he have any other problems – mentally, perhaps?'

'Not in the way you mean,' Sylvia replied. 'He's actually pretty
normal in other ways, and he's bright. But he gets frustrated
easily, and he can be hard to handle then.'

'Does he become violent?'

'Oh, no, he's never been violent. He gets upset when he can't
make himself understood, but it's more like a tantrum. He sort
of huddles up and beats his fists on his knees. Justine knows
how to handle him, but he's not the same with me. Actually, I've
only seen it happen a couple of times, and one of them was this
morning. We don't see much of him over there in the office. Mrs
Lorrimer is very strict about that. I suppose she's right; it *is* a
business office, and we do have all sorts of people coming in,
and not everyone appreciates a small boy running around.' She
sighed. 'Still, it's a pity they have to spend so much time up
here.' She waved a hand to encompass the heavily panelled walls
and even darker floor of the corridor. Narrow windows, set in
alcoves some fifteen feet apart, spread pallid pools of light across
the boards, but there was no warmth to the place.

'Odd sort of place, though, isn't it?' Tregalles observed. 'This
house, I mean. Does that door lead to the stairs we saw outside?'
He didn't wait for an answer, but walked over to take a closer
look. The door was made of metal. It certainly wasn't part of

the original structure, and the glass in the small window looked as if might be unbreakable. He grasped the handle and opened it, then stepped out on to a platform at the top of solid wooden steps. A cool breeze swept into the corridor, prompting Sylvia to shiver and draw the cardigan tighter around her shoulders.

'Would Justine use that door to come and go, rather than go down the main stairs?' Molly asked.

'I suppose she might,' the girl said, 'but I really don't know. I've never been out that way myself. In fact, this is only about the fourth or fifth time I've been up here since I started last year. I work in the office, not here in the house.'

'Can't say I'd like to spend much time up here,' Tregalles said with a mock shiver as he rejoined them. 'I think Mrs Lorrimer was right: this house has had its day.'

'The office downstairs is a lot brighter than this,' the girl said. 'They had to knock a few walls down, and it's a bit of a maze, but at least we have some daylight. The house was modelled on some sort of army barracks in India where an ancestor of Mr Lorrimer's was stationed. There's a picture of it downstairs on the office wall.'

Tregalles looked pointedly at his watch. 'We'll take a look at it when we go down,' he said, 'but I'd like to get back to why we're here. What can you tell us about Justine Delgado? I'm sure Mrs Lorrimer has asked you this already, but do you have any idea where she might have gone? Were you friends? You work here in the same house, so if you can think of anything Justine said that might help us find her, now is the time to tell us.'

The girl was shaking her head. 'We weren't friends,' she said, 'at least, not in the way you mean. Justine's a lot older than me for a start, and she works full-time here in the house. I work for Mrs Lorrimer in the office – she's the office manager – so I don't see much of Justine at all in the normal way.'

Molly looked puzzled. 'But surely there were times when the two of you would have a coffee together, or lunch, perhaps?'

Once again, the girl shook her head. 'You don't understand,' she said. 'As I said, Justine works in the house and I work in the office. I bring my lunch with me and eat it in the office or outside on the veranda when the weather's nice, and she and

Michael eat up here in the classroom. They have everything they need in there: stove, fridge, microwave; it's set up really well, so there's no need for them to come downstairs for meals, except when Mr Lorrimer's home, of course, but that's not very often. Michael loves that; he gets so excited when his dad comes home.'

Molly looked puzzled. 'Am I missing something here, Sylvia?' she asked. 'Where is Michael's mother in all this? A few moments ago, you said we could come back up here later, *because Mrs Lorrimer would be out*, and you could take Michael downstairs. Why does she have to be out before you can take her son downstairs? Does he live up here all the time with Justine?'

'Oh, no. They do go downstairs sometimes. Like when Justine is doing some washing or ironing and things like that, Michael has the run of the house while she's down there.'

'But not while his mother is there. Right?' Molly waited, but Sylvia took refuge in wiping her eyes and rubbing her cheeks. 'So let me get this straight,' Molly persisted. 'Michael loves his dad, who is away most of the time, but he seldom sees his mother, who is here all the time. Isn't that just a little bit odd?'

The girl avoided Molly's eyes. 'It's just that . . .' She took a deep breath, then leaned closer and dropped her voice to little more than a whisper. 'I probably shouldn't be telling you this,' she said, 'and don't take it for gospel because I wasn't even here back then, but they say Mrs Lorrimer nearly died when she had Michael. They say she had a breakdown and wasn't even allowed to see her new baby for ever such a long time, and when they told her he couldn't see and couldn't talk, it did something to her mind, and she's had trouble dealing with the boy ever since. Which is why Justine is here.'

Molly frowned. 'Trouble dealing with the boy in what way, exactly?'

Sylvia Lamb wrinkled her nose. 'It's not that she doesn't *care*,' she said carefully. 'I think she does, but she can't stand the funny sort of growling noises Michael makes. I'll admit it's not very nice to listen to, but it does something to her nerves. Same with the cane. Michael uses a folding cane to find his way around the place, and Mrs Lorrimer can't stand the sound of it on the tiles and the wooden floors. In fact, she had a rubber tip put on it to deaden the sound.'

   A muffled burst of chimes, sounding like the arrival of an ice-cream van, prompted Sylvia to thrust her hand into the pocket of her cardigan. She took out her phone and scanned the screen, then put it back in her pocket. 'That was Mr Lorrimer,' she said with obvious relief. 'He's ready for you now, so if you would like to come with me . . . ?' Without waiting for a reply, she set off briskly down the corridor, pausing only briefly at the head of the stairs to make sure that they were following.

FOUR

'Sorry to have kept you waiting,' Stephen Lorrimer said when Sylvia Lamb ushered Tregalles and Forsythe into his office, and they introduced themselves. He pushed some papers aside, took off his glasses and came out from behind his desk to greet them both with a handshake. 'Julia said you were in Justine's room. Did you find anything?' He searched their faces anxiously for an answer.

'I'm afraid not,' Tregalles said, 'but we'll be taking some of Miss Delgado's things back to the office for further examination.' He indicated the evidence bag Molly was carrying. 'However, we still have to look in the classroom before we go, so we may be luckier there. Do you know if Miss Delgado has a computer? We didn't see one in her room.'

'She has a laptop,' Lorrimer said. 'Have you seen it, Sylvia?'

She shook her head and said, 'I haven't, Mr Lorrimer, but it might be in one of the drawers.'

Lorrimer nodded. 'Take a look when you go back and call me.'

'I'd prefer that everything be left as it is,' Tregalles cut in quickly as Sylvia turned to leave. 'We'll be up there in a few minutes ourselves,' he added as a reminder to Sylvia that they wanted the room to be clear. 'In the meantime, Mr Lorrimer, we would like to ask you a few questions about events leading up to Miss Delgado's disappearance.'

'Then please sit down.' Lorrimer waved a hand in the direction of a couple of well-worn leather chairs facing the desk. 'And I'll let you get back upstairs,' he told Sylvia. 'Michael's behaving himself, is he? Not making any fuss?'

'He's listening to one of his books at the moment,' Sylvia replied, avoiding a direct answer, 'but we'll be coming downstairs for toast and jam in a few minutes. So, if you need me back in the office, I'm sure Betty could keep an eye on him.'

'I think Michael would be more comfortable with you, under

the circumstances,' Lorrimer said firmly. 'And I rang Carole to ask her to come in to cover for you; in fact, she should be here any minute now, so there's no need to worry about things down here.' He put his hand on Sylvia's shoulder and steered her gently toward the door. 'But before you do *anything* else,' he said sternly, 'for God's sake, get rid of those contact lenses before you go blind!'

He closed the door, then stood there for a moment, shaking his head. 'Stubborn girl!' he muttered as he walked over to take his seat behind the desk. 'I shouldn't go on at her like that, but somebody needs to. Sylvia's a good girl and a good worker, and she's worn glasses for most of her life . . . until last week, when my stepson came down from university and Julia put him to work in the office. Sebastian's a handsome young man and suddenly the glasses disappeared and contacts were in, and you can see the result. However' – he paused to rub his face vigorously with both hands as if trying to stir up the blood and bring some colour to his pallid features – 'that's not why you're here, is it? I'm not sure I can add anything to what my wife told Chief Inspector Paget, so what do you want, exactly?'

Molly had never met Stephen Lorrimer before – at least not face to face. She had seen him on television, and his picture appeared quite regularly in the local papers. Invariably smartly dressed – dark suit, white shirt and tie – Molly had always thought he looked young for his age, which had to be close to fifty. Lorrimer was not a big man, nor was he a particularly handsome man, but there was something about the broad forehead, set of the eyes and determined line of the jaw that had appealed to Molly. Call it charm, charisma – she wasn't sure herself what the attraction was – but she had voted for Stephen Lorrimer in the last two general elections.

But the man facing them across the desk looked his age and more. The lines around the eyes and mouth were deeper; his eyes lacked lustre, and the dark patches beneath them suggested a lack of sleep. He was making a valiant attempt to hide it, but, to Molly's eyes at least, Stephen Lorrimer appeared to be a very worried man.

Tregalles began with the usual questions. Had Lorrimer noticed any changes in Justine's behaviour? Did she appear to be worried about anything? Had she been in an argument with anyone recently? Had his son, Michael, behaved any differently towards his nanny? And were he and Mrs Lorrimer satisfied with Justine's work? All questions that had been put to Julia Lorrimer by Paget, but there was always a chance that Lorrimer would add something new.

As expected, the answer was no to everything except the last question. 'We've been more than satisfied,' Lorrimer said earnestly. 'Michael adores Justine, and she has quite literally become one of the family.'

'When did you last see Miss Delgado?' Tregalles asked.

'The last time I saw *Justine*,' Lorrimer said, with emphasis on her first name, 'was last Saturday lunchtime. It was just before Terry and I left for Worcester. Terry Baxter is a young intern who works for me in London,' he explained. 'As you probably know, we are on our Easter break from our parliamentary duties, and I invited Terry to spend a few days down here before going on to see friends in Penzance. I took him into Worcester just after lunch on Saturday, and we stayed there overnight. I came home the next morning, and Terry caught the noon train to Exeter and Penzance.'

Molly looked up from her notes. 'So you weren't here when Justine left for church on Sunday morning, Mr Lorrimer?'

'No. As I said, I stayed in Worcester overnight, and arrived back here just in time to pick up Julia before going on to church ourselves. We went to the ten o'clock service at All Saints'.'

Tregalles frowned. 'Would you mind telling us why you went to Worcester on Saturday, when Mr Baxter's train didn't leave till noon on Sunday?' he asked. 'I mean it's barely an hour's drive.'

'Is that relevant?' asked Lorrimer. 'I don't see what my visit to Worcester has to do with Justine's disappearance?'

'We don't know what may prove to be relevant at this point,' Tregalles conceded. 'From what we've been told about Justine, though, her disappearance is totally out of character. So, if she is as devoted to your son as we're told, I can't see her staying away this long without so much as a phone call . . . at least, not voluntarily.'

Lorrimer's eyes narrowed. 'I'm still not sure I see the relevance,' he said. 'What, *exactly*, are you saying, Sergeant?'

'I'm saying, sir, that, while we can still *hope* that Justine will turn up safe and sound, we have to treat her disappearance as suspicious. If she did leave voluntarily, she may have said something to someone about where she was going. On the other hand, if Justine is being detained against her will, we can't rule out the possibility that someone she knows is involved. So, the sooner we can establish where everyone was, their relationship with Justine and what they were doing when she left here on Sunday morning, the sooner we can eliminate them from our enquiries . . . or not.'

'Well, that's certainly plain enough,' Lorrimer said tightly. He flicked a look at Molly with her hand poised above her notebook, then turned back to face Tregalles. 'Very well, then,' he said. 'As you may or may not know, there is to be a by-election in Worcester later this year, and they have an unusually large number of candidates jockeying for the nomination. So the local committee arranged an informal gathering last Saturday afternoon, to meet and get acquainted with the aspiring candidates. To put it bluntly, it was to winnow the wheat from the chaff, and I was invited to attend and offer my thoughts on their various strengths and weaknesses to the committee. It's by no means the deciding factor in the ultimate selection, but it does help to narrow the field. Following that, there was a dinner, to which Terry and I were invited, and the inevitable drinking session followed. Terry was staying over because he had to catch his train the next morning, so I decided to stay on as well. I hadn't had that much to drink, but I thought it best not to take a chance of being picked up for drink driving on the way home, so I phoned Julia to let her know so she wouldn't worry when I didn't turn up.'

'The name of the hotel?' Molly prompted. 'If you don't mind, sir?' She indicated her notes.

'The Raebourne,' he said, spelling it out while giving Molly a look that said she was trying his patience. 'It's a small hotel just off the Oxford Road, and, yes, before you ask, I can give you the names of more than half a dozen people who will verify that I was there.'

'That would be very helpful,' Tregalles broke in quickly before

Molly could reply. 'Perhaps you could let us have them before
we leave. But I'd like to get back to last Saturday lunchtime.
Can you tell us what you and Justine talked about?'

Lorrimer frowned into the distance as if picturing the scene
in his mind. 'Actually,' he said, 'I don't think I had more than
a dozen words with Justine all through lunch. Julia and I were
talking about my brother and his family coming to dinner on
Sunday, so it was Terry who was doing all the talking to Justine.
He spent a month in Manila during his gap year, and he was
trying to impress her with his knowledge of the Philippines. I
think he was quite smitten with her, but he was pushing it a bit.'

'How would you say Justine responded?' Tregalles asked.

'I think she was embarrassed,' said Lorrimer. 'Young Terry
had been trying to engage her in conversation every chance he
got from the time he arrived here, and I think she was getting
tired of it. She'd tried to be polite, but I think she was glad to
see him leave.'

Molly looked up from her notes. 'This may sound ridiculous,'
she said hesitantly, 'but is it possible that Justine *was* interested
in Terry, but for some reason didn't like to show it, and the two
of them have gone off somewhere together?'

Lorrimer scoffed at the idea. 'Justine was definitely not interested in Terry,' he said firmly, 'so I think you can safely forget
that line of enquiry.'

'No doubt you're right, sir,' said Molly diplomatically.
'Alternatively, Justine may have said something to him about
what she would be doing at the weekend to put him off. As you
said yourself, they were talking together for quite some time, so
I think we should at least find out what they talked about.'

'It was Terry who was doing all the talking,' Lorrimer countered.

'Even so—' Molly began, only to be cut off by Tregalles.

'The fact is, Mr Lorrimer, that if there is even the slightest
chance that Justine told Baxter something of consequence, then
we need to talk to him. Do you have an address or phone number
where he can be reached?'

Tregalles had been quite happy to let Molly ask a few questions, but he had no intention of letting her take over. As a newly
appointed detective sergeant, he knew she was anxious to make

a good impression, and he didn't object to that, but there was no need for her to be quite so aggressive. He liked Molly; they had worked well together when she was a DC, but things were different now. Molly Forsythe wasn't just a colleague and friend; *DS* Forsythe was the *competition*, because there wasn't room for two detective sergeants on Paget's team. One of them would have to move. Normally, it would be up to Molly to seek a posting, but Paget had been relying on her more and more for some time now, and Tregalles couldn't help wondering if he was being nudged aside.

His wife, Audrey, had scoffed at the idea. 'Mr Paget's always done right by you,' she had reminded him, 'and Molly's not one to go behind your back. Besides, if you carry on with the course and become an inspector, it will all work out for the best anyway. You'll see, love.'

But Tregalles wasn't convinced. Sometimes promotion did strange things to people, and even friends could change.

'I don't have the address where he's staying,' Lorrimer was saying, 'but no matter where Terry is, he never turns his phone off, so I'll give you his number.' He consulted his BlackBerry, then wrote down a number on the back of a business card and passed it across the desk to Tregalles. The sergeant glanced at it briefly, then handed it to Molly, who slipped it between the pages of her notebook.

'Do you know if Justine attended mass regularly, sir?' Molly asked. 'Or was she going because it was Easter Sunday?'

Lorrimer stared at her for several seconds, brow furrowed as if he didn't understand the question; when he did speak, he seemed to have to force the words out. 'Justine goes to mass every Sunday,' he said. 'She takes her religion very seriously indeed.'

Molly thought about the crucifix, wrapped and hidden away in a drawer upstairs, and wondered again why it wasn't out in plain sight. 'And, from what we've heard about her character, she is normally truthful and trustworthy?' she asked.

Lorrimer bristled. 'I thought that had been made very clear,' he said. 'Just what are you driving at, Sergeant . . . ?'

'Forsythe, sir,' Molly supplied. 'It's just that I can't help wondering why someone who takes her religion seriously would

lie to your wife about who she was going to see that day. Do
you have any thoughts about that, sir?'

'No, I don't,' Lorrimer said coldly, 'and I'm as mystified as
you, because it is not like Justine at all.'

Molly was about to ask another question, but Tregalles inter-
vened by saying, 'There is one other avenue I'd like to explore,
sir. I hope there's nothing to it, but it is just possible that Justine
has been abducted, so I have to ask if you have been contacted
by anyone demanding money for her safe return?'

Lorrimer squinted at the sergeant as if he didn't quite believe
what he was hearing. 'That's preposterous,' he said dismissively.
'You can't be serious?'

'As I said, sir, I sincerely hope that is *not* the case, but I don't
think we can dismiss it out of hand. You are in the public eye,
you are a relatively wealthy man, and, apart from anything else,
it would be very hard on your son if anything happened to Justine.
So, I must ask you again: has there been any contact?'

'Absolutely not! And from what little I know about such
matters, isn't contacting the police the last thing we would do if
we had received a demand? The whole idea is absurd!'

'Absurd or not, the fact of the matter is that Justine Delgado
has been missing now for more than forty-eight hours, and both
you and your wife tell us that it is completely out of character.
So we can't discount anything until proven otherwise. As for
contacting the police, it was your wife who came to us, and we
assume she did so in good faith. But that's not to say that *you*
have not been contacted and, for whatever reason, didn't tell Mrs
Lorrimer. I'm not suggesting that *is* the case, but I am asking
you to tell us now if you have been holding anything back?'

'No, I have not, and you'll just have to take my word for it.'
Lorrimer pushed his chair back as if preparing to stand, then
appeared to change his mind. He slumped down in his seat and
pressed his hands to his face and rubbed his eyes. 'Look,' he
said, 'I'm sorry if I sound boorish; I *know* you have a job to do,
I *know* you have to ask these questions, but these past few days
have been extremely stressful.' He drew in a long breath and let
it out again slowly. 'So, now what happens?'

'Do you have CCTV cameras covering the approaches to the
house?' Tregalles asked.

'No,' said Lorrimer wearily. 'Jim Bradley was pushing the idea because of what happened to the member from Birmingham Selly Oak last year, but we've never had any trouble here, so I didn't think we needed it. Perhaps I should have listened to him.'

'Can't anticipate everything,' Tregalles said solicitously as he got to his feet. 'And thank you for your time, sir.'

Lorrimer came out from behind his desk. 'So where are you going now?' he asked.

'We'll split up,' Tregalles replied, ignoring the look of surprise on Molly's face. They'd come in his car, and he was leaving her here with the evidence bag and whatever else she might find in the classroom, but he needed the car, and she could always call the office and get someone to pick her up. 'DS Forsythe will go back upstairs to look for Justine's computer, and anything else that might prove useful, while I'll be talking to the priest at St Joseph's to see if he remembers seeing Justine at mass last Sunday. But before we go, is there anyone else here in the house we should be talking to? I heard you mention someone called Carole, and Jim Bradley. And I believe Sylvia mentioned someone called Betty. Are they here now?'

'Carole used to work here, but she left long before Justine came to work for us,' Lorrimer explained. 'We call her in from time to time, as I did today, when we need an extra hand, but this is the first time she has been in the office for months, so I don't think she will be able to help you. As for Jim, the only time he's here on a regular basis is when we are gearing up for an election, and while I'm sure he knows who Justine is, I don't think their paths have crossed more than half a dozen times, if that. As for Betty Jacobs, our housekeeper and cook, you can give it a try, but she's as deaf as a post, and "independent", if you know what I mean, so a conversation with Betty is usually limited to basic instructions about what we'll be having for dinner.'

Molly tucked her notebook in her bag, then slung it over her shoulder and picked up the evidence bag. 'And Sebastian Mills?' she prompted as they walked to the door. 'Would he be available, Mr Lorrimer?'

'He's . . . not here at the moment,' Lorrimer said after a moment's hesitation. 'In fact, I'm not sure where he is. To be honest, I don't think he can tell you any more than Julia and I have told you. He's only been here a few days.'

Tregalles took out a card. 'We'd still like to talk to him,' he said, 'so perhaps you would ask him to give us a call when he returns. And if you should happen to think of anything that might help, no matter how insignificant it might seem, please give us a call at that number, day or night. And thank you for your patience, Mr Lorrimer. We will be in touch.'

'And I'd appreciate it if you could have those names for me when I'm finished upstairs,' Molly prompted gently. 'The people you were with in Worcester on Saturday, if you don't mind, sir?'

FIVE

'Will you please tell me exactly how you managed to get yourself involved in what appears to be a routine missing person case, Neil?' Detective Superintendent Amanda Pierce slipped off her reading glasses and sat back in her chair. She looked comfortable in that chair, thought Paget, which was more than he would have said when she'd first taken the job eight months ago – the job that everyone, including himself, thought would be his following the departure of the late Detective Superintendent Thomas Alcott. She had faced hostility and resentment on every side, and the fact that Paget held her responsible for the death of his late wife's younger brother, and had arrived like a ghost from the past, had not made things any easier. But Amanda had fought back. He'd learned the truth about his brother-in-law's death, and he had to give her credit for the way she'd tackled the job. Even Chief Superintendent Morgan Brock, with his seemingly never-ending sniping, using figures from his beloved charts and graphs for bullets, had grudgingly acknowledged that she had met and, in some cases, surpassed most of his arbitrary targets.

'According to the overnight activity report,' Pierce continued, 'you told PC Mercer that you would deal with it personally before he'd even had a chance to put it into the system. Do you not have enough to do down there as it is?'

'I know it's not much of an excuse,' said Paget, 'but I was more or less ambushed by Julia Lorrimer as I was coming in this morning. She didn't strike me as the sort of person who panics easily, but she was certainly worried when she spoke to me. According to her, Justine Delgado is a very responsible young woman, and this is totally out of character. I didn't like the sound of it, so I sent Tregalles and Forsythe over to Simla House to take a look at the missing woman's room and talk to—'

'*Both* of them?' Pierce broke in. 'Was that really necessary?'

'I thought it might save time in the long run,' Paget replied.

'Tregalles is perfectly capable of interviewing Lorrimer and anyone else in the house, but I sent Forsythe along because she has a keen eye for detail, and I thought she might spot something in Justine Delgado's room that might not register in quite the same way with Tregalles.'

Amanda Pierce eyed him thoughtfully. 'Are you quite sure you're not giving the case – if there is a case – special treatment because Stephen Lorrimer is an MP?'

'I'll admit it had a bearing,' Paget conceded, 'but I wasn't so much concerned about Stephen Lorrimer being an MP as I was about the fact that he is also a very rich man. And, if this young woman is so highly thought of by the Lorrimers, and so important to the wellbeing of their son, I couldn't dismiss the possibility of an abduction.'

'Possibly set up by Justine Delgado herself,' Pierce suggested. 'She lied about where she was going to spend the day when she left the house on Sunday morning, which Mrs Lorrimer says is totally out of character, so Delgado was clearly up to something. Which makes her disappearance all the more suspicious. Perhaps you were right to send Forsythe along as well. Have you heard back from either of them yet?'

'I have,' Paget said. 'As far as the abduction theory is concerned, Stephen Lorrimer insists that he hasn't been contacted, and both Tregalles and Forsythe believe he's telling the truth. Tregalles is going on to St Joseph's to see if the priest remembers seeing Justine at the early-morning mass last Sunday, and Forsythe is still at the house. They found nothing in Justine's room to indicate where she might have gone, so Forsythe is searching the classroom, which is where Justine and the boy spend much of their time. She's looking for Justine's laptop and anything else that might tell us where she's gone. Meanwhile, I'll have someone get started on checking phone records, bank statements and so on.' Paget glanced at his watch. 'Tregalles said he'll be going on to talk to Justine's friend at the hospital after he's finished at St Joseph's, but I'm wondering if it might save time if I—'

'Don't even think about it,' Pierce warned, reading his mind. 'Leave the man alone. I know how much you'd like to get out there yourself, but unless you think he needs your support in the field, let him get on with it. And if he *does* need your support, then I would question your judgement in encouraging him to take the inspector's exam. Has he said how he's getting on with his studies?'

'It took him a while to get used to studying again, as you know, but he tells me that his wife, Audrey, has taken to working with him, and that has helped a lot. He said she's getting to know the material so well that she might sit the exam herself, and she wondered if we would take her on if she passed.'

Pierce's mouth twitched. 'I'm not sure we are quite ready for *two* Tregalleses on the team,' she said, 'but it's nice to know that he has her support.'

The phone rang. Paget shot an enquiring glance at Pierce, who shook her head and dismissed him with a wave of the hand. 'But keep me informed,' she said as she picked up the phone.

Church Street was well named, with the Baptists at one end, Anglicans at the other, and the Roman Catholics roughly in the middle. St Joseph's looked quite small, hemmed in as it was by the post office on one side and a three-storied house converted into offices on the other. Built of brick and stone, and with a steeple higher than its neighbours, however, it had managed to hold its own.

Parking on the short street was reserved for weddings, baptisms and funerals, according to the signs. Regular churchgoers knew to leave their cars in Market Square, which was empty on a Sunday morning, and walk the short distance to the church. Not so today, though; every space was filled, so Tregalles parked on a double yellow line and crossed his fingers as he walked away.

Having telephoned ahead, he expected to meet Father Leonard inside the church, but as he walked up the steps, he heard someone call his name. He turned to see a tall, young, fair-haired man, wearing a sweatshirt, shorts and trainers, getting off a high-end racing bike. The man had broad shoulders, a narrow waist, and legs like young saplings, and he couldn't have been more than thirty.

'Sergeant Tregalles?' the man said again, and grinned. 'Not quite what you were expecting, I can see,' he said, extending his hand when Tregalles came back down the steps. 'Father Leonard,' he said. 'Sorry if I kept you waiting; I was at the top of Long

Hill when you called. I thought I would have plenty of time to get back, but traffic was heavy in the valley.' He took a smartphone from a leather pouch on the handlebars. 'Makes for uncomfortable riding when it's in the back pocket,' he said, 'but you have to stay in touch in this job.' He looked up as rain began to fall. 'So, if you'd like to go into the church and take a pew, I'll get rid of the bike and meet you in there in about five minutes . . . or maybe ten.' Without waiting for a reply, he wheeled the bike towards a narrow passage between the church and the building next door and disappeared.

Some fifteen minutes later, the priest reappeared, wearing a simple cassock. Walking up the aisle to where Tregalles sat waiting, he looked too young to be called Father. Handsome devil, too, Tregalles thought irreverently.

The priest sat down and ran his fingers through damp hair. 'Sorry to keep you waiting,' he said, 'but it was a bit sticky riding this morning, so I took a quick shower. Now, you said on the phone that you wanted to talk to me about one of my parishioners? Who are we talking about?'

'Justine Delgado,' Tregalles said. 'Do you recall if she attended the eight o'clock mass last Sunday?'

'Justine?' Father Leonard shot him a questioning look. 'Mrs Lorrimer rang me yesterday to ask the very same question,' he said. 'Has something happened to Justine? Is she all right?'

'She's missing,' Tregalles said. 'According to Mrs Lorrimer, Justine left the house to attend the eight o'clock mass last Sunday morning, and she hasn't been seen since. Do you recall seeing her at mass that morning?'

The priest shook his head. 'I'm afraid I have to tell you the same as I told Mrs Lorrimer,' he said. 'There were so many people here that morning, I honestly can't remember if she was among them or not. I asked Mrs Lorrimer why she wanted to know, but she just muttered something I couldn't catch, then apologized for troubling me and rang off. Mind you, it's not like Justine to miss a Sunday, so she probably *was* here.'

'Unfortunately, "probably" isn't good enough,' Tregalles said. 'I need to know for certain when she was last seen. Do you remember the last time you *did* see her? I mean, wouldn't she have to come to confession?'

Father Leonard smiled indulgently. 'No one *has* to come to confession,' he said. 'It is their choice, but, yes, as it happens, Justine was here last week, but not for confession. She was here in the church, praying, and young Michael Lorrimer was with her.'

'Praying? Did you talk to her?'

'No. I stopped and had a whispered word with Michael, but I left Justine to her prayers.'

'Is that something she was in the habit of doing?'

'Not that I'm aware of. That's not to say she *hasn't* been coming here to pray, but I haven't seen her.' He paused, eyes narrowed in concentration. 'Except once,' he continued slowly. 'I saw her here around the beginning of the year, but I didn't speak to her. She gave me the impression that she didn't want to be disturbed.'

'Did you know her well? Can you tell me anything about her?' Tregalles asked. 'We have so little to work with, so anything you can tell me would be appreciated.'

The priest was shaking his head. 'I can't say I know her well,' he said. 'The reason I know her at all is because she is here as regular as clockwork every Sunday, but I doubt if we've exchanged more than a few dozen words since she started coming. She's always struck me as a very private person.'

'You say you had a word with Michael?' Tregalles said. 'We've been led to believe he doesn't speak.'

The priest smiled. 'He doesn't, but Justine must have told him to be quiet in church, so he shushed me by putting his fingers against his lips and shaking his head when I spoke to him.'

Tregalles tried to think of a more productive line of questioning. 'I know you can't tell me *what* Justine said when she was last here for confession,' he said, 'but can you at least tell me if she seemed to be worried or concerned about anything?'

Father Leonard shook his head. 'I'm afraid I can't tell you that,' he said. 'Not because of the constraints of the confessional,' he added quickly, 'but because Justine Delgado has not made her confession – at least not to me – since before last Christmas.'

The classroom was much larger than Molly had imagined. Situated as it was at the end of the house, the east-facing windows looked out across the river valley to a row of once stately homes, now turned into flats, lining the hill on the far side. The river itself was hidden from view by the crest of the hill, but it could be seen from the south-facing windows as it wound its way down to the George IV bridge and beyond.

Sylvia Lamb had told them that Simla House was divided into two parts: 'the house' and 'the office'. As Molly wandered around the room, she couldn't help wondering if it was really divided into three parts, the third part being the first floor of the south wing, where a small boy was being kept in virtual confinement, with only his nanny for company, because his father was away and his mother had never accepted him. Molly had encountered some strange family relationships in her time, but never one like this.

Now, after an hour of fruitless searching, not just for the laptop, but anything else that might give her a clue to where Justine had gone, Molly was preparing to leave when she heard someone say, 'Oh, it's you. I thought I heard someone moving about in here.' She turned to face the speaker who stood in the open doorway; a tall, dark-haired young man was eyeing her speculatively. 'You must be the copper my mother was talking about,' he said. 'And a very nice one, too, I must say,' he added appreciatively as he entered the room and stuck out his hand. 'I'm Sebastian Mills, and you are . . . ?'

'Detective Sergeant Forsythe,' said Molly, ignoring the hand, 'and since you're here, Mr Mills, is there anything you can tell me that might explain the disappearance of Justine Delgado?'

'Sebastian, please,' he said, then shook his head. 'Sorry, but I barely knew the woman. I only came down from Leeds last week, so I'm afraid I can't help you.'

'But she has been here for almost a year,' said Molly, 'so you must have some knowledge of her.'

'Justine wasn't the easiest person to get to know,' he said. 'She wasn't interested in anything beyond her work up here with the kid. And, to be honest, not my type at all.'

Sebastian Mills was an attractive man, but there was something about the way he looked at her, a sort of insolence behind predatory eyes that put her on her guard. Wearing a black T-shirt, shorts and trainers, there was a slight sheen to his well-muscled body that suggested he'd either been running or working out in the gym downstairs. He reminded Molly of his mother; again, it was the eyes – dark and expressive with long lashes of which any woman would be proud. But there was nothing effeminate about Sebastian Mills. He was all male . . . and didn't he just know it!

His lips curled ever so slightly; it was as if he were reading her thoughts, and Molly could feel her face becoming uncomfortably warm.

'Even so,' she said quickly, 'living here under the same roof, if only for a few days, there must have been some contact between you. So if there is anything you can recall that Justine said or did that might help, please tell me.'

He shook his head. 'I don't think I saw her more than two or three times last week,' he said, 'and we certainly didn't have any conversations. She spent most of her time up here, and I was downstairs or out somewhere, so I really can't help you.'

'What about last year? Holidays and Christmas?' Molly persisted doggedly. 'I know you were at university, but weren't you here during the holidays?'

'Part of the time, yes, but even then our paths seldom crossed.'

'When was the last time you saw her?'

Sebastian pursed his lips. 'Last Saturday afternoon, about . . .' He stopped. 'Actually,' he said, 'the very *last* time I saw her was Sunday morning when I was getting dressed. She was going through the gate, trotting off to church like a good little Catholic.'

'What time was that?'

'Seven thirty, maybe quarter to eight.'

'And you are quite sure it was Justine you saw?'

A flicker of irritation crossed Sebastian's face. 'I'll admit I only saw the back of her, but nobody else around here has long black hair like that, so, yes, I'm sure it was Justine.'

'Do you recall what she was wearing?'

Sebastian squeezed his eyes shut and hung his head like a child pretending to think hard. 'She was wearing a coat,' he said, 'a light-coloured coat, but don't ask me what colour it was because I couldn't tell you. And black stockings . . . well, tights, I suppose they are. She has quite decent legs, actually.'

Trust him to zero in on Justine's legs, thought Molly. 'Did

you happen to notice anyone else out there? On the road or in the car park?'

'No. But then I can't see the road from my room because of the hedge.' He smiled. 'I can show you if you like; my room's just down the corridor.'

'Thank you, Mr Mills, but I'll take your word for it,' Molly said crisply. 'Do you remember if Justine was carrying anything?'

'Such as?'

'Anything,' Molly repeated as she picked up her handbag and slung it over her shoulder.

Sebastian thought about that, then shook his head. 'If she was, I don't remember. Sorry.'

'No need to be,' Molly said, moving towards the door. 'Every scrap of information helps, so thank you, Mr Mills. Now, if you'll excuse me . . . ?'

Sebastian moved aside, but left only just enough room for her to get through the doorway without actually touching him. 'I'll walk with you,' he said, falling into step beside her. 'Do you have a number where I can call you? In case I think of anything that might help,' he added quickly. 'As I said, I didn't really know Justine well, but I might think of something. And if there is anything you would like to ask me, I can give you my number.'

'I don't think that will be necessary,' Molly said as she took out a card and handed it to him. 'But there is one thing you can help me with. It's about your brother.'

'My bro—?' Sebastian stared at her. 'Oh, you mean Michael?' The corners of his mouth turned down in a grimace of distaste. 'He may be my *half*-brother,' he said coldly, 'but with almost twenty years between us, we hardly have anything in common. And why my mother ever agreed to have him at her age, God only knows. She wanted to abort, but Stephen talked her round, and you can see how that turned out. Damn near killed her, and for what? You have seen him, haven't you?'

They paused at the head of the stairs.

'No, I haven't,' Molly said. 'Your mother doesn't want us to talk to him for fear of upsetting him, but it's just possible that Justine told the boy something about where she was going on Sunday. So I was wondering . . .'

Sebastian Mills shook his head. 'If you're looking to me to

put a word in, forget it!' he said. 'Besides, I know Stephen quizzed him when they realized she might be missing, but the kid didn't know anything.'

Molly frowned. 'Quizzed him how, exactly?' she asked.

'The kid can hear and understand everything you say to him, and he's been trained to use a phone or laptop to type replies. He's actually quite good at it,' Sebastian added grudgingly, 'but he still makes those godawful noises when he tries to talk.' Sebastian made a face. 'Justine is supposed to have training in speech therapy, but I can't see much difference in the kid since I was here last Christmas. God knows what sort of state he'll be in when he finds out that Justine isn't . . . well . . . might not be coming back at all.'

'You don't think she's coming back?' asked Molly sharply.

Sebastian shrugged. 'I could be wrong,' he said, 'but say what you like about Justine, she was more than attached to the kid; she hardly ever left him out of her sight, so I can't see her just taking off like that and lying to my mother about going to see a friend without something pretty serious going on in her life.'

'Such as?'

'Not the foggiest,' he said with a shrug, 'but my guess is that wherever she is, she isn't there voluntarily or she'd have been in touch.'

SIX

Maria Navarro was a slight, dark-haired young woman who looked extremely tired. 'Not a very good day in Casualty,' she told Tregalles as she filled a large mug with coffee from the urn, then selected a blueberry muffin and two pats of butter. 'I need a jolt,' she confided with a weary smile. 'It was a madhouse. I don't know what was happening out there on the streets, but we had three accident victims with multiple injuries, a heart attack, and a patient we had to helicopter to Birmingham, plus all the usual stuff, *and* we're a doctor short.' She brushed a wisp of hair away from her eyes. 'So this is my lunch,' she ended, holding up her plate.

Tregalles filled a mug himself and moved ahead of her to pay for both at the till. 'Are you sure you wouldn't like anything else?' he asked before he handed over the money.

The young nurse smiled and shook her head. 'Thanks, but this is all I need for now.' She led the way to a quiet corner and sat down. Her eyes were troubled as she met those of Tregalles across the table. 'So, Justine is still missing,' she said softly. 'When Mrs Lorrimer telephoned yesterday to ask me if I knew where Justine was, I thought it was strange that she would go off like that, but when *you* rang the hospital and said you wanted to talk to me, I *really* began to worry. Do you have *any* idea what could have happened to her?' She took a tentative sip of coffee, then proceeded to pull the muffin apart and butter it.

'I'm afraid we've very little to go on,' Tregalles replied, 'which is why I'm here, hoping that you might be able to help me. Did you see or hear from Justine at all last Sunday?' He tried his own coffee, winced and set it down again.

'Mrs Lorrimer asked me the same thing yesterday,' Maria said, 'and I told her I haven't seen or spoken to Justine for more than a week. And when she told me that Justine had said she was spending the day with me on Sunday, I couldn't believe it. I was

working on Sunday, and we had no plans to meet, so I don't
understand why Justine would say that.'

'Do you attend St Joseph's?' he asked.

Maria grimaced guiltily. 'Sometimes,' she said cautiously.
'Why?'

'What about last Sunday? Did you attend mass before coming
to work?'

'No, I was on the same shift as I am today – seven till three,
although it was more like half past five by the time I got back
to the house that day. I was supposed to be doing some of the
preparations for our Easter dinner, but I had to phone and let the
others know I'd be late.'

'The house?' Tregalles queried. 'You don't live in the resi-
dence?'

'No. I live in an old house in Cogshill Lane. There are six of
us. We share the work and share the rent. It's like a mini co-op.'

'Did Justine have any other close friends?' he asked. 'Mrs
Lorrimer seems quite certain that Justine said she would be
spending the day with you, but she could have been mistaken
– perhaps Justine was talking about some other friend?'

Maria shook her head slowly. 'She isn't what you would call
a social person; she keeps pretty much to herself, and she's never
mentioned anyone to me.'

'What about a boyfriend? Did she ever speak of a man? Perhaps
someone she'd met recently?'

'No. Justine doesn't have time for them,' she said. 'I mean
that literally; I don't mean she's gay or anything like that. It's
just that she's too immersed in her work. That's all she ever talks
about . . . well, except when we start talking about things back
home.' Maria's eyes drifted away. 'I'm afraid we're both a little
homesick, but when the jobs and the money are here, what can
you do? I'm hoping to go home for a visit next year, but I know
Justine intends to keep working here as long as she can. She
works very hard, but the Lorrimers have been extremely good
to her, and they pay her well, which is how she is able to support
her grandfather in the care home in Manila. But she really should
get out more. I almost have to bully her into coming out with
me at times. The thing is, I know she enjoys herself when she
does come out, but you can see she's anxious to get back after

she's been out for a couple of hours. She's mother, father, teacher, nurse, you name it, to Michael Lorrimer.'

'What about his own mother?' Tregalles asked. 'We're getting the impression that she doesn't want anything to do with the boy. Has Justine talked to you about that?'

Maria picked up her mug with both hands and propped her elbows on the table. 'Mr Lorrimer told Justine that his wife almost died when she was having Michael. There were complications; she had a fever and had to be kept in hospital for weeks, so she never even saw her baby until he was about six weeks old. And when she discovered that Michael was disabled, she couldn't handle it; she had a breakdown and spent quite some time in therapy, but it didn't help. She still couldn't bring herself to treat the boy as her own. Anyway, that's why they hired a nanny.' Maria set her mug down. 'But I don't see how any of what I'm telling you is going to help you find Justine.'

'To be honest, I don't know either,' Tregalles confessed. 'The only way we can approach this is to find out as much about Justine as possible in the hope that it will give us a lead. Now, I know you don't seem to think it likely, but let's assume for a moment that the reason Justine lied to Mrs Lorrimer about who she was spending the day with was because she was meeting a man. Can you think of where or how she might have met him? Did she belong to any groups in town? Social, political, church, perhaps? Any ideas, Maria?'

The young nurse shook her head once again. 'As I said, Justine doesn't really have a social life. To the best of my knowledge, she wasn't a member of anything, and I think I would have known. We are good friends and we share stuff like that. Actually, although she always seems to be very confident, she's really quite shy. She doesn't mix well in groups; I think there are times when she would like to, but she doesn't quite know how. I know there are times when I've had the feeling that she is a little bit envious of my relationship with Paul. Not that she's ever said anything. It's more in the way she looks when I talk about something that Paul and I have done together. It's as if she wishes she could do something like that herself.'

'And Paul is . . . ?'

'Paul Wheeler. Another member of our little co-op at the house.

He's in the first year of the Foundation Programme. It's a programme they have to go through before going on to become a GP or continue on to specialize,' she explained. 'Paul wants to get into cardiology.'

Tregalles couldn't put his finger on it, but he had the feeling that Maria was holding something back. 'Look, Maria,' he said, lowering his voice to match her own, 'I know Justine is your friend, and perhaps she's shared secrets with you that you feel obliged to keep to yourself, but this is no time to hold back. So please tell me if Justine has ever said or even hinted that she has a lover?'

'A lover?' Maria stared at him, then dismissed the idea with an emphatic shake of her head. 'That's . . . well, it's ridiculous,' she said.

'Ridiculous or not, we have good reason to believe that Justine may have a lover, and since she's been missing for close to three days now, we have to explore every possibility. So please think hard before you answer: has Justine ever said anything that might lead you to believe she was involved with a man?'

The young nurse drew back to study him through narrowed eyes. 'You really *are* serious, aren't you?' she said. 'But why are you so sure she was seeing someone?'

'I'm afraid I can't tell you that,' Tregalles said. He tried his coffee again; it was lukewarm. He grimaced at the taste. Maria must be used to it, he decided, because she had almost finished hers. He set his mug aside.

Maria looked perplexed. 'I don't know what to say,' she said. 'Honestly, Sergeant, the only other thing Justine had any time for, apart from when we were able to get together, was the church. She always has time for that. She hardly ever misses going to mass on Sundays and sometimes on holy days in the middle of the week as well. Father Leonard runs fitness classes in the gym in the basement of the church, and Justine even talked about taking Tai Chi at one point last year, but I don't think she ever did. In fact, I tease her that she goes because she's got a thing for Father Leonard—'

She stopped abruptly as she saw the expression on Tregalles's face. 'Oh, no,' she whispered, horrified at the unintended impli-cation. 'I didn't mean . . . It was a joke. Honestly!'

'But *could* there be some truth to it?' Tregalles persisted.

'No! No, absolutely not,' Maria said flatly. 'I only meant it in fun, because Father Leonard is young and good-looking.'

'How did Justine respond to your teasing?' Tregalles asked.

'She didn't like it,' Maria said softly. 'Justine said I shouldn't be saying things like that about a priest. I only meant it in fun, but I could see she was quite annoyed, so I never mentioned it again. She doesn't take kindly to jokes, even mild ones, about her faith.'

Or perhaps Maria had come too close to the truth, Tregalles thought. But there was nothing to be gained by pursuing that line of questioning with Maria.

'All right, then,' he said, 'what can you tell me about this chap, Sebastian Mills? Mrs Lorrimer's older son. I haven't met him yet, but I've been told he's a good-looking man. Do you know if Justine has shown any interest in him?'

Maria shook her head. 'Besides, he's in university. Leeds, I think Justine said, and she doesn't like him. I met him briefly last Christmas when I called for Justine, and I didn't like him either. He's too . . .' She searched for a word. 'Smarmy? Is that the right word?'

'It could be,' Tregalles said. 'Thinks a lot of himself? God's gift to women? That sort of thing?' Maria gave an emphatic nod. 'He's back home now,' Tregalles told her. 'Came home last week.'

Maria looked at her watch. 'I don't know what else I can tell you,' she said, 'and I really should be getting back.'

'Then I won't keep you,' Tregalles said. 'And thank you for your time and patience. If you should happen to think of anything, no matter how small, please call this number.' He handed her his card, then got to his feet.

Maria took it and had started to get up when her eyes filled with tears, and she sat down again. 'I really wish I could help you,' she said plaintively. 'I've been trying not to think about it, but I'm so afraid that something bad has happened to Justine. I know she wouldn't just leave that little boy. Not like that, not without . . .' Eyes glistening, she looked up at Tregalles. 'You think she's dead, don't you?' she whispered. 'You haven't said it, but that's what you think, isn't it?'

'It's far too early to be thinking along those lines,' Tregalles told her. 'I'm sure there is some reasonable explanation, and we'll do everything we can to find her.' He offered his hand to help Maria to her feet. She flashed him a grateful smile and took his hand. 'Tell me,' he said as they made their way to the door, 'have you ever been in Justine's room in Simla House?'

'A couple of times, yes. Why?'

'Did you ever see a crucifix there?'

Maria nodded. 'Oh, yes. It belonged to Justine's grandfather. He gave it to her when she left Manila. It's on the wall above her bed.'

'When was the last time you were in her room?'

Maria thought back. 'It was the Saturday before Christmas. I called for her and we went out to a pre-Christmas lunch together.'

'And it was there then?'

'Of course, but why do you want to know that?'

'Just checking,' Tregalles said vaguely. 'Just checking.'

SEVEN

Tregalles shouldered the door open and entered the office, a Styrofoam cup of coffee in one hand and a packaged sandwich in the other. 'Late lunch,' he explained as he set both on the edge of Molly's desk. He took off his coat, flung it over a vacant chair, pried the top off the coffee, then sat down and set about unwrapping the sandwiches. 'Supposed to be tuna,' he confided as he examined one. He took a tentative bite, then wrinkled his nose and shrugged. 'Anyway,' he said, 'I saw the priest, and he couldn't say if Justine attended mass or not on Easter morning, but he is going to ask the people who assisted him that morning if they remember seeing her. He's also going to talk to members of the choir, especially the men, because they have a good view of everyone as they come up to take the sacrament, and Justine is a good-looking woman.'

Molly eyed him sceptically. 'That doesn't sound like something a priest would say,' she said. 'That sounds more like DS Tregalles. What sort of man is he, anyway?'

Tregalles grinned. 'Believe it or not, that's exactly what he did say,' he said. 'As for what sort of man he is, let's just say that Father Leonard is not your typical priest. He's young, he's good-looking, he rides a racing bike, and I imagine there's more than one of his female parishioners attending mass a bit more often than they used to before he came to town.' He became serious. 'But one thing he did tell me was that although Justine has attended mass regularly, she hasn't been to confession since the beginning of the year.'

'She got the prescription for Yasmin a day or two after New Year,' Molly said thoughtfully. 'I wonder if that had anything to do with it. Any luck with Justine's friend, Maria?'

Tregalles shook his head. 'She was quite shocked when I asked her if Justine had a lover, and even more shocked when I asked if she thought there might be something going on between Justine and Father Leonard.'

'Hardly surprising,' Molly observed drily, 'especially if she's a Catholic herself.'

'True, but, funnily enough, Maria said she had teased Justine about that very thing, suggesting – jokingly, of course – that the reason she was going to church so regularly was because Father Leonard was so good-looking, and Justine more or less rounded on her for even suggesting it in fun.' Tregalles sighed. 'I just don't get it,' he confessed. 'Justine Delgado doesn't seem to have anything remotely resembling a social life. She's young, she's pretty, she's obviously intelligent, and yet her entire life appears to be centred around Michael Lorrimer. She shows no interest in mixing socially. Doesn't that sound odd to you, Molly?'

Sounds a bit like my life, thought Molly, but she nodded. 'On the other hand, maybe she's just shy?'

'Maria said that, too, but I still think it's odd. Let's leave that for the moment. Did you find anything in that classroom upstairs?'

'No sign of a laptop or anything of a personal nature in there, I'm afraid,' Molly said. 'Michael Lorrimer has his own Braille computer and an audio reader; I suppose it's *possible* there is something on it to do with Justine's intentions, but I very much doubt it.'

'Why don't you go back there tomorrow with a tech to have a look at it. And while you're there, try to talk to anyone else who's around, regardless of what Stephen Lorrimer said about them not knowing anything.'

'I've already spoken to Mrs Lorrimer's older son, Sebastian Mills,' Molly told him, 'and he confirms what his mother said about seeing Justine as she was leaving Sunday morning. Other than that, he claims he barely noticed her, which I find hard to believe, since she's an attractive young woman, and he seems to think of himself as irresistible to women.'

'Sounds like he's made a hit with young Sylvia, though,' Tregalles observed. 'Come on to you, did he, Molly?'

She made a face. 'Not exactly,' she said, 'but I had the feeling that he might if given half a chance.'

'You could always give him a trial run if he asked you out?' Tregalles suggested slyly. 'After all, it's been a long time since I've heard you say anything about your boyfriend in Hong Kong. Perhaps it's time to think about—'

'I rang that number Mr Lorrimer gave us,' Molly cut in sharply. 'The one for Terry Baxter in Penzance. He confirmed that the last time he saw Justine was at lunch on Saturday before leaving for Worcester. When I asked him what they talked about, he said it was a bit one-sided and he'd realized, belatedly, that Justine was barely listening. He told me it was as if she had something much more serious on her mind, and he'd felt a bit of a fool for not recognizing that earlier.'

'So, if Terry Baxter, a total stranger, noticed that, why didn't those who knew her notice it as well?' Tregalles wondered aloud.

'It just might be that Justine was simply fed up with Baxter's persistent attentions and deliberately shut him out.'

'Could be,' Tregalles agreed, 'but it's worth keeping in mind. Now,' he pointed to the papers spread out on Molly's desk. 'Anything worthwhile in that lot?'

'Nothing out of the ordinary, I'm afraid. Justine's pretty careful with her money. She transfers at least half of her salary to an account in Manila every month. Don't know yet if it goes to her own bank account in Manila, or—'

'Maria Navarro told me Justine helps pays for her grandfather's care in a home in Manila,' Tregalles broke in. 'We can check that out once we gain access to her bank records.'

'No need,' said Molly. 'The boss is already taking care of that himself.'

'*Paget*?' Tregalles stared at Molly. 'How did that happen?'

'He came down here after talking to you when you were leaving the hospital, and asked me what I thought. He wanted to know what was in the papers I'd brought back, and when I mentioned bank statements and Manila, he said it might save time if he spoke to the bank and the police in Manila. Not only that, but he said he's been on to the agency in Birmingham that handled Justine's placement, requesting any information they have on her background and previous employment.'

Tregalles eyed Molly suspiciously. 'Now, why would he do that?' he asked softly. 'Did you *ask* him to do it? Did you suggest . . . ?' He stopped when he saw the look on Molly's face.

'I did *not* ask or suggest that he do *anything*,' Molly said coldly. 'He just took the bank statements and said he'd take care of them. I was just as surprised as you are, but I could hardly say no, could I? Personally, I think Mr Paget is just dying to get back into the nuts and bolts of the job, instead of sitting behind a desk all day. I think he wants to be involved in things the way he used to be.'

'Could be, I suppose,' Tregalles said grudgingly. 'It's just that . . .' He shook his head as if trying to rid himself of an unwelcome thought, and fell silent.

Molly thought she understood what was going through the sergeant's mind. Tregalles was the senior investigating officer on what could turn out to be a major case, and he didn't want Paget or anyone else taking over.

'Anything else?' he asked.

Molly ran through the rest of her notes, but she had the feeling that Tregalles was only half listening. The request for Justine's mobile telephone and internet records had gone in, but wouldn't be available until tomorrow, she told him, and Paget had authorized the release of Justine Delgado's picture to the media. 'In time for the evening news and the morning papers,' she concluded.

Lingering in the back of her mind was the vivid memory of a case last year where victims had been literally plucked off the streets to be murdered in the most brutal way. The killer was dead, but that didn't mean there couldn't be another predator out there. She shared her thoughts with Tregalles.

'On the other hand,' Tregalles countered, 'it could be as simple as someone trying to snatch Justine's handbag or mobile phone. There'd be very few people about at that time on a Sunday morning. She tries to hang on to it, and is either hit or falls and hits her head, and suddenly her attacker has a body on his hands. He panics, and perhaps he and a mate conceal her body or drag it to a car or van and take it away.'

'If it were me, I don't think I'd spend much time hiding the body,' said Molly. 'I'd get as far away from the scene as fast as I could, rather than risk someone seeing me.'

'Either way,' Tregalles said, 'we need a team out there to search the area and do a door-to-door between Simla House and St Joseph's first thing tomorrow morning. And we're going to need some help, so give Uniforms a call and see how many bodies they're prepared to give us.'

'Pretty girl,' Audrey Tregalles observed sadly as she switched off the television set and the picture of Justine Delgado faded to black. 'What *could* have happened to her at that time of morning? I mean, it's not like a weekday when there'd be all sorts of people on their way to work, is it, love? So where could she have gone?'

'We'll be doing a sweep through the area first thing tomorrow morning,' Tregalles told her. 'The priest can't remember if she was at mass that morning or not, so we don't know if something happened to her on the way to church or after she left there. I've asked him for the names of everyone he *does* remember being there that morning, so we can question them.'

Audrey picked up the knitting that was lying in her lap. 'What do *you* think happened?' she asked. 'I mean, I know you don't *know*, but any ideas at all?'

Tregalles stared at the blank screen. 'To tell the truth, I'm beginning to wonder if she went to mass at all. Somebody with a car could have been waiting to pick her up, or she may have gone off in another direction entirely. She did lie about where she was going, and I wonder if that was so she wouldn't be missed until late Sunday night or Monday morning.'

'Maybe she never left that funny old house at all,' Audrey suggested darkly. 'Have you thought of that?'

'I have, but considering the state Mrs Lorrimer was in when she talked to Paget this morning, and how much they rely on Justine to look after the boy, I don't see a motive if you're suggesting they did away with her.'

'Oh, I wasn't suggesting anything like that,' Audrey said hastily, 'but it is a bit of a mystery, isn't it? What does Mr Paget think? I haven't heard you say much about him lately, until today. It must be nice for the two of you, working together again like you used to.'

'We're not,' Tregalles said tightly. 'At least not the way we used to. He was involved in the beginning because Mrs Lorrimer happened to catch him when he came in first thing this morning, but Superintendent Pierce still has him chained to his desk. I still report to him, but out on the street it's just been me and Molly these past few months.'

'So you're like partners now that she's a detective sergeant as well?'

'Except I'm still senior,' Tregalles pointed out. 'The trouble is, Molly's anxious to get on, so it's a bit of a competition between us. Normally, she would have been gone by now, but with all the cutbacks, there aren't any openings.'

'I shouldn't worry about it,' Audrey said placidly. 'You'll be an inspector soon, and she'll still be a sergeant. Anyway, what about that young man she was going out with?' Audrey liked to keep up to date with what was going on at work. 'You haven't mentioned him for ages. The one who went to China.'

'Hong Kong,' Tregalles corrected. 'And I think things might be a little dicey in that direction. Not that Molly's ever said anything, but when I happened to mention him today, she got a little frosty, so I didn't push it.'

'Pity,' Audrey sighed. 'She's a nice girl, is Molly. It would be good to see her settled, but if it's not to be, then it's not to be. So, what will you be doing tomorrow about the missing girl?'

'As I said, we'll be doing a sweep of the route we think Justine took, and Molly will be back at the house talking to the staff, and I think I'll get her to have another word with Mrs Lorrimer's older son, Sebastian Mills.'

Audrey looked up from her knitting. 'Mrs Lorrimer's been married before, then?' she said, probing. 'How old is the son?'

'A lot older than her five-year-old son,' Tregalles told her. 'He's twenty-four.'

'Sebastian,' Audrey said slowly. 'Now there's a name you don't hear very often. Mrs Lorrimer must have been quite young when she had him. What would she be now? Forty-three or four?'

'If she is, she's in pretty good nick for her age,' Tregalles said. 'I'd have put her closer to thirty-five.'

Audrey laughed. 'With a twenty-four-year-old son? Some detective you are!' she said.

'Well, it's not the sort of thing you ask a woman like her, is it?' he said. 'But I'll do that first thing tomorrow. I'll tell her my wife wants to know. All right?'

'No need for sarcasm,' Audrey said. 'I was just curious, that's all. It seems to me that nineteen years between kids is stretching it a bit, if you'll pardon the pun. I mean, why would she want another child at that age?'

'From what I heard today, I don't think she did,' Tregalles said soberly.

'Could have been an accident, I suppose.' Frowning, Audrey thrust the needles into the ball of wool and set them aside. 'And what, exactly, did you mean when you said Mrs Lorrimer's in "good nick" for her age?'

'Come to think of it, love, she's a lot like you in a way,' he said, grinning as he got to his feet. 'Looks young for her age, kind of sexy . . . and hard as nails underneath.' He raised his arms and stretched. 'Dunno about you, love, but I'm ready for bed. What do you say?'

EIGHT

Wednesday, 4 April

Beginning at seven o'clock the following morning, two WPCs patrolled the route between Simla House and St Joseph's Church. Armed with pictures of Justine Delgado, they stopped every man and woman setting off for work to ask if they had seen Justine on Easter Sunday. Later, it was older children on their way to school, and, as the day wore on, anyone who happened to pass by. They went in and out of shops and left posters in the windows. Some people glanced at the picture, then shook their heads and continued on; some stopped and took their time. Some scurried by, avoiding eye contact as if afraid they might be accused of something if they so much as paused, while others saw it as an opportunity to complain about something completely unrelated.

Meanwhile, a team of searchers, working in pairs, were knocking on doors and probing every dark corner, rubbish bin and possible hiding place along the same route. But, as Tregalles told Molly when he called her as she was leaving Simla House, they'd found nothing. 'The trouble is,' he said, 'it was Easter Sunday so the shops were closed. There aren't many private houses along the route, and there weren't many people about that early in the morning. We're not finished yet, but I think we'll just have to hope that someone sees the picture and comes forward.'

'You're assuming Justine did actually go to church that morning,' Molly said. 'After all, she lied about where she was going afterwards.'

'Like I needed reminding,' Tregalles groaned. 'So, how did you make out at the house?'

'Didn't get to see Michael Lorrimer,' said Molly. 'He's been farmed out for the day with the woman who lives next door. Apparently, he gets on well with her, but neither of the Lorrimers

want the boy upset over Justine's disappearance any more than
he is already. However, they did agree to let us look at his
computer, so I've arranged for someone from Forensic to take a
look at it. Also, I had a few words with Betty Jacobs, the woman
who cooks and cleans. At least, I tried to, but she is hard of
hearing, so it was a bit of a slog, and she couldn't add anything
to what we already know. And Sebastian's out, so I'm on my
way back to Charter Lane to check on Justine's phone and internet
records.'

'Get someone else to do that,' Tregalles said, 'because I'd like
you to do me a favour. Father Leonard just rang with the names
of several people who might remember seeing Justine at mass
last Sunday, and I was hoping that you could call in and pick
them up on your way?'

'And you'd like me to go round and talk to those people as
well, I suppose?'

'That's the favour, Molly. I'm going to be tied up here for the
rest of the day and most of the evening on callbacks, and the
sooner someone talks to the church people, the better. All right?'

'No problem,' she said. 'And good luck . . . boss.' Molly
smiled as she dropped her phone into her bag. Tregalles would
like that. As her father used to tell her, it costs nothing to be nice
to people, so why not?

As long as it didn't go to Tregalles's head, she thought belatedly.

Thursday, 5 April

Molly arrived early the following morning, but both Paget and
Tregalles were already there, waiting for the rest of the staff to
trickle in. But Paget was impatient, and, with ten minutes still
to go to the top of the hour, he told Tregalles to begin.

'I'm afraid we've drawn a complete blank on every possible
street and back alley that Justine might have taken on her way
to church,' he said. 'We've knocked on almost every door, with
callbacks last evening to catch most of the ones we missed
during the day, and we should be all caught up by noon today.
We've shown Justine's picture to just about everyone in the
area; we've stopped people in the street, and we've not had so

much as a flicker of recognition from anyone. And we've found nothing on the ground. No evidence of a struggle having taken place anywhere along the route. But then, it's been raining on and off since the weekend, so any physical evidence there may have been could have been washed away by now.'

Paget shot Molly an enquiring look.

'I don't think Justine went to church,' she said. 'I spoke to the two Eucharistic ministers who assisted Father Leonard, as well as several members of the choir, and the organist. All of them say they know Justine by sight, because she rarely misses a Sunday, but none of them can recall seeing her there last Sunday at either service. I've left pictures of Justine in the church, together with a note asking anyone who has seen her to contact us, but, to be honest, I'm not holding my breath. I think something happened to her long before she got to the church, assuming she intended to go there in the first place.'

Tregalles was nodding. 'I'm beginning to think along the same lines myself,' he said. 'I mean, everyone we've talked to tells us that Justine is a devout Catholic, dedicated to her job, devoted to the boy, supports her poor old granddad back in Manila, and butter wouldn't melt in her mouth. Yet she lied when she said she was going to spend Sunday with her friend, Maria Navarro. So who *was* she going to meet? If she's being that secretive about it, it has to be a man.'

It was Molly's turn to nod agreement. 'The date on the prescription for the pill is the third of January,' she said. 'Her doctor wasn't all that helpful, but he did say that Justine had quizzed him pretty thoroughly about side effects, so I'm pretty sure it was the first time she'd used them. Funny thing is, she's only used one pill out of three months' supply.'

'Maybe they didn't agree with her,' Tregalles suggested. 'Whatever the explanation, it still brings us back to a man as the reason for her disappearance. And both Maria and Father Leonard said they noticed a change in Justine shortly after Christmas.'

'It could explain why that crucifix was wrapped and hidden away,' said Molly. 'A sign that Justine was struggling with guilt.'

'Maria told me the crucifix was on the wall above Justine's bed the week before Christmas,' Tregalles said. 'I didn't tell her it had been taken down.'

'What about Miss Navarro?' asked Paget. 'Do you think that *she* knows more than she's telling?'

Tregalles shook his head. 'I don't think so,' he said. 'She seems to be as baffled as we are, and I think she is genuinely worried about her friend. She is also concerned about Justine's grandfather. As I was leaving, she asked if anyone had contacted him. She said she didn't know the man, but she knew that he and Justine were very close, and she thought he should be told.'

'I've taken care of that,' Paget said. 'Sorry, I should have mentioned it earlier. I spoke to the Manila police, and they told me that the old man is in a home. His name is Raul Aquino; he's the girl's grandfather on her mother's side, and he's in poor health. The man I spoke to got back to me late last night, and said that, on the advice of Mr Aquino's doctor, he did not tell the old man that his granddaughter was missing, but presented himself as a friend of Justine's asking if he had heard from her recently. He said Mr Aquino is mentally alert, but his memory is going, and he wasn't able to say with any certainty when he had last spoken to Justine, nor did he give any indication that he thought anything was wrong. But the phone records should tell us.' He looked at Molly. 'Do we have anything back on that yet?'

Tregalles and Molly exchanged glances. DS Pierce might think she had Paget chained to his desk, but it looked as if he'd slipped his leash and was back in the field again.

'The last call Justine made to Manila from the landline in her room was two weeks ago last Sunday,' Molly said in answer to Paget's question, 'but we don't have anything back yet on calls she may have made on her mobile phone, sir.'

'Still no sign of her mobile or her laptop,' said Paget. 'What about CCTV coverage of the area? How is that coming along?'

'No sign of her so far, sir,' Molly said, 'but we're still looking.'

'Good luck, then,' Paget said, 'and let me know if you do find anything. I'll be in my office if you need me.'

'Got a minute, Sarge? I think you might want to see this.'

Molly looked up to see a slim, dark-skinned young woman standing beside her desk. She smiled. 'No need for the "Sarge", Sophie,' she said. 'The name's still Molly when the brass isn't around.'

DC Sophie Kajura smiled in return. 'I know,' she said, 'but I thought it's still new enough that you might like to hear your title used. I have something on screen that I think you should see.'

Sophie had only recently transferred in from Uniforms, a replacement for DC Tony Brooks, who had decided to take early retirement, at age twenty-nine, to become a househusband, staying home to look after their two children when his wife, a solicitor, was offered an extremely well-paid position with a law firm in Birmingham. 'Why not?' he'd said to colleagues who had tried to dissuade him. 'She's making more money than I'll ever make if I stay here. Besides, I like being with my kids, and I'm a better cook than she is.'

'It's footage from the traffic camera monitoring the north end of Edge Hill Road,' Sophie explained as they sat down in front of the screen. 'You can just see the entrance to Lorrimer Drive. Unfortunately, you can't see the whole entrance because the road turns to the right at that point. But if Justine was going to church, she would come out of Lorrimer Drive and we would have a clear view of her coming towards the camera. But if she was going the other way down into Edge Hill *Crescent*, we wouldn't see her on camera.'

'Right,' said Molly. 'I understand what you're saying because I've been there. So, what is it you want me to see?'

Sophie ran the tape forward. 'I've been over it several times,' she said, 'but there's nothing between seven and eight that morning. At twenty minutes *past* eight, however, we have a white Ford Transit van parking just this side of the entrance to Lorrimer Drive. There! See?' Sophie let the tape run. 'As you can see, a man gets out and walks to the corner, where he seems to be looking for someone, then he walks back and gets in the van and just sits there.' She ran the tape forward. 'Then, at twenty-two minutes to nine, he gets out again and does the same thing. Then he's back in the van, when a BMW comes out of Lorrimer Drive at nine minutes to nine, and comes towards the camera, then disappears beneath it. You can see the driver as he makes the turn – not all that clearly, but he appears to be the only one in the car. I can check the number plate to see—'

'No need,' said Molly. 'That's Sebastian Mills's car, and it looks like him driving it. Let's run that again, Sophie. Slowly. I'd like to see if Justine could be hidden in the back of the car.' They both watched intently, but the reflections on the windows blocked a view of the interior of the car.

They watched together as the tape rolled on, but there was no more activity until two minutes to nine, when the man got out of the van and stood looking down Lorrimer Drive for almost five minutes, then returned to the van and drove off. Sophie ran the tape forward again. 'And there you see Mr Lorrimer's car turning in at nine fourteen, returning from Worcester, which matches what he told you. Then he and his wife come out again at nine forty-six, presumably on their way to church.'

Molly had Sophie run the tape again up to where the white van drove off, then slumped back in her chair. 'It could be anybody under that jacket and hood,' she complained. 'He never looks up once. That camera must be fifty or sixty yards away, but it's almost as if he knows it's there. And the black-and-white picture doesn't exactly help with the clothing, either. Is this the best we can do for clarity?'

'It gets more grainy if I enlarge it,' Sophie explained, 'and because of the way the van is parked, the number plate is unreadable. But if you look closely' – she ran the tape back – 'there's a dark strip that looks like rust along the bottom of the rear doors, and you can just see marks that could be scratches or grazes beside the right rear light. Forensic may be able to do something with the picture, and, if we can find the van, at least we know what to look for.'

Sophie sat back. 'And just in case Justine did go down Edge Hill Crescent and was picked up by someone in a car, I'm running a check on all the cars on camera around the time she disappeared. There aren't many; traffic was pretty light that early in the morning, but you never know.'

Molly's mind was running ahead. 'He got the time wrong,' she said. 'He was expecting Justine to be going to the *nine* o'clock mass as she usually did, assuming it was Justine he was waiting for, and I can't think who else it would be, so it has to be someone who knows her and her habits.' Molly continued to stare at the screen. 'I wonder who was looking after Michael Lorrimer while the Lorrimers were at church,' she said softly. 'I doubt if they would have taken him with them, and there was no one else in the house.'

'Didn't I see something in the notes about the woman in the cottage next door looking after the boy?' Sophie ventured.

'That's right, a Mrs Tillman,' Molly said, 'and thanks for reminding me. I think it's time I had a chat with her.'

NINE

'It's Tilly,' the woman said firmly when Molly introduced herself and addressed her as Mrs Tillman. 'And you'll be here about Justine, no doubt. Is there any news, Sergeant?'

'I'm afraid not,' said Molly, 'which is why I'd like to ask you a few questions, if you don't mind? And my name is Molly.'

'Then you'd best come inside and I'll put the kettle on,' said Tilly, dusting off her hands.

Tilly was a small woman, dark-haired, weathered face, arms lean and sinewy, as were her hands, roughened by years of working with the soil.

They were standing between the back door of the cottage and a large greenhouse. Molly had tried the front door without success, so she had come around to the back where she'd found Tilly potting up seedlings.

The cottage was small. 'Lieutenant Colonel Lorrimer had it built at the same time as Simla House,' Tilly told Molly. 'Built it for his batman and his wife. Like a lot of others in those days, the colonel brought his batman with him when he retired and returned to England, and he left the cottage and this bit of land to them in his will. Of course, it's changed hands a good many times since then. We came here nine years ago when Fred, my late husband, retired from the nursery in Pond Street.' She cast an enquiring glance at Molly. 'It's Stirling's now.'

Molly nodded. 'I've bought several plants from there,' she said. Most of which had died from neglect, she thought guiltily, but better not mention that.

'This place is small,' Tilly continued, 'but it suited Fred and me, because we spent most of our time in the greenhouse or the garden anyway. Fred was quite a bit older than me, but he was still only seventy-two when cancer took him, so I've been on my own now for the past five years.' She waved Molly to a seat at the kitchen table. 'Sit yourself down and I'll get the tea made.

It's not often I have company, but I'm sure I have a few biscuits in the cupboard.'

'Now,' Tilly said a few minutes later, as she poured tea and sat down facing Molly across the kitchen table, 'you were asking about Justine.' She pushed a plate of biscuits towards Molly. 'Lovely girl, and I don't just mean her looks; I mean as a person. Michael is so lucky to have her as a teacher – well, she's more than that to him. More like his mother, as far as he's concerned.'

Molly had intended to concentrate on whether or not Tilly had seen Justine last Sunday morning, but perhaps she would learn more if she allowed the woman to talk about the missing girl. 'Funny you should say that,' she said cautiously, 'but young Sylvia Lamb said much the same thing. Are you saying that Justine has literally taken his mother's place?'

Tilly dipped a biscuit in her tea. 'Bound to happen when your mother pays you no attention, and someone else does,' she said.

'I don't understand how any mother could do that,' said Molly, shaking her head.

'Well, now, don't be too quick to judge,' Tilly cautioned. 'It hasn't been easy for Julia. She started having morning sickness within three weeks of getting pregnant, and I don't mean just a little bit. It's called *hyperemesis* something or other. Like the duchess had, if you remember?'

'*Gravidarum*,' Molly supplied, 'and, yes, I do remember. It can be quite deadly, I understand.'

'And it nearly was in Julia's case,' said Tilly. 'That poor woman was as sick as a dog for eight long months, and then everything went wrong at the birth. They nearly lost her, and she was so ill she never so much as saw her baby until he was more than a month old. And when they told her he was partly blind, and had something wrong with his throat, she couldn't take it. She insisted he wasn't hers; said they'd made a mistake. She told the nurse to take him back to the nursery.' Tilly shook her head sadly. 'She was seeing a psychiatrist for months after she left hospital, but it didn't help. There was nothing there between her and the boy – no bond, no love. Nothing! Mind you, she'll deal with him if she must. I mean she'd never let him go hungry or anything, but she avoids contact with him if she can.' She sighed again. 'It's not the boy's fault, but there you are.'

'Where is Michael now?' asked Molly. 'I thought he might be here with you.'

Tilly used her spoon to fish a piece of soggy biscuit from her tea. 'He's gone out in the car with his dad,' she said. 'Michael loves riding in the car. At least the boy has one parent who loves him very much. Pity Stephen is away so much. Still—' Tilly stopped short. 'But here's me going on about things that are none of my business,' she said, 'and that's not what you came to talk about, is it?'

'We never know what might help in a case like this,' Molly told her. 'You seem to know Justine pretty well. How would you describe her?'

Tilly cocked her head on one side. 'She's bright, clever, very serious about her work, and completely dedicated to working with Michael. She enjoys her work. She told me that it's the best job she's ever had.' Tilly's face clouded. 'But she's not happy – at least, she hasn't been recently. I don't know if it's because she's worried about her grandfather in Manila, or what it is. She used to stop and chat and have a cup of tea, like we're doing now, but she hasn't been the same this past while. Preoccupied, as if there's something preying on her mind. Only last week, I told her she should spend some time over here with me in the garden and the greenhouse. It's a great way to relax. And I told her she should get out more, meet more people. She's too young to be cooped up in that old house all day, every day. She promised me she would, but . . .' Tilly wrinkled her nose and shook her head, 'I don't think she was *really* listening to what I said.'

'You say Justine *used* to stop and chat and have a cup of tea,' said Molly. 'Do you remember when that changed?'

'Yes, I do, as a matter of fact,' Tilly said slowly. 'It was around New Year when I first noticed it. I remember her bringing Michael over here the day after New Year, and she barely spoke two words. Just left the boy and scooted back next door as if someone was after her. I never did find out why.'

'How does Justine get along with Mrs Lorrimer?' asked Molly. 'It must be a bit difficult under the circumstances.'

Tilly took a few moments to answer. 'Now, isn't that strange?' she said. 'I've never given it much thought before, but they get along very well. Surprising, that, when you think about it.'

Maybe not so surprising, thought Molly, considering that Justine had relieved Julia of any responsibility for Michael.

'We know that Justine has one friend – Maria Navarro,' Molly said, 'but do you know of any others? Has she ever mentioned a boyfriend, for example?'

'She wouldn't have time for one,' Tilly said dismissively, 'and she certainly never mentioned one to me.'

'When was the last time you saw Justine?'

'Thursday. Last Thursday afternoon. She left Michael with me while she went off to the shops to buy Easter eggs for the children's hunt on Sunday afternoon. She said Stephen's brother and his wife – that's Richard and Eloise Lorrimer – and their two girls were coming back to the house after church on Sunday to have dinner with them, and they were going to have the Easter egg hunt in the afternoon.'

'Was Michael to be included?'

'Oh, yes. Michael gets on very well with Richard and Eloise's children. Chelsea's eight and Loren is six, and they don't seem a bit bothered by the sounds Michael makes, or the fact that he's blind . . . well, he has a little vision. He can see some things if he holds his head in a certain way, and he knows his colours.'

'But Justine wouldn't be there,' said Molly.

'I must say I am surprised she wasn't there,' Tilly said. 'She didn't actually *say* she would be, but it's not like her to miss something like that when Michael's involved.'

'So she didn't say anything to you about being away on Sunday?'

'Not a word. That's why I was so surprised when Julia brought Michael over before they went to church that morning.'

'Do you remember what time that was?' asked Molly, pen poised over her notebook.

Tilly thought. 'Half past eight – maybe quarter to nine,' she said. 'Julia said he'd had his breakfast, but the poor lad was still half asleep. That's when she told me that Justine was spending the day with her friend, the nurse, and she thought Justine had arranged for me to have the boy for the day. I told her Justine hadn't mentioned it when she was here last Thursday, which was a bit odd, because she was usually very good about that sort of thing, so something must have come up after that. Not that I minded having Michael, of course, but I'd planned to spend the day with my granddaughter, so I told Julia she would have to pick Michael up as soon as they got back from church.'

'Did she?' asked Molly.

'Actually, it was Stephen who came over,' Tilly said. 'Julia must have said something, because he apologized for dropping Michael off at short notice.' She lifted troubled eyes to meet Molly's own. 'Then, Monday afternoon, when Julia telephoned to ask if I had seen Justine or heard from her, I couldn't believe it when she told me Justine hadn't returned on Sunday night. It was so . . . so unlike her.'

So unlike her. How many times had Molly heard that before?

'I know you said the last time you saw Justine was last Thursday, when she brought Michael over, but I'm wondering if you might have caught sight of her going off to church on Sunday. Around twenty minutes to eight?'

'I'd be here having breakfast,' Tilly said, 'and you can't see anything of the house and the road from here. Why? Is it important?'

'It's just that we can't find anyone who saw her that morning, including people who know her at St Joseph's. Someone mentioned a path leading down to the river. Could Justine have gone into town that way?'

Tilly all but snorted. 'Have you *seen* the path?' she asked. 'It's steep and it's overgrown. I doubt if anyone's been down it for years, so I can't see Justine trying it in her Sunday clothes. No, I think you can forget that, Molly.'

'Do you know of any reason why Justine might have gone down Edge Hill Crescent instead of going uptown to church?'

Tilly's mouth turned down. 'There's nothing down there except those big houses above the road, so no, I don't know why she would go that way. Doesn't make sense to me.' She picked up her cup and put it down again, frowning as she did so. 'You asked me when I last *saw* Justine,' she said slowly, 'and I told you Thursday, but the last time I *spoke* to her was Saturday evening just before eight. See, I happened to mention some time back that I liked to watch *Midsomer Murders*, but I keep falling asleep in front of the telly before it comes on, so she phoned me just before eight to see if I was awake.' Tilly grimaced guiltily.

'Good job she did, because I was fast asleep when she rang, but I made a point of staying awake since she'd gone to the trouble to remind me. Not that it would have mattered; they're all reruns now, aren't they?'

'Did she say anything else?' Molly asked, suddenly hopeful, but Tilly was shaking her head. 'She just said, "Wake up, Tilly. Time for your show." So I thanked her and we both laughed and she rang off.' Tilly shrugged her narrow shoulders apologetically, 'Sorry, Molly, I know it doesn't help, but I thought I should mention it.'

'Don't apologize,' Molly told her. 'We never know what might help, so thanks for telling me.'

The expression on Tilly's lined face changed. Her mouth tightened into a thin line, and her eyes were bleak as she said, 'It's bad, isn't it, Molly? I mean, being gone this long without a word?'

'It doesn't look good, I'm afraid,' Molly conceded as she got to her feet, 'but we'll do our very best to find her. And thank you very much for your help, and for the tea and biscuits.'

Tilly rose and walked with Molly to the door. They stepped outside into the sun, and the fresh smell of bark mulch rose to meet them. Rhododendrons and azaleas, some in full bloom, lined the short walk to the greenhouse and the garden beyond, and for the first time that year Molly heard the soft sound of bees going about their business.

Impulsively, she turned to Tilly. 'You said you invited Justine to come here to relax, and I can see why. Would you think me cheeky if I asked if I could come and visit you sometime? It's so peaceful here.'

Tilly smiled. 'Any time,' she said. 'I'll put you to work, mind, but you'll enjoy it. Just don't forget once you leave here.' Her expression changed as she reached out to put a hand on Molly's arm. 'But find Justine first,' she said earnestly. 'Please.' She turned abruptly and walked away, but not before Molly caught the gleam of tears on Tilly's weathered cheeks.

Molly returned to where she'd left her car in the parking area below Simla House. But instead of getting in, she walked to the far end of the hardstanding to the break in the wall where the path began its zigzag descent to the river below. Began and ended, Molly thought, because the path soon disappeared into a tangle of spiky shrubs that would tear clothes to ribbons within a few feet of the descent.

So we can forget that, she told herself as she turned away. She checked the time. No excuses; she might as well get on with it. There was more than enough time to find Sebastian Mills and take a look at his car.

It was mid-afternoon when Tregalles came into the office, shrugged off his coat and flopped into a chair to face Molly across the desk.

'Bad as that, is it?' asked Molly, not unkindly.

'Dead end,' he said wearily. 'As you said on the phone, Justine must have gone down Edge Hill Crescent, probably to be met by someone with a car, but God knows where they went from there.'

'Sophie is already checking out cars that show up on the Edge Hill Road camera around the time Justine left the house,' Molly told him, 'but maybe we should be talking to the people in the houses above the crescent as well. It's a bit of a long shot, but someone might have seen Justine, or noticed a car parked there.'

'Already thought of that,' said Tregalles, 'but that can wait till morning. How did you get on with Mrs Tillman? And did you manage to get a look at Sebastian's car?'

'*Tilly*, as she calls herself, said she noticed a change in Justine just after New Year, but other than that . . . .' Molly shook her head. 'As for Sebastian's car, I'd be very surprised if Justine left that way. For one thing, Sebastian has long legs, so both his and the passenger's seat sit well back, leaving very little room behind the seats. I suppose it's *possible* that Justine was hidden on the back seat, but it would have been extremely uncomfortable.'

'Assuming she was alive.'

Molly grimaced. 'That's a bit of a leap, isn't it?'

Tregalles shrugged. 'Can't rule it out,' he said, 'but you're probably right. Did you look in the boot?'

'Of course I looked in the boot,' Molly shot back, annoyed that he should feel it necessary to ask the question. 'It was full of junk that didn't look as if it had been shifted for ages. There was even a box of empty beer cans in there, along with one of those bikes that comes apart in three pieces. It seems Sebastian is a bit of a health nut. He made a point of telling me he works out in the gym every day.'

'But he likes his beer,' Tregalles said. 'How did he react when you asked to look at his car?'

Molly smiled. 'He offered to take me for a spin, and he invited me out to dinner, not just once but twice during our conversation.'

'Did you accept?' Tregalles grinned wolfishly. 'I mean, a free dinner and a chance to do a little discreet questioning, perhaps? You could learn something.'

'Oh, I'm sure I would,' said Molly, rolling her eyes, 'but I doubt if it would have anything to do with the disappearance of Justine Delgado. Anyway, that's enough about Sebastian Mills; let's talk about something positive.'

'Such as?' Tregalles looked sceptical.

'Well, thanks to Sophie, I think we may be a bit closer to identifying the man I told you about on the phone. The one in the white Ford Transit. We don't know *who* he is, but I think we're close to tracking down the van.'

'A white Ford Transit with no markings?' Tregalles eyed Molly suspiciously. 'Get a tip, did you?'

'No tip,' Molly told him. 'Just some good work by Sophie when she realized that the van isn't entirely without markings.' She pulled out one of the stills taken from the tape. 'As you can see, there's a line of what looks like rust along the bottom of the rear doors, and some damage around one of the lights, so she started with that, and got a printout from the DVLA of all the Ford Transits registered to owners in this area. Once she had that, she eliminated all those owned by bakeries, florists, plumbers, contractors and other businesses, because they would have logos or lettering of some sort on them. Then she eliminated anything less than four years old, because of the rust beneath the doors, which left her with a grand total of eight, and I think there's a good chance that one of those eight will match the one on the tape.' Molly pushed a single sheet of paper across the desk. 'That's a list of the owners and their addresses,' she said, 'and I intend to start on them first thing tomorrow morning.'

Tregalles picked up the list. 'How'd she get DVLA to react

so fast?' he asked as he scanned the names. 'They've never done that for me.'

'Maybe it's because you're not Sophie, and you don't have that lovely Welsh accent,' said Molly, grinning. 'She can be very persuasive when there's a young man on the other end of the line.'

'None of the names ring a bell,' Tregalles said as he started to hand the list back, then paused to look at it again and sat up straight. 'I don't recognize the *name* – Mullen,' he said softly, 'but his address in Cogshill Lane is interesting. *Very* interesting.' He took out his own notebook and flipped the pages until he found what he was looking for. 'Yes, here it is. Maria Navarro, The Larches, Cogshill Lane. It's the same address!'

He snapped the notebook shut and looked at the time. 'I know it's late in the day, but I don't think we should wait till morning; I think we should go out there now. Maria told me that everyone in that house works at the hospital, so I think there's a better chance of finding this man, Gary Mullen, at home now, rather than tomorrow. Before we go, though, I'd better have a word with the boss and bring him up to speed, so I'll see you in fifteen minutes at the car. And give Audrey a ring for me, will you? Tell her I'll be a bit late home. Don't suppose you've got anything special on tonight, have you?' he asked belatedly.

No, nothing special on tonight, thought Molly bleakly as she watched him leave the room. Tonight or any other night for that matter, apart from her visits to the gym, and even they were becoming less frequent. Even so, the fact that Tregalles had assumed so casually that she would be free really irked her. He hadn't even waited for an answer.

Muttering beneath her breath, Molly took out her phone and scrolled to *Tregalles Home.*

TEN

There were only four houses in Cogshill Lane; all were on one side of the dead-end lane, all large, rambling old places, each with its own half acre of land. On the other side of the lane was a high brick wall, the rear boundary of a small industrial park.

The Larches was the third house down, half hidden behind a hedge that looked as if it hadn't been trimmed for years. Tregalles turned in and followed the short, once gravelled, rutted driveway to a grassy patch in front of the house on which three vehicles were parked – two cars and a white Ford Transit van.

'Just take a look at that little beauty!' Tregalles said as he got out of the car. 'That's a Porsche Carrera 911 convertible,' he continued almost reverently. 'Take a good look, Molly, because I guarantee you won't see many of those around here.' He glanced up at the house. 'I wonder who it belongs to. I got the impression from Maria that these people were all trainees like herself, and they'd joined forces to keep their costs down. But somebody's doing all right by the look of it. Whoever owns this car isn't some poor struggling student.'

'Could be struggling to make the payments, though,' said Molly. 'But it's the van we came to see,' she reminded him.

'Bit of a comedown, isn't it?' Tregalles said as they walked past the second car, an eight-year-old Renault Clio, to take a close look at the van beside it. 'Oh, yes, this is it,' he declared. 'Rust along the bottom, and there's the scrape next to the tail light. Let's go and see what this Gary Mullen has to say for himself.'

They mounted the wooden steps leading up to the front door and Molly rang the bell. From inside they heard someone yell, 'Somebody get that. I'm busy.'

The woman who opened the door was older than Tregalles had expected. At least ten years older than Maria Navarro. Dressed in an old shirt, jeans and a pair of well-worn Birkenstocks on bare feet, the woman looked as if she had been working hard. Her fair hair was pulled back and tied with a bit of cloth, and there was a faint sheen of perspiration on the broad brow above pale blue eyes. Molly's own eyes moved to the woman's hands. Capable hands, nails neatly trimmed and, like her toenails, varnished and clear, and there was a faint pale circle on the third finger of her left hand.

Holding up his warrant card, Tregalles introduced himself and Molly. 'And you are . . . ?' he asked.

'Linda Carr,' the woman said cautiously. 'What's this about?'

'We'd like a word with Gary Mullen,' Tregalles said. 'Is he in?'

The woman nodded. 'He's upstairs in his—' She stopped. 'Tregalles,' she said slowly. 'You're the one Maria told us about, aren't you? You're looking for Justine, right? Are you *sure* it's Gary you want?'

'Mind if we come in?' Tregalles stepped forward as he spoke, leaving the woman little choice but to step back. 'Perhaps you could call Gary,' he said as Molly followed him in, 'but no need to be specific. Just tell him he has visitors. Or we could go up,' he suggested when the woman hesitated.

'No, no need for that,' she said tartly. 'I'll get him down.' She walked back down the hall and climbed partway up the stairs and stopped. 'Gary?' she called. 'Someone to see you. Come on down.' She listened for a moment, then came back down the stairs.

'He'll be down in a minute,' she said. Then, 'There's nobody in the front room. You can use it if you like?'

Tregalles shook his head. 'This will be fine,' he assured her. 'And don't let us keep you. We'll just wait for Gary to come down.'

Linda Carr seemed unwilling to leave. '*Is* there any news about Justine?' she asked.

'You know her?' Tregalles countered.

'She's been here a few times, but I don't really know her. It's just . . . well, I mean, people don't just *disappear* like that, do they? Not on their own. So something must have happened to her. Maria's been *really* worried about her. They come from the same place, you know.'

'When you say Justine has been here a few times, how often would that be?' asked Molly.

Linda shook her head. 'I don't know, exactly,' she said. 'Three, maybe four times that I know of, but she may have been here at other times when I wasn't here.'

'You work at the hospital, do you?'

Linda nodded. 'Twelve years now,' she said. 'I'm a registered nurse.' She flicked her head towards the stairs. 'Gary's supposed to be training to be a nurse.'

Molly raised an eyebrow. 'Supposed to be?'

Linda Carr lowered her voice. 'He's young and still likes to burn the candle at both ends, and you can't do that if you're really serious about the work.'

A young man appeared at the top of the stairs: pudgy, pale, round face, dark hair and the beginnings of a stubbly beard. 'This them?' he asked Linda when he reached the bottom.

'Detective Sergeant Tregalles and DS Forsythe,' Tregalles said, holding up his warrant card once more. 'Mr Mullen?'

'That's right,' Mullen said warily. 'What's this about?'

Tregalles looked at Linda Carr and said, 'Thank you for your help, I think we can take it from here.'

'Take what from here?' Mullen asked truculently as Linda moved off down the hall. 'I haven't done anything wrong.'

'No one said you have,' Tregalles said mildly. 'But we would like to ask you a few questions. Is that your van outside? The Ford Transit?'

Mullen's eyes flicked from Tregalles to Molly and back again. 'Yeah,' he said cautiously. 'What of it?'

'Can you tell me where you were between the hours of eight and ten last Sunday morning?'

'I was here,' said Mullen. 'Sleeping it off, if you must know. There was a wedding party going on at the Three Crowns on Saturday night. Nobody seemed to care about who was ordering, so me and some of my mates crashed it. Don't know what they were serving, but it had a hell of a kick to it, because I don't remember anything much until Linda came in Sunday afternoon and started pouring coffee into me.'

'Do you remember what time you left the party?' asked Molly.

'I told you, I don't remember much of anything until—'

'Yes, we heard that,' Molly broke in, 'but we would still like to know where you were and what you were doing between the hours of eight and ten last Sunday morning. And "I don't remember" is not the answer we are looking for, so perhaps you could try harder, Mr Mullen.'

'But I *don't* remember!' Mullen protested. 'I don't even remember driving ho—' He stopped, squeezed his eyes shut and said, 'Oh, shit!' He opened them again. 'So *that's* what this is about,' he said with an air of resignation. 'But I got home all right. I mean, I know I probably shouldn't have been driving, but there's almost no one on the road at that time in the morning, so—'

'So you do remember what time it was when you drove home?' Tregalles broke in.

'Well, yeah . . . sort of. I'm not sure, but it wasn't anywhere near what you said: eight and ten? No way. More like midnight or maybe one? Check with some of the others here in the house. They were complaining about me waking them up when I came in.' He grinned weakly. 'I sort of fell up the stairs. They'll tell you.'

'So how do you explain the fact that your van was parked near the corner of Edge Hill Road and Lorrimer Drive between the hours of eight and ten last Sunday morning?'

'Couldn't have been my van,' said Mullen defiantly. 'You've got the wrong one. There's thousands of vans like mine out there.'

'There are a few,' Tregalles agreed, 'but not with the same band of rust along the bottom of the doors and a damaged panel by the tail light. So, I'll ask you again: what were you doing there?'

Mullen closed his eyes and clenched his fists. 'I keep *telling* you, I wasn't bloody there! I was here in my room, sleeping off one of the worst hangovers I've ever had. We shouldn't have tried to finish off the wine, but the others were swigging it down, and there was so much there it seemed a shame to waste it.' He put his hands to his head. 'My head hurts just thinking about it.'

'All right,' Tregalles said, 'then tell me who can verify that you were here?'

Mullen stared at him. 'I told you, I was in my bloody room!' he said through gritted teeth. 'I mean, the others heard me come in. They knew I'd had a bit too much to drink, so no one was going to come into my room. At least, not until Linda came in to make sure I was all right, and that was sometime in the afternoon. She'll tell you I was still suffering.'

'Who else has access to your van?'

'No one.' Mullen said.

'Anyone else have a spare set of keys?'

'No.'

'Do you leave a spare set where someone else could find them and use them?'

'Of course I don't. Do you think I'm daft? It's not much of a van, but it's all I've got, so I'm not going to leave keys lying about, am I?'

'Then I come back to my first question,' Tregalles said. 'If you are the only one with keys to the van, and the van was parked on Edge Hill Road for roughly an hour last Sunday morning, what were you doing there?'

Mullen threw up his hands. 'I've had enough of this,' he said. 'I'm going back upstairs and you can let yourselves out.'

Tregalles took one of Sophie's still photographs from his pocket. 'Before you go, take a look at this and tell me that's not your van. And then we'll go outside and see which one of us is right.'

'I don't need to go outside, because I know it's not mine,' Mullen said stubbornly. He looked at the picture, then shoved it back at Tregalles. 'And that's not me, either. I don't know who it is, but it's not me.'

'In that case, I think we should continue this conversation down at the station,' Tregalles said. 'And we will need to impound the van, of course.'

'I don't believe this.' Mullen put both hands to his head. 'Why won't you believe me? I haven't *done* anything, for Christ's sake!'

Tregalles sighed and shook his head as if weary of the conversation.

Molly stepped forward. 'The choice is yours, of course, Mr Mullen,' she said, keeping her voice calm and level, 'but it really comes down to this: you can cooperate with us here, or we will have to take you in for further questioning. So, since you are convinced that this is *not* your van in the picture, I suggest we go outside and compare it with the van itself. If you're right, you have nothing to worry about.'

Mullen eyed her suspiciously. 'I *was* here all day,' he said. 'I'm not lying.' He spoke earnestly as if he felt that if he could convince Molly, they might both go away.

'Then let's go and prove it,' Molly said. She opened the door. 'Do you have the keys with you?'

Mullen gave a grudging nod, then sidled past Tregalles and allowed Molly to shepherd him out of the house.

'Who does the Porsche belong to?' Tregalles asked as they passed the car.

'Oh, that's Paul's car,' Mullen said. 'His father gave it to him. The family's got pots of money.'

'So why is he staying here?' Tregalles asked. 'I thought you were all staying here because it's one way of keeping your living expenses down.'

'The *family* has money,' Mullen said, emphasizing the word, 'but Paul doesn't. His old man gave him the car, but that was it. As far as his father is concerned, Paul has to make it on his own. He has the car but it sits idle most of the time because he can't afford the petrol.'

They came to a halt in front of the van. Tregalles handed the picture to Mullen and said, 'Right. Take a good look at this, then compare it with the van, and show me where we're wrong. We'll wait.'

Three minutes later, a shaken Gary Mullen handed the picture back to Tregalles. 'It–it's the same van,' he said huskily,' but I swear that isn't me. And why would I be there anyway?'

'You know Justine Delgado?' Molly asked.

'Maria's friend?' he said. 'The one who went missing, right? So what's that got to do with me?'

'Do you know where she lives?'

Mullen shook his head. 'I only met her once, and that was here. I was just going out when she came to call for Maria. Maria introduced us as I was leaving.'

'Do you know who she works for and what she does?'

'Yeah, Maria told us. She's a nanny for some MP's kid.'

'Is that all you know about her?'

Mullen shrugged. 'I know she's been missing since Sunday,

and Maria's been worried about her, but that's—' He broke off
to stare at each of them in turn. 'You think *I* had something to
with that?' His voice rose. 'Is that what this is all about?' He
snatched the picture back from Tregalles and stared at it. His
already pale face turned even paler, and he looked as if he were
about to burst into tears. He appealed to Molly. 'Please, come
back in the house and talk to the others. They heard me come
in; they know the state I was in. I was out cold most of the day.'

'The keys, please,' said Tregalles.

Mullen started to reach for them, then stopped. 'What do you
want them for?' he asked.

'We need to take a look inside.'

'Don't see why you need to. I can tell you there's nothing
there. What do you expect to find anyway?'

'Possibly evidence relating to the abduction of Justine Delgado,'
Tregalles said. His voice hardened. 'Now, stop messing us about
and give me the keys!'

The clock on the mantelpiece was striking the half hour as Molly
let herself into the flat. Eight thirty, and all she wanted to do was
flop into a chair and put her feet up. At least she didn't have to
prepare a meal. She'd intended to pick up a takeaway from the
Mumbai Lotus on the way home, but once she was inside, the
food had smelled so good she'd changed her mind and treated
herself to a sit-down meal instead.

Molly took off her coat and kicked off her shoes. She was
tired, and she would have liked nothing better than to forget
about work for a while, but she couldn't. Like an endless tape,
the events of the day kept playing over and over again inside her
head.

They had gone back to the house where Molly had met Maria
Navarro, and all but one of the other members of the small
community. The missing member was Brigit Lystrom, another
student nurse, who was on the four-till-midnight shift.

Maria said that she and Brigit were both working the same
shift on Easter Sunday, so they had left the house together just
after six thirty that morning, and Gary's van was parked in the
middle of the driveway. She said that one of the doors was open,
so she closed it before going on to work. 'We heard Gary come

in earlier,' she told them, 'so I wasn't surprised to find the van where it was. He's done that before.'

'We?' Tregalles queried. 'You said, "*We* heard Gary come in"?'

'That's right,' Maria said calmly. 'We have our own rooms, but Paul and I sleep together in my room.'

'What about the keys? Were they still in the van?'

Maria shrugged. 'I didn't look,' she said. 'The door was hanging open, so I just pushed it shut as I went by.'

When Molly asked how she and Brigit had travelled to work, Maria said they'd cycled. 'Gary has his van, of course, and Chandra has his little car, but the rest of us have bikes – even Paul. That fancy car out there, the Porsche, is his, but he's been biking to work because the car is so expensive to run.'

Paul Wheeler had red hair, an infectious grin and an easy-going manner. As far as image was concerned, Molly thought, he'd do very well as a doctor. He told them that, as he'd had the Sunday and Monday off, he'd gone back to bed when Maria left for work on Sunday morning. Chandra Lali, another Foundation doctor, had had the weekend off as well, but he'd left the house on Friday evening to visit relatives in Birmingham.

'So, Linda and I were the only two people in the house that morning,' Wheeler explained. 'I'd had a tough week, so I thought I'd catch up on some sleep, but I'd forgotten that Sunday morning is when Linda does her washing, cleaning and vacuuming. Her room is downstairs at the back, and our bedroom is upstairs at the front, but this old place isn't exactly soundproof, so I finally gave up and got up around ten.'

'Just you and Linda?' Tregalles queried. 'What about Gary?'

'Well, yes, that's right, he was here – dead to the world, I should imagine, judging by the way he looked when he finally staggered out that afternoon.'

When he was asked if he had gone outside at any time, Paul said, 'Yes, I did. I went out to check the petrol gauge in the car. Maria and I were planning to go over to Ludlow for lunch on the Monday, and I wanted to make sure I had enough in the tank.'

'What time was this?'

'When I went out? Ten, ten thirty. I'm not sure exactly. Why?'

'Was Mullen's van out there?'

Wheeler hesitated. 'Why are you so interested in Gary's van?' he asked. 'Did something happen on his way home from the pub?'

'Where, exactly, was the van?' Tregalles asked, ignoring Wheeler's question.

'In the middle of the driveway where Gary left it. At least he hadn't left it running like he did the last time. And it's a good thing we're in a dead-end lane and very few people come down here, because the keys were still in it, and anyone could have taken it. Not that it's worth taking, but still . . . Anyway, I shifted it on to the grass and left the keys on the hall table.'

Tregalles had gone on to ask Wheeler about Justine. Did he know her? Yes, he said, he'd met her several times when Maria had brought her to the house. In fact, he'd driven her home once to save her the walk. But, as for knowing anything else about her, he said all he knew was what Maria had told him, and what he had seen about her disappearance in the papers and on TV.

Tregalles had switched back to Mullen. Had Wheeler seen him that morning? How did he know he was in his room? And could Mullen have been faking? Wheeler admitted he hadn't actually seen Gary until later in the day. 'But believe me,' he said, 'Gary wasn't faking; he was in rough shape.'

Chandra Lali, tall, lean-faced and very thin, confirmed that he had been away in Birmingham on the long weekend, so he knew nothing about what had gone on while he was away. He said he had met Justine only once, but he'd made it very clear to Molly and Tregalles that he took little interest in what the others did.

'I like my privacy,' he told them, 'and just because we live under the same roof does not mean that we have to share each other's company or activities. They have their lives; I have mine.'

Bedside manner zero, Molly remembered thinking. Lali's only comment about Gary Mullen was that he couldn't understand why the hospital allowed him to remain in the training programme, when he was so plainly unsuited for the job.

Molly's mouth was dry. She'd ordered the hot and spicy Lamb Biryani, a dish she'd had a number of times before, but someone in the kitchen must have spiked the sauce with extra-hot chilli peppers, because it had made her eyes water, and now it was repeating. She went to the kitchen and ran the water until it was very cold, then sipped it, holding it in her mouth for a few seconds before swallowing. It helped . . . but not much.

She refilled the glass and sat down again. Her body might be here at home, but her mind was still at work, or, to be precise, in the house in Cogshill Lane.

Tregalles had left the questioning of Linda Carr to Molly while he arranged for Gary Mullen's van to be towed in for forensic examination. 'I know it only arrived there well after Justine had left the house,' he'd said when Molly asked why, 'but that van has to be connected somehow. Mullen, or whoever it is in that video, was up to no good, so I want Forensic to go through it from stem to stern.'

Molly found Linda in the garden at the back of the house. She was weeding. 'It's not much of a garden,' she said apologetically, 'but we'll get a few vegetables off it, and I enjoy coming out here.' She flicked a nod in the direction of the house. 'They're a good bunch, by and large, but they're all quite a bit younger than me, and I like a bit of peace and quiet now and then.'

She stood up and dusted her hands off. 'But I'm sure you didn't come out here to chat, so what is it you want? Is this about Gary's driving the other night? Did something happen on his way home?'

'Let's just say we are more interested in what he did *after* he came home on Sunday morning,' Molly said. 'He claims he passed out in his room and remembers nothing until you came in to see how he was on Sunday afternoon.'

Linda sighed. 'He's his own worst enemy, that boy,' she said. 'He knows how drink affects him, yet he will go out and drink more than is good for him. My room is at the back, but I still heard him come in. It's a wonder he didn't do himself a serious injury on those stairs. He insisted later that he hadn't hurt himself, but he had a pretty good scrape on both knees when I took his jeans off him.'

Molly's eyebrows shot up. 'You took his *jeans* off him?' she said. 'When was this?'

Linda laughed. 'I couldn't go back to sleep without checking on him,' she said, 'and it was a good thing I did because he would never have made it to his bed. He was out cold on the floor. So I stripped him off and got him into bed.'

'By yourself?' Gary Mullen was no lightweight.

'I am a trained nurse,' Linda reminded her, 'and I've wrestled bigger men than Gary into bed.' Her expression changed as she caught the amused look on Molly's face. 'I could have put that better, couldn't I?' she said. 'But you know what I mean.'

'You didn't happen to look in on him later, did you?'

'Of course I looked in on him,' she said. 'I checked on him when I got up about seven thirty, and then later in the morning around ten.'

Molly took another sip of water and thought about Tregalles's reaction when she told him what she'd learned. 'And you're *buying* that?' he'd said. 'Stripping off his clothes and putting him to bed like he's some little kid? And then saying she checked on him in the morning?' He'd shaken his head. 'Can't see it myself. Mullen's not exactly an attractive specimen when he's sober; God know what he looks like when he's drunk. They aren't related, are they? I mean she's not his mother, is she?'

Molly assumed it was a rhetorical question, but she answered it anyway. 'Mullen is twenty-three and Linda Carr is thirty-seven,' she said. 'She's a registered nurse; she cares for people. And I think it has less to do with Gary needing someone to look after him than her need to look after someone.'

Tregalles grunted. 'So why is she living there with a bunch of students? Registered nurses are paid a decent wage, aren't they?'

'Decent wage or not, she's there for the same reason as the others,' Molly told him. 'Low rent. After fifteen years of marriage, her husband, a doctor, cleaned out their joint bank account and took off with a nurse ten years younger than Linda. She can't afford anything better.'

'But we know it's Mullen's van in the video,' Tregalles persisted, 'so if Mullen wasn't the driver, who the hell was it? And what was he doing there?'

'According to Maria, the van was sitting there when she and Brigit went to work that morning,' Molly reminded him. 'Later, when Wheeler went out to check his own car for petrol, he said the van was in the middle of the drive; the keys were still in it, so he moved it on to the grass and left the keys on the hall table. But that was sometime around ten o'clock, so – in theory at least – anyone could have taken the van between the time Maria left and Paul Wheeler moved it from the driveway.'

'We'll see,' Tregalles said stubbornly, 'but my money's still on Mullen, and I think the Carr woman is covering for him.'

There had been no point in continuing the discussion, so the rest of the journey was driven in silence. Molly had worked with Tregalles long enough to know that once he'd made up his mind about a suspect, he hated to let go. But, given time to think about it, reason usually prevailed, and they would start afresh tomorrow.

Molly stifled a yawned. Give it a rest, she told herself, and settled down to watch TV. She was asleep in less than twenty minutes.

ELEVEN

Friday, 6 April

Tregalles was busy writing on the whiteboards as Molly fed him information from her own handwritten notes on Friday morning, when Paget came looking for a progress report. 'I have a meeting with DS Pierce in about twenty minutes,' he explained, 'so how did you get on yesterday afternoon?'

'We've tracked down the owner of the Ford Transit van that was sitting out there on Edge Hill Road last Sunday,' Tregalles told him. 'His name is Gary Mullen; he's not much more than a kid really, but according to Linda Carr, a registered nurse, he spent the morning in bed with the mother of all hangovers, after crashing a wedding party and drinking himself legless the night before. We've checked and verified that he was at the party with two of his mates, who both spent the best part of Sunday in much the same condition. They both live at home, and their parents confirm their story.'

Molly, who had moved back to her desk to take a phone call, rejoined them. 'That was a callback from the Birmingham police,' she told them. 'They've given me the names of thirteen witnesses – aunts, uncles, cousins and friends – who are prepared to swear that Chandra Lali was with some or all of them throughout the Easter weekend, so I think it's safe to say it isn't him on the tape.'

'So, with Maria Navarro and Brigit Lystrom both at work, that only leaves Linda Carr and Paul Wheeler,' said Tregalles. 'The van was sitting there in the yard; the keys were in it, so, theoretically, anyone could have wandered in and taken it. But it had to be someone who knew where Justine lived, and also knew that she usually goes to mass at nine on Sunday morning. Wheeler admitted to driving Justine home on one occasion, so he knew where she lived, and he could have learned about Justine's regular attendance at church from Maria. He volunteered the information that he had moved the van from where Mullen had left it, but he may have done that deliberately to account for any prints he might have left behind.'

Tregalles picked up a marker pen and put crosses against the names of everyone living at The Larches in Cogshill Lane, except Wheeler's, then stepped back and folded his arms. 'It has to be him,' he muttered, more to himself than the others, 'but I'll be damned if I can see the connection between him sitting out there in Mullen's van, waiting, we *assume*, for Justine, and her disappearance an hour earlier.'

'I wonder if Wheeler was stalking her,' said Molly. 'Maybe he'd tried it on with Justine at some time in the past, perhaps when he drove her home, but when she told him she wasn't interested, maybe he started stalking her. We've been told that Justine appeared to be worried about something, yet she wouldn't talk to anyone about it. If she was being stalked by Maria's boyfriend, she may have been trying to find a way out of the situation without hurting Maria. But if Wheeler was persistent, perhaps even threatening, Justine might have suspected that he would be waiting for her on Sunday, and decided to leave earlier to avoid him. And, just to be sure, she went down Edge Hill Crescent instead of taking her usual route, which is why she doesn't show up on camera.'

'To where?' Tregalles demanded. 'It would take her half an hour or more to get to St Joseph's that way, *if* she was going to church at all.' He stood back to eye the board. 'Do you know what I think?' he asked, then went on to answer his own question. 'I think Justine Delgado set this whole thing up. I think she'd arranged to meet someone – probably a man she didn't want anyone to know about. She probably knew about the traffic camera just up the road from Lorrimer Drive, because she'd pass it every time she went into town, so she arranged for this person to pick her up in the crescent. The question is: did they ride off into the sunset together, or was the boyfriend just bait for an abduction?'

'We have people tracking down the owners of the cars that appear on camera around the time Justine disappeared,' Molly reminded him, 'but no luck so far.'

'I'd like to see if there is anything to this stalking theory of yours,' said Paget, 'so I think the sooner you talk to this man Wheeler, the better.'

Paget climbed the stairs to the second floor and was heading for the partly open door of DS Pierce's office, when he was stopped by Fiona McRae, Pierce's secretary.

'She's on the phone,' she said. 'I don't think she'll be much longer' – Fiona indicated one of the lights on her phone and lowered her voice – 'it's Chief Superintendent Brock,' she said, 'and he doesn't usually stay on very long.'

Just long enough to tell you he was displeased with something, Paget thought. He couldn't remember having a conversation with Morgan Brock when the man wasn't complaining about something.

'Any news about the missing girl?' Fiona asked. 'They had her picture on TV again last night. Such a pretty girl.'

'Afraid not, but we're still hopeful,' he said.

Was he still hopeful? Or was it just something you said, when all the time that inner voice was telling you that the chances of a happy outcome were fading rapidly with every passing hour?

'But five days . . .' Fiona shook her head. It was as if she had read his thoughts. The light on the phone went out. Paget tapped on the door and went in.

The sun had broken through, and Amanda Pierce had risen from her desk to adjust the Venetian blinds to make the most of it. Impeccably dressed as usual, this morning she was wearing a two-piece suit in soft greys with contrasting touches of charcoal on the collar, pockets and cuffs of the jacket, over a plain white blouse and straight skirt. And with the sunlight on her face, Paget was transported back to when he'd first set eyes on her almost twenty years ago. Amanda Pierce and Jill Hambledon were two young, enthusiastic probationers, and he'd been attracted to them both. In the end, he'd married Jill, and it had been the right decision, but as he looked at Amanda now, he couldn't help thinking how easily it could have gone the other way.

'Anything new on the Justine Delgado case since this morning?' she asked as she returned to her seat and motioned for him to sit down.

'We have one new line of enquiry regarding the driver of the

Ford Transit van,' he said. 'We think it could be Paul Wheeler, Maria Navarro's boyfriend, and Forsythe wondered if he was stalking Justine. If she's right, and Justine knew or suspected that Wheeler – assuming it *was* Wheeler – was waiting for her out there, that could be the reason she decided to leave early and take evasive action to avoid him. But that doesn't explain why she is still missing.'

Pierce's blue-grey eyes held his own for a long moment. 'Do I detect a change in tone in this investigation?' she asked.

Paget nodded slowly. 'The trouble is, I don't know whether this is something Justine planned, or if it's something she *thought* she'd planned, but it all went wrong.' He hunched forward in his chair. 'You see, the thing I keep coming back to is this: apart from the clothes she was wearing, and a handbag, Justine Delgado took nothing with her that suggests she intended to be away for more than the day. In fact, given what we've been told about her attachment to the boy, everything suggests that she had every intention of returning to the house that evening. Forsythe mentions unfinished knitting on the girl's bed, which is another indication that Justine intended to return. So, what may have started out as a secret assignation, or whatever you wish to call it, something or someone prevented her from coming back as planned.'

Amanda Pierce was nodding her agreement even before he had finished speaking, but Paget had the feeling that there was something else on her mind. 'I've just had a phone call from Mr Brock,' she said, confirming his suspicions. 'He is questioning the use of our resources on a missing persons case, and I'm afraid I didn't have much of an answer. I did point out that it was Mrs Lorrimer, wife of our MP and friend of the chief constable, who had appealed to you directly, but I had to agree: it's not really our case.'

'I don't agree,' said Paget. 'I think this young woman could be in danger, if she isn't already.'

Amanda Pierce slid her glasses into place. 'Sorry, Neil,' she said, sounding as if she really meant it, 'but this is not negotiable. So, as we're coming to the end of the week, I think this would be a good time to start getting the paperwork together so that Missing Persons can be fully briefed on Monday morning.'

Paget had been gone for several minutes, but the image of him lingered in Amanda's mind. For one brief moment when he'd first come in, it had seemed as if all those years apart had disappeared, and they were back to a time when things were different. There had been something about the way he had looked at her. It was gone in an instant, but, in that fleeting moment, memories and feelings she'd long thought dead had shouldered their persistent way into her consciousness . . . again.

She closed her eyes, but if she thought by doing so she could shut out the past, she was mistaken. Images long suppressed came back to life: images of herself and her best friend Jill, and Neil and Matthew, Jill's younger brother. The four of them had been almost inseparable back then, but while neither she nor Jill would ever admit it, it had always been a contest for Neil's attention. Jill had won, and Amanda had been her maid of honour at the wedding. A short time later, she'd married Matthew, convinced that she was in love with him. It was only later that she realized her mistake.

Amanda shook the image away, annoyed with herself for allowing her mind to drift. So much had changed since then: Jill was dead, Matthew was dead, and Neil was married to Grace Lovett . . . well, *living with*, which amounted to the same thing, she supposed, suddenly irritable.

This was her life now, she told herself sharply, and the sooner she stopped thinking about what might have been, the better.

TWELVE

'He should be out in about fifteen minutes,' they were told when Tregalles and Molly finally tracked Paul Wheeler to one of the lecture rooms on the second floor of the hospital. Tregalles was all for having Wheeler called out, but Molly persuaded him to wait. 'We don't know for certain that it is Wheeler in the video,' she said, less confident now than she had been when she had first voiced her suspicions about the doctor, 'and pulling him out in the middle of a lecture could make us look bad if we're wrong. And it is only fifteen minutes.'

In the event, it was closer to half an hour before the door opened and a stream of young men and woman filed out. Wheeler spotted them as soon as he came out, but quickly averted his eyes. He began talking animatedly to the young woman beside him, and would have walked past them if Tregalles hadn't stepped forward to intercept him.

'Sergeant,' he said, feigning surprise. 'I didn't expect to see you here at the hospital.' His expression changed to one of concern. 'I hope everything is all right?'

'That rather depends on your answers to some questions we have,' Tregalles told him. Wheeler turned to the young woman beside him. 'You go ahead,' he said, lowering his voice to a confidential tone. 'I'll be along in a few minutes.' He reached out, and for a moment it looked as if he was about to pat the young woman on the bottom, then changed his mind and moved his hand up to rest lightly on her shoulder. 'Really, it's all right, Jenny,' he assured her. 'I'll be there in a few minutes.'

'We're running late as it is,' she warned, looking at her watch and then at Tregalles to make sure he got the message. 'I'll save you a seat.'

Wheeler watched her go, then turned back to Tregalles. 'That's quite true,' he said, 'we are running late, so if you could be brief . . .'

'We've taken a closer look at the tape taken last Sunday of Mr Mullen's van and the driver on Edge Hill Road,' Tregalles said. 'We now believe that the man on the tape is you, Doctor Wheeler, so we would like you to come with us to the station to answer a few questions.'

Wheeler drew back, brow furrowed as if he couldn't believe what he was hearing, then shook his head. 'That's quite, impossible,' he said. 'I can't just leave the hospital. I'm part of a team, and we still have some practical work to do.' He moved in closer and lowered his voice as three young nurses walked by. 'As for your tape, I was nowhere near Edge Hill Road last Sunday, so I'm afraid you must be mistaken.'

'Oh, I don't think we are,' said Molly. She had been watching Wheeler closely, and she'd seen the way the young nurses had looked at him as they went by, and how their heads went together to whisper once out of earshot. 'The images on the tape itself were a bit grainy, but Forensic has a programme that enhances images, bringing everything into sharper focus. The driver of the van is wearing a hooded jacket, and I suspect we might find one to match it if we were to search your room. Or perhaps you have it here today?'

Wheeler's eyes narrowed, moving from Molly to Tregalles and back again. 'Let's go and find out, shall we?' Tregalles said. 'Where do you keep your street clothes, Doctor?' He reached out to take Wheeler by the arm, but the doctor stepped back and held up his hands in a gesture of surrender. 'All right, all right!' he said. 'So perhaps I did hold out on you a bit yesterday, but there's no need to go all officious about it. I had a good reason. I can explain.' He glanced up and down the hall, then moved in closer. 'But not here.' He nodded in the direction of the lecture room behind him. 'This room is free now, so why don't we go in and clear up this misunderstanding like civilized people?'

'Misunderstanding?' Tregalles said as they moved inside. 'I don't think so, Doctor Wheeler. You lied to us and you could be charged with obstruction, so whatever your explanation, it had better be a good one.' He pulled one of the metal chairs from the end of a row, and thrust it at Wheeler. He pushed another chair in Molly's direction, then sat down himself.

The doctor looked pained. 'I didn't have much choice,' he

said, 'not with Maria there. I mean, it's not as if I've done anyone any harm, is it?'

'You lied to us, which is an offence,' Tregalles said. 'Wasted police time, which is also an offence; interfered with an investigation into the disappearance of Justine Delgado . . . Would you like me to go on, Doctor?'

Wheeler shook his head impatiently. 'I'm sorry,' he said, 'but it would have been hard to explain with Maria there. She might not have understood—'

'Might not have understood why you were out there waiting for Justine shortly after getting out of Maria's bed?' Molly cut in coldly.

'It wasn't like that,' Wheeler snapped.

'Then tell us what it *was* like,' Tregalles said. 'Tell us why you were stalking her. How long has this been going on?'

Wheeler pulled back as if he'd been stung. 'I was *not* stalking her,' he said. 'I was hoping to catch her on her way to mass to . . . well, to apologize.'

'For . . . ?'

Wheeler shifted uncomfortably in his seat. 'It's . . . it's embarrassing,' he said sheepishly. 'I mean, I really thought . . . well, the truth of the matter is, when I drove Justine home the first time, she gave me a sort of peck on the cheek when she thanked me and said how much she appreciated the ride, so when she did it again the second time, I thought . . . well, I kissed her back, and . . .'

'And what?' Tregalles demanded harshly.

Wheeler glanced at Molly, then looked away. 'I didn't mean anything by it,' he said, 'but there she was in the car, close, leaning over me, and I got a bit carried away.' Wheeler turned his attention to Tregalles and said, 'You know how it is? These things happen, don't they?'

'Not to me, they don't,' the sergeant snapped. 'You groped her, didn't you?'

'I wouldn't call it that,' Wheeler protested. 'I mean, it was just a bit of fun, and—'

'To you, perhaps, but not to her. What did Justine do?'

'She punched me,' he said. 'Hard. Made my nose bleed.'

'When was this?' Tregalles asked.

'A couple of weeks ago.' Wheeler sat up straighter in his chair. 'I've been trying to get hold of her to apologize,' he said, 'but she wouldn't answer my phone calls, so I went over there on Sunday because I knew she always went to mass at nine, but she didn't show.'

'To apologize?' Tregalles said. 'Or to teach her a lesson? Teach her that she couldn't do that to you and get away with it?'

Wheeler was shaking his head. 'No, no, it wasn't like that,' he said. 'I really did want to apologize. Honestly, I swear. I didn't mean her any harm.'

'But apologizing wasn't the only reason you were there, was it, Doctor?' Molly said. 'You were scared to death that she would say something to Maria. So, how far were you prepared to go to make sure she didn't tell her friend?'

'Honest to God, I just wanted to talk to her,' said Wheeler. 'Maria had told me how religious Justine was, so I thought that might work in my favour if I asked her to forgive me. Really, that's all I intended to do, but, as I said, she didn't show.' He looked at each of them in turn. 'That's it,' he said, 'I've told you everything, so can I go now?'

Tregalles shook his head. 'It doesn't work that way,' he said. 'You're coming with us to Charter Lane to make a formal statement.'

'Just one question,' said Molly. 'Why did you use Gary's van and not your own car?'

'Oh, that,' said Wheeler. 'I thought if Justine spotted my car, she might take off before I could talk to her. But the main reason was because my car takes too much petrol, so I thought I might as well use Gary's. He'd never miss it.'

So there it was, thought Molly as she entered her flat and dropped her keys on the hall table. Case closed. At least, that's what it amounted to as far as they were concerned. Paget had broken the news to them on their return from the hospital. Tregalles had protested loudly, but, as Paget said, it wasn't open for discussion. Move on, he'd said. But it wasn't that easy. How long, she wondered, would it be before she stopped scanning the missing person reports or running a quick check on HOLMES 2?

She shrugged out of her coat and jacket and hung them up.

She stood for a moment, inhaling and exhaling rhythmically, while stretching sinuously like a cat. It was hard to imagine, but she had a whole weekend to herself. She could do what she liked, so she would have to give that serious thought while she made dinner. Italian tonight, and she'd picked up a bottle of wine on the way home to go with it.

She switched on her computer on her way to the kitchen, returning a few minutes later to see if she had any messages. Receiving mail. Just spam, she thought. She'd been getting more and more of it lately, and she was about to turn away when a word caught her eye. Two words, actually: Hong Kong!

Molly dropped into the chair and clicked on the message.

PART 2

THIRTEEN

Wednesday, 9 May

Twenty minutes till midnight. Close enough, thought George Holland as he took a last look around the yard. The overhead lights were on – not that they would deter anyone who was determined to climb the wall to search through the bins in the hope of salvaging something of value. They did, regularly, and George couldn't see the harm in it. If something had been tossed away that someone else could use, why not let them take it? Wasn't that what recycling was all about? As far as he was concerned, the best thing about the yard lights was that they saved the scavengers from stumbling about in the dark and injuring themselves.

The rest of the evening crew had already gone. They'd worked hard tonight, shifting more than a ton of materials into boxes, bins and special containers, so he'd let them go early. He took one last glance around the yard, checked that the big gates were secure, then left by the side gate, locking it behind him.

George paused to stretch and look up at the sky. It was a clear night; the moon had yet to rise, but the stars were pinpricks of light in the night sky. He inhaled deeply, then let his breath out slowly. Funny how different it felt. The yard was just as open to the stars, but somehow it was different on this side of the high brick wall of Broadminster's recycling depot.

The rest of the crew had cars or bikes, but George walked to and from work, a ten-minute stroll down River Road, and on a night like this it was good to be out.

Headlights appeared at the bottom of the hill, and George could hear the heavy beat of throbbing music attempting to compete with the roar of the engine of the fast accelerating car coming like a rocket up the middle of the road. Arms were waving through open windows and voices screamed in time with the mind-numbing beat. Teenagers on a drunken joyride.

George stopped in the shadow of the wall. You never knew what kids would do – they could be out of their minds on drugs – so he stood still and hoped they wouldn't notice him. They were almost past, when suddenly one of the voices rose, not singing now but screaming! He looked back and saw a car had come round the corner at the top of the hill, and was coming fast down the centre of the road! George squeezed his eyes shut, clenched his fists and waited for the crash. Tyres screamed in protest; a horn blared. George opened his eyes to see the second car had swerved and was bearing down on him. Blinded by the headlights, he flattened himself against the wall. Something brushed against his coat . . . He opened his eyes in time to see the car bounce off the wall ten feet beyond him. He watched, paralyzed with fear, as the driver fought to gain control. The car zigzagged back and forth across the road before it finally straightened out. George expected it to stop; expected the driver to get out to see if he was all right. But it didn't stop. Instead, it picked up speed and kept on going down the hill to disappear around the corner at the bottom. He looked back up the hill. The other car was gone. Wouldn't you know it? He was almost killed, and that carload of idiots had made it without a scratch!

He stood there shaking. If ever he wished he had a mobile phone, now was the time. His daughter had been after him to get one for years, but he'd always said he didn't need one. His legs were shaking, and it took him a couple of minutes of deep breathing before he could trust them not to give way beneath him. He'd call the police when he got home. He might have been scared shitless, but at least he'd kept his wits about him, and he could tell them the make and more or less the model of the car. And he could give them the number plate – not all of it, but enough for them to trace the bastard who had almost killed him.

Thursday, 10 May

The call was logged in at 06:19. A fisherman by the name of Alan Hughes said there was a car in the river near an abandoned boathouse below River Road. The PC who took the call was having trouble finding the location on the map until Hughes told him to look for a small road leading from River Road to the boathouse, and ended by saying, 'It's more or less opposite the recycling depot.'

That rang a bell. The PC recalled a report he'd received just after midnight from a man who said he'd come close to being killed outside the recycling depot when a car swerved to avoid a head-on collision with another car full of hooligans. He asked Hughes to stay there, and said he would have someone there within ten minutes.

Hughes, a man in his late sixties, and in good shape for his age, had climbed the hill and was waiting on River Road for them when the patrol car arrived and PCs Perry and Lancaster got out. 'You can see for yourselves where the car went over,' he told them. 'It looks like it got partway down the track, then got too close to the edge, and the ground gave way. The car rolled and finished up in the river. It's hard to see it because the water's not all that clear, but you can see where it went in, and I found one of the doors and some bits and pieces on the side of the hill when I was climbing up here.'

Hughes pointed to the door as they made their way down the hill, and was about to continue on down when Lancaster shouted, 'Hey! Look over there!' They followed the line of his pointing finger, then all three men began to scramble crabwise across the face of the hill to where a body lay partly concealed by bushes. Lancaster, the younger and more agile of the three, reached the body first – a boy, seventeen or eighteen perhaps, dressed in torn jeans, sweatshirt, socks and one shoe. His hair and face were covered in dried blood, and there was more blood and dirt on his sweatshirt. The young policemen checked for a pulse, then snatched his hand away as if he'd been stung. 'He's alive, for Christ's sake!' he croaked hoarsely. 'We need an ambulance.'

The ambulance arrived twelve minutes later, but it took the combined efforts of the police and the medics almost half an hour to get the injured youth wrapped warmly, strapped on to a stretcher and carried to the waiting ambulance. When they checked his pockets for ID, they found nothing except thirteen pounds and change, together with a clear plastic envelope containing half a dozen tablets, concealed in the waistband pocket of his jeans.

'Ecstasy,' the older of the two medics declared, and added it to the rest of the information on his clipboard.

More police arrived. The entire area was cordoned off, and two men in a boat probed the water with poles until they determined that the car was resting right side up some thirty feet from shore. 'The top is about four feet under water, but the current's strong, so we can't do anything without divers.'

'Not going in to work this morning, then, Ron?' Vera Styles asked her husband innocently as he came out of the bathroom. She looked pointedly at her watch. 'A bit hung-over, are we, after last night's bash at Harry's?' Try as she might, she couldn't keep the smile out of her voice.

Ron Styles shook his head. 'I think the steak was a bit off,' he said. 'I don't think Harry had the barbecue hot enough. Or it could have been the sauce.'

'Sauce as in drink, maybe?'

He scowled. Vera didn't like Harry, which was why she hadn't gone with him last night. She hadn't wanted him to go either, but Harry was a mate he'd known since school, so he said he was going whether she wanted to come or not, and now she was giving him a hard time. 'So we had a few beers,' he muttered as he brushed past.

Vera followed him down the stairs. 'Well, don't expect me to phone your boss and lie for you,' she said. 'You can do that yourself. Anyway, if you're feeling so bad, why did you get up and get dressed?'

'I have to take the car in,' he said tersely.

'Why? What's the matter with it? It was all right yesterday.'

'It . . . it's the brakes. I think they're losing fluid. It could be dangerous, so I'm taking it in this morning.' Brakes should be a safe excuse, he thought, praying silently that Vera wouldn't go out to the garage to take a look for herself.

'Well, I suppose,' Vera said grudgingly. 'You going into work after you take it in to Tony's?'

He wasn't going to Tony's, but he didn't intend to tell Vera that. Almost anywhere *but* Tony's in fact. Tony would want to know every last detail, and he'd share the information freely with anyone who came into his garage. Besides, Tony didn't do bodywork.

'Maybe,' he said. 'I'll see what I feel like.'

'So, how long will it be in the shop? Brakes shouldn't take long, should they? I need to go shopping this afternoon.'

'Depends how busy he is.' God! He wished she'd shut up.

'Do you want some breakfast before you go?'

'Don't feel like eating,' he said. 'Anyway, time's getting on, so I'd better be off.'

The front doorbell rang. They could see a shadow through the frosted glass at the end of the hall.

'See who that is, Ron,' Vera said. 'I don't want to go to the door looking like this.'

He walked to the door and opened it. 'Mr Styles?' The uniformed policeman was big. Pleasant-faced, but big! 'Mr Ronald Styles?' he said. Ron nodded. 'Tell me, sir, do you own a six-year-old Volvo, registration number . . . ?'

There was a sudden roaring in his ears and he didn't hear the rest.

It was almost eleven o'clock by the time the regional dive team arrived and were satisfied that all precautions had been taken before they entered the water. Once there, it took only a few minutes to establish that there were three bodies trapped in the car. One, apparently the driver, later identified as eighteen-year-old Gerry Slater, had become entangled in the airbag in his struggle to get out through the window. In the passenger seat was sixteen-year-old Debbie Woodruff, trapped when her seat had come forward to jam her legs beneath the dash. And behind the driver's seat, face down on the floor, was fifteen-year-old Barbara Hodge, with what appeared to be a broken neck. None of the three had been wearing seatbelts, although whether they would have saved anyone was open to question.

Paget, who had been monitoring the situation since his arrival at work that morning, decided to visit the scene himself, and he was there when the divers arrived. There was no indication that a crime had been committed, but there was a report of a near head-on collision, and if that was what had forced this car full of teenagers off the road, there would be an investigation.

'From what we're told by the man who says he was almost killed last night, and the tyre tracks on the road, it looks as if the car coming up the hill swerved to avoid a head-on with the car coming down,' one of the white-suited men explained to Paget. 'And the only option he had was to take the opening to the track leading down to the old Broadminster Rowing Club boathouse. Trouble is, the track is in poor shape, and it's in even worse shape now, because the car took out a chunk of it when it went over.'

Carved out of the hillside, the gravelled track seemed solid enough to begin with as Paget started down, but he hadn't gone far before he saw potholes and cracks where tufts of grass had broken through, and the outer edge was crumbling in several places. It was probably safe enough for a car driven slowly, but at high speed? There was no way! He paused to look at where the front wheel had slipped over the edge and the car had rolled.

A trail of debris marked its path before plunging into the river: a blanket, maps, first-aid kit, a cushion, papers caught in bushes, an umbrella, tools, sunglasses, a plastic container half full of windscreen washer, and the rear door from the passenger's side of the car.

One of the white-suited men approached Paget when he reached the bottom. 'Lucky this didn't go into the water with the car,' the man said. 'Saved you a bit of time and trouble.' He handed Paget a log book identifying the owner of the vehicle as Dr Lydia Bryant, who lived on Falcon Ridge, an affluent area of Broadminster.

So, unless one of the teenagers was a member of the Bryant family, the car was probably stolen, and when Paget called back to the station to check, he was told that Dr Bryant had reported her fifteen-year-old Audi A4 stolen from the driveway outside her home. The report was logged in at three minutes past nine that morning, but she said the car could have been stolen at any time after eight o'clock the previous evening. 'It was locked, and I didn't hear anything,' she'd said, 'so I didn't know it had been taken until I went out this morning.'

When Paget was asked if Dr Bryant should be notified that her car had been found, he said, 'No. Let's wait until the car is out before we notify her.'

The bodies had been laid out on plastic sheets on the narrow footpath and a makeshift screen set up around them. But when Dr Reginald Starkie arrived, there was little he could do beyond taking temperatures and directing the photographer to take pictures of the injuries before ordering the bodies to be covered and carried up to the road.

'Are you quite sure that no one else is trapped down there?' Paget asked one of the divers. 'The report we had from the man who claims he was nearly killed last night said that one of the cars was full of screaming teenagers, so I'd like you to go as far as the next bend in the river, just to be sure.' If there had been others in the car, and they had been swept beyond the bend, they could be anywhere downstream, so there was nothing to be gained by extending the search until they knew more.

The divers slid into the water, and Paget made his way along the bank to take a look at the old boathouse that was once the home of the Broadminster Rowing Club. The clubhouse itself was tucked into a fold in the hill, with a canopied extension, supported by pilings, jutting some twenty to thirty feet into the river. It was a sad-looking building: the paint on the warped wooden siding was peeling, the glass in some of the windows was gone, and some of the pilings needed replacing. The tunnel-like canopy over the water was made of heavy canvas; once taut and tight-laced, it was now ragged and sagging between rusting metal ribs.

He was about to turn back when he noticed a man sitting quietly on a large slab of rock, smoking a pipe. A folded fishing rod and basket lay in the grass beside him. Paget recognized the man as the fisherman who had reported the car in the river.

'Mr Hughes,' Paget said. 'I thought you'd gone home. I must thank you for bringing this to our attention.'

'Can't fish, so I thought I'd just sit here and watch for a while,' the man said. 'Haven't seen this much activity along here in many a year. Old hat to you, no doubt, but all new to me.'

'Do you fish here regularly?' Paget asked.

'Used to come the odd Sunday when I was working,' Hughes told him, 'but now that I'm retired I try to get down here two or three times a week. Gets me out for a walk and a bit of fresh air.' A sly smile touched his lips. 'And I can smoke my pipe.'

'I thought the boathouse was no longer in use,' said Paget, 'but I see two skiffs moored to the pilings down there, and they don't look very old.'

'The rowing club moved out a couple of years ago,' Hughes said. 'The place was falling apart, and the road was in need of repair. They couldn't afford to fix everything up, so they packed up and left. But there are still a few who moor their boats here from time to time because it's free.'

Paget's mobile phone rang. 'PC Thomas, sir, up here on the road,' a voice said when he answered. Paget looked up and saw a man in uniform give a brief wave. 'It's about the crane, sir,' Thomas continued. 'It's here, as you can see, but there's a problem. I'll hand you over to the operator and he can explain it better than I can. His name is Carter. Here he is now.'

Paget could see a man wearing a hardhat take the phone from the constable and put it to his ear. 'What's the problem, Mr Carter?' Paget asked.

'The problem is the distance between where I'm standing and the river,' said Carter. He looked like a big man, but he had a thin, asthmatic voice. 'Even with the extension, the boom of my crane won't reach far enough out to lift the car straight up in a sling, and there's not enough room down where you are to get equipment in, so we'll have to do it in two goes, if that's all right with you, sir?'

'When you say "two goes", will you explain that to me, Mr Carter?'

'Right. What I mean is, if the divers can attach the cable well enough to take the weight of the car, I can winch it on to the bank and drag it partway up the hill to that bit of a flat spot over to your right. That will bring it within reach, so, when you've done whatever you have to do, we can get a sling under it and I can lift it straight up and on to the trailer.'

Paget could see the problem, and Carter was right: there was no other practical way to lift the car out of the river. 'Very well, then,' he said, 'we'll do it your way, Mr Carter. However, the divers still have some preliminary work to do before we stir up the mud by moving the car, so I'll have to ask you to be patient. Shouldn't be too long.'

'It's all the same to me, sir,' the man said. 'We bill by the hour, so take as long as you like.'

Paget heard a shout as he pocketed the phone. One of the divers was making his way to shore. He pulled himself out and gestured for Paget to join him.

'We've found another body,' the man said as Paget approached. 'It's only a few yards away from the car, but we almost missed it because it was half buried in the mud. But this one comes gift-wrapped, and it's held down by a couple of what looks like ten-kilo barbell plates; one's wired to the neck, the other to the feet.'

'Could the body have been thrown from the car?'

'It's . . . possible,' the diver said doubtfully. 'As I said, it's half buried in the mud, so it looks to me as if it's been there for some time. But, if it *was* slung from the car, what with the weights and all, I suppose it could have buried itself. But which-ever it is,' he continued, 'we could do a lot of damage to the body if we try to bring it up with the weights attached, so I'd like to cut them off and bring them and the body up separately. We can do that without unwrapping the wire; there must be at least ten feet of it around the neck and legs.'

'In that case, go ahead and do it that way,' said Paget, 'but I want the body and the weights kept below the surface of the water until they can be brought on to the bank under cover of the screens. There are too many people up there on the road with mobile phones and cameras, and I'd like to keep this one from public view until we've had a chance to see what we've got. And bring up anything else you find that looks as if it might be relevant.'

Paget took out his phone and called Tregalles. What had begun as an almost routine investigation into the cause of a tragic acci-dent had changed with the discovery of the additional body. 'We have the accident on one hand,' he told Tregalles, 'and a suspi-cious death on the other, and I don't know whether they're linked or not. An autopsy could settle it, but that will take time, so I'm going to assume, for the moment at least, that the body could have been thrown out of the boot of the car. Anyway, that will be for you to follow up, so you'd better bring Forsythe with you.'

The body was wrapped in layers of black plastic. Industrial-strength bin liners, it was determined later, held together with what must have been at least one full roll of duct tape, and possibly more. It was bound so tightly that Paget wondered if any water had managed to get in at all. But that was for Starkie to find out, and the doctor was not in the best of humours when he was called back to the scene. In fact, when Paget described the body, Starkie flatly refused to come down the hill to examine it. 'There is no way I'm going to take that plastic off down there,' he told Paget, 'but tell the divers I need to know the temperature of the water where it was found. And tell them to handle the body very carefully.'

Easier said than done. The narrow hillside road was too rough for the small wheels of an ambulance trolley, so, like the others, anonymous in a body bag, the plastic-wrapped body was carried up on a stretcher by four sturdy constables.

'Let's hope that's the last of them,' Starkie muttered as the body was being loaded into the van. 'There's not much doubt about the way the rest of them died, but the coroner will probably want autopsies done on all three, so you may have to wait a bit for this one. In any case, I won't be able to do a PM until Monday at the earliest, because we're closed until then for the quarterly inspection and decontamination.'

'You have a problem?' asked Paget.

'The place is old and hard to keep as clean as it should be,' Starkie told him. 'You've seen it. They keep saying they're going to build a new facility, but it never happens, so I have the place scrubbed from top to bottom every three months.'

Paget remained on site only long enough to brief Tregalles and Forsythe when they arrived, and to watch as the car was pulled ashore. The divers had tied the boot and the rest of the doors shut so they wouldn't be torn off or damaged further when the car was dragged on to the bank. 'Everything was open when the divers first found it,' Paget explained, 'so it's possible that the body was thrown from the boot when the car went in. The divers think not, but it's something to keep in mind.'

Paget turned to leave, then paused. 'I'm going to the hospital to see how the young chap is doing – the one who was thrown clear and spent the night up there.' He pointed to a marker halfway up the hillside. 'I'll have a word with him if he's in a fit state, and find out what happened.'

Tregalles and Molly exchanged glances as Paget moved away.

'Looks like he's back in the saddle again,' Molly observed drily. 'I wonder what happened to spending more time in the office.' She saw the flush of disappointment on Tregalles's face, and wished she'd bitten her tongue. She had assumed that Paget was handing the investigation over to Tregalles. Clearly, Tregalles had thought the same, but, whether Paget realized it or not, he'd assumed command, and it didn't look as if he intended to give it up. Was it force of habit, Molly wondered, or was there some other reason? She could almost see the same thoughts going through Tregalles's mind, and she wished there were something she could say. But that might make it even worse, so she decided to say nothing.

FOURTEEN

'Fortunately, it wasn't very cold last night,' the doctor said, 'so Mr Kendrick is warming up quite nicely. We're keeping an eye on him, of course, because he did suffer a mild concussion, but it would seem that his fall was cushioned by bushes; he has cuts and scratches all over his body, but nothing too serious. And being either drunk or stoned – I don't know which, because I haven't seen the blood tests yet – probably helped. It would keep him relaxed when he tumbled out of the car. Barring the unforeseen, he'll be as right as rain in a couple of days: bruised and sore, but no broken bones.'

'You say his name is Kendrick? There was no identification on him when he was found.'

'A and E recognized him,' the doctor said. 'His name is Walter Kendrick; he lives by his wits on the streets, and he's been in several times with food poisoning. He's one of these people who will eat anything that appears to be remotely edible, and I suspect his main source of food comes from bin diving, and that, together with drugs and alcohol, when he can afford them, can be a very unhealthy combination. I'd be surprised if he hasn't been in your care at one time or another.'

'Is he conscious?' asked Paget. 'The sooner I can speak to him, the better, because he is the only one who can tell me exactly what happened when that car went over the edge and into the river. The boy isn't in any trouble as far as we're concerned, so there will be no pressure on him. I just want to know what happened.'

'In that case, I can't see any harm in it,' the doctor said. 'His injuries aren't serious, but he is under light sedation until we're satisfied that there are no after-effects from the concussion, so he might be a bit groggy. But you're welcome to try as long as you don't press him too hard. I'll have a nurse accompany you, and it will be up to her to decide if you are putting too much pressure on the boy.'

Kendrick was dozing, twitching restlessly. There was almost no colour in his face and he was painfully thin. It had taken only one phone call to the office while Paget was making his way upstairs to learn that boy had been living on the streets since he was fourteen. Walter Kendrick, he was told, had gone to bed as usual one night, but when he got up the following morning, his parents had disappeared, taking all their worldly goods with them, together with as much of the landlord's small furniture as they could pack into their battered van. The boy had been taken into care, but he didn't like that, so he had ended up on the streets, where he joined a group of tearaways led by Gerry Slater.

Now, seated beside Kendrick's bed, Paget coaxed the boy awake. 'I won't keep you long,' he promised when he'd introduced himself and had the boy's attention, 'so if you can just tell me what happened when the car you were in went off the road, I'll let you go back to sleep.'

'Gerry was driving,' Kendrick said quickly. He might not be fully awake, but his brain was alert enough to tell him to push whatever blame there might be on to someone else. 'I just went along for the ride. He swerved to avoid a head-on, and the next thing I knew the car was doing somersaults. My door came off – just disappeared – and I was flying . . .' His eyes slipped out of focus. 'Flying,' he repeated lazily. 'Never felt like that before. It was cool, man.'

'And you landed in the bushes,' Paget said.

'Suppose so.' A pale hand came out from under the covers to touch his face, and his voice took on a stronger tone. 'How does it look?' he asked anxiously. 'I mean, what's it going to look like? Will there be marks?'

'I shouldn't think so,' Paget told him. 'Your nose is swollen, but it will go down, and the scratches will heal. You were very lucky.'

'Yeah.' Kendrick closed his eyes. 'They told me the car went in the river, and they're all dead. They *really* dead, or were they just shittin' me?'

'You are the only survivor, I'm afraid,' Paget told him. 'But tell me, how many were there in the car when it went off the road?'

'Gerry and Debbie and Barbie Doll.' Kendrick screwed up his face to peer intently at Paget. 'You *sure* they're gone?' he asked. 'I mean, we were just having fun. Gerry was driving. Geez! That car went up the hill like a rocket. Flattened me back in my seat like I couldn't breathe. Debbie was hammering her fist on the dash and yelling for Gerry to go faster, and Barbie Doll was screaming her head off. Then this car comes outa nowhere. Gerry swerved—'

'Are you quite sure that there was no one else in the car?' Paget cut in.

The boy shook his head and winced. 'No, that was it, man. Piggy wanted to come, but Gerry wouldn't let him.' Kendrick's face clouded. 'He shoulda let him come, because it was him who found the car back of Parkside Place and brought it round. Wide open, he said it was, just asking to be taken.' Kendrick snickered. 'Said he'd come to give Gerry a ride in his new car, but Gerry tossed him out and we all piled in.' Kendrick frowned, and his watery blue eyes drifted away from Paget's face. 'But then Piggy'd be dead as well if Gerry had let him come, wouldn't he?' he said sadly.

'Piggy?' Paget said. 'Does he have another name?'

'Ummm.' The boy was beginning to drift. Paget reached out and shook his shoulder gently. 'Don't do that, man,' Kendrick chided sleepily. 'That hurts.'

'I need a name,' said Paget. 'What is Piggy's real name?'

'Sammy, Sammy Pollock.'

'Where did he get the car? Come on, Walter, stay with me for a couple of minutes, and then I'll let you go back to sleep. Where can I find Sammy Pollock?'

Kendrick tried to focus his eyes on Paget, but they wouldn't stay open. 'Joyride,' he muttered sleepily, and giggled.

'Joyride?' Paget echoed sharply. 'Please, Walter, just answer the question. Where can I find him?'

'Who?'

'Pollock. Sammy Pollock.'

'Dunno. We left him. Gerry shouldn't't've done tha . . .'

There were other questions Paget wanted to ask, but Walter was fast asleep, and he had enough to be going on with. Time enough for a formal statement from the boy when he was fully recovered. But first things first: he needed to talk to Sammy Pollock.

Arriving back in Charter Lane, Paget was about to enter the building when the custody officer, Sergeant Sam Broughton, came down the steps. 'Finished for the day,' he announced with some satisfaction when they met at the bottom. 'I'll be glad to get home and put my feet up.'

'Bad day, Sam?' Paget asked.

'It's the knees,' Broughton said, glancing up at the sky. 'Weather's going to change and the buggers are letting me know it.' Sam had arthritis in both knees, and there were days when he found it almost too much to stand up.

Paget was about to continue on his way, but the name "Sam" triggered an association with the name Walter Kendrick had given him. 'What do you know about a kid by the name of Sammy Pollock?' he asked the sergeant.

'Piggy Pollock?' Broughton sighed and shook his head. 'Oh, yes, we've had him in a few times. What's he done now? Something to do with cars—' He stopped, eyes narrowing. 'Oh, don't tell me he was in the car that went into the river?'

'No, he wasn't one of them,' said Paget, 'but I'm told by the boy who was thrown out of the car, Walter Kendrick, that it was Pollock who stole the car in the first place. It was a boy by the name of Gerry Slater who was driving when it went into the river.'

'I heard,' Broughton said heavily. 'We've had Slater and Kendrick in a few times as well. So, what do you want to know about Piggy?'

'First of all, why is he called Piggy?'

'It's his nose. It's sort of turned-up and flattened out a bit. It's really not that bad, but somebody started calling him Piggy and it stuck. He's not a bad kid if we could just find a way to stop him nicking cars. Drives his mother crazy. She tries, but nothing seems to work.'

'How old is he?'

'Fifteen, maybe sixteen by now.'

'Where would I find him?'

'His mum lives over the other side of the river in the Flats, but Piggy's never there. You'll probably find him down the bottom end of Bridge Street in the arcade. He's crazy about video games. You could try Zapp or Joyride, which is where Slater and Kendrick usually hang out. Sammy's always trying to get in with some of the older crowd down there by giving them stuff he nicks from cars, but they just use him to run errands and things like that.'

'So that's what Kendrick was telling me when he mentioned Joyride,' said Paget. 'He told me that young Pollock said he found the car behind Parkside Place, that block of flats facing Victoria Park, but Doctor Bryant said it was stolen from her driveway on Falcon Ridge. That's right, isn't it, Sam? You must have seen the report.'

Broughton nodded. 'That's right. Sometime after eight o'clock last night. And now you come to mention it, I can't see it being Piggy. I've never known him to go any further afield than King's Road and the station for a car. I doubt if he's ever *been* up there to Falcon Ridge, so either Kendrick was having you on, or someone else stole it in the first place and Piggy picked it up later.'

'I don't think Kendrick was lying,' said Paget. 'He'd been sedated, but he seemed lucid enough. And I find it hard to believe there were two separate thefts, which leaves me wondering . . .'

'If Doctor Bryant was telling the truth about where it was taken from?' Broughton finished for him. 'Do you want Piggy brought in?' The sergeant made to turn and go back up the steps, but Paget stopped him. 'Thanks just the same, Sam,' he said, 'but your shift is over, so go home and give those knees a rest.'

He was toying with the idea of leaving Sammy Pollock until the following day, but when he spotted one of the junior DCs trying to make himself invisible behind a police car while he enjoyed a smoke, Paget changed his mind. 'Cruickshank!' he called loudly. 'Just the man. I have a job for you.'

Friday, 11 May

'The divers seem to think that the body with the weights attached to it had been down there for some time,' said Paget as they were wrapping up the Friday morning briefing. 'They said it was half buried in the mud, and they'd have missed it altogether if it hadn't been for the gold coating on the weights catching the light when they were searching the area for things thrown from the car. And, until I spoke to Sammy Pollock, I was almost prepared to accept that, but Pollock insists that he took the car from where it was parked in the lane next to the back door of Parkside Place, whereas Doctor Bryant claims her car was stolen from outside her home on Falcon Ridge. Now, when it comes to credibility, normally I would go with Doctor Bryant's version, but I can't see any reason for Pollock to lie, and Falcon Ridge is certainly well beyond his normal stamping ground. However, since we have virtually nothing else to go on until we have the results of the autopsy next week, we might as well work with what we have, so I suggest we start with a visit to Doctor Bryant.'

'Wouldn't the boy look in the boot to see if there was anything worth stealing?' asked Molly.

'He claims he didn't,' Paget replied. 'He says all he wanted to do was show it off to Slater and his mates, and take them for a ride. But Slater pushed Sammy out of the car and took off with the others. So,' he concluded, turning to Tregalles, 'I'd like you to go and talk to Doctor Bryant and see if she can offer an explanation. But don't mention the fourth body – at least not yet. When I spoke to her yesterday afternoon to tell her that her car had been recovered, I told her someone would be coming out to talk to her today, so she is expecting you.'

'What do we know about Doctor Bryant, other than what's in the report on the theft of her car?' Tregalles asked. 'What kind of a doctor is she?'

'She's a consultant psychiatrist,' said Paget. 'Her husband is Geoffrey Bryant, a psychotherapist. You may remember there was a piece in the paper about him a couple of months ago. He has a private practice here in town, but he donates a couple of days each week to work with traumatized military servicemen and women in the Queen Elizabeth Hospital in Birmingham. Doctor Lydia Bryant works from home. She told me she has appointments beginning at two this afternoon, but she is free this morning.'

The driveway curved gently upward beneath a canopy of arching trees, opening out to reveal the house itself. Faux Georgian was what they were calling them these days, Tregalles recalled, although this particular house was on a smaller scale, and looked the better for it. Small stands of fir and spruce bracketed the house like bookends, to 'ground' it, in the parlance of estate agents, and make it look as if the house and trees were part of the natural landscape. But the trees would have to grow a bit before that happened, he decided as he got out of the car.

He mounted the shallow steps and rang the bell, then turned to admire the view of the town on the far side of the river valley, with the hills of Wales as a backdrop. The sun glinted on windows of houses, and he realized that one of those houses was Simla House. Strange the way that young woman had disappeared without a trace, he thought sadly, and felt a twinge of guilt for having allowed it to slip so easily from his mind in recent weeks.

The door opened behind him, and a pleasant voice said, 'DS Tregalles, I presume?'

Surprised, as much by the form of address as the greeting itself, he turned to see a slight, neatly dressed young woman looking at him with amusement. 'DS?' he echoed.

Her smile grew wider. 'I have a brother-in-law in the West Yorkshire Police,' she said. 'He's also a detective sergeant, so I'm familiar with the ranks. My name is Naomi. I'm Doctor Bryant's secretary. Please come in. Doctor Bryant will be with you in a couple of minutes.' She led Tregalles across the spacious hall and into what he guessed was a comfortably furnished waiting room for Doctor Bryant's clients. 'Can I get you something? Coffee . . . tea, perhaps?'

'I imagine the sergeant will be far too busy for that, Naomi,' a voice said briskly, 'so let's not detain him unnecessarily.'

The woman who had entered the room so silently was tall, slim, beautifully made-up and expensively dressed. Good-looking, classical features, in fact, but there was no softness to them. 'Professional' was the word he used to describe her later. Fortyish, perhaps? He looked at her hands. Older, he decided.

'Good morning, Sergeant. I'm Doctor Bryant,' she said. 'Now, how can I help you?' She didn't offer him a seat.

'About your car,' Tregalles began, only to be interrupted by Dr Bryant saying, 'Ah, yes, my car. I saw the poor thing on TV last night. I suppose it is a complete write-off?'

'I'm afraid so, Doctor,' Tregalles took a folded paper from his jacket pocket. 'This is a list of items that were either in the car or close by in the water, or scattered about the hillside before it entered the water. Obviously, anything that would float is gone, and there may be things the divers recovered that didn't come from your car. Perhaps you could take a look to see if anything significant is missing?'

A pair of glasses hung from a thin gold chain around Lydia Bryant's neck, and she put them on before taking the paper from him. 'They asked me what was in the car when I reported it missing,' she said as she scanned the page, 'but I had no idea there were so many bits and pieces in there. All I can say is this looks about right.'

'Nothing missing that you can think of?'

Dr Bryant shook her head. 'I can't think of anything.'

'The car was locked, was it, when you left it the other evening?'

'Of course. I believe I made that clear when I reported it.'

'Could I see the keys?'

Lydia Bryant's eyes narrowed. 'Are you doubting my word, Sergeant?'

'Not at all, Doctor. The insurance claims adjuster will want to know if we checked, and Forensic will need them when they examine the car, so if you wouldn't mind . . .'

'I see. In that case, I'll give them to you when you leave. Anything else?'

'You said the car could have been taken at any time after eight o'clock on Wednesday evening, but you didn't hear anything?'

'That's right. As I explained, I was either in the back of the house or in the den with the television on, so I wouldn't have heard it in either case.'

'But the alarm?' Tregalles said. 'I'm not familiar with the alarm on your particular car, but I'm sure it must be pretty loud.'

'The car is fifteen years old,' Lydia Bryant reminded him, 'so I don't know if it even *has* an alarm. I can't recall ever hearing it.' She took off her glasses to look directly at Tregalles. 'And I believe I answered those questions when I reported the car missing. So why are we going through this again, Sergeant?'

'Well, to be honest, Doctor, we have a bit of a problem,' he said. 'You see, we've been told by the sole surviving joyrider that the car was stolen from behind Parkside Place in town.'

'Really?' Lydia Bryant frowned. 'Then either your informant is wrong or the car was stolen twice in one evening.'

'Who else was in the house on Wednesday evening? Your husband, perhaps? Children? Anyone else?'

The doctor shook her head. 'My husband is a psychotherapist,' she said, 'and he spends every Wednesday and Thursday in Birmingham. He stays in town overnight on Wednesday and comes back Thursday evening. We have no children, so I was here alone.'

Tregalles looked surprised. 'No live-in help, then?' he asked.

'I have a housekeeper who comes in daily, as does Naomi, and I'm not entirely helpless myself,' the doctor said drily. 'And I can't quite see what my staffing arrangements have to do with the theft of my car. What, exactly, is your point, Sergeant?'

'I'm just trying to account for how the car came to be stolen from here in the first place, and how it ended up behind Parkside Place,' Tregalles said, 'and one of the possibilities I was considering was that someone from here – a young person, perhaps – might have "borrowed" it to go into town, but was afraid to admit it.'

Lydia Bryant looked pointedly at her watch. 'As I said, Sergeant, I was here alone, so I'm afraid you will have to work that one out for yourself. Is there anything I have to do about my car? Or will that be dealt with between you – that is, the police – and the insurance company?'

'We'll take care of that, and you will be kept informed,' Tregalles assured her as he made a move towards the door. 'And the keys?' he reminded her.

'Oh, yes, the keys,' Dr Bryant repeated. 'We mustn't forget the keys, must we? I presume you would like both sets?'

Lydia Bryant waited until she was sure the car was gone before picking up her mobile phone and scrolling through the list of contacts until she reached *Podiatrist*. She had never been to a podiatrist in her life, and the person at that number was certainly not in that profession, but it served as a cover in case someone – someone like her husband – happened to pick up her phone and started searching for names.

FIFTEEN

Tregalles wasn't buying it. Lydia Bryant was lying about the car being stolen from her driveway. It was a fifteen-year-old car, so why would someone go out of their way to go up a driveway to steal a car that he or she couldn't see from the road, and risk being seen from the house, when the neighbourhood was practically littered with much newer Mercs, Beamers and Jags?

Having read Sammy Pollock's statement before going to see Lydia Bryant, Tregalles decided to take a look at Parkside Place for himself. The block of flats faced Victoria Park, but it was the lane behind the building that interested him. Pollock had said he'd found the Audi 'sort of tucked out of sight next to the bins at the back'. And there they were: two large bins, one for waste and one for recycled materials, and next to them was a space marked *SERVICE VEHICLES ONLY*. More than enough room for Dr Bryant's car.

Tregalles circled the block. A ramp at the side of the building led down to secure underground parking for the residents of Parkside Place, and there were two parking spaces reserved for visitors at the front of the building. Both were occupied, so he took a chance and parked in a loading zone close to the entrance.

There were thirty-two units in the four-storey building. Tregalles ran down the list until he came to one marked *SALES/ MANAGER*. He entered the number, and was rewarded by a pleasant female voice saying, 'Can I help you, sir?'

He realized that he was on camera and held up his warrant card. 'Detective Sergeant Tregalles, Broadminster police,' he said. 'I'd like a word if you don't mind?'

'Of course. Please come in.' A buzzer sounded softly. He pushed open the heavy glass door and found himself in a spacious entrance hall paved with blue-grey marble tiles flecked with gold. Oak-panelled walls rose to meet a twelve-foot-high ceiling from which hung a chandelier, and facing him was the door of a lift.

Carpeted corridors ran to right and left, and Tregalles had the feeling that, if he spoke at all, it shouldn't be above a whisper.

'Sergeant?'

He turned to see a young woman standing in the entrance to one of the hallways. She extended a hand as she crossed the floor. 'Loretta Hythe,' she said, smiling, but there was a question in her eyes as they shook hands. 'Are you here on police business, or are you interested in one of our suites?'

Chance would be a fine thing, Tregalles thought. If Loretta Hythe knew anything about a sergeant's pay, she would know the answer to that question. 'Police business, I'm afraid,' he said. 'It's concerning a car that was stolen from behind this building on Wednesday night?'

'Really?' Loretta frowned. 'Behind this building? This is news to me.'

Through the glass doors, Tregalles saw a woman coming up the steps with a key in her hand. 'Perhaps we can go inside?' he suggested.

'Of course.' Loretta Hythe turned to lead the way to the first door they came to down the hall. 'This used to be the sales office and show suite,' she explained, 'but now that things have more or less settled down, this is actually my apartment.' She stood aside to let Tregalles through, then closed the door behind them. 'I keep this room as an office,' she explained, 'because I'm a sales rep for the company as well as the manager of the building.' With a graceful wave of the hand, Loretta Hythe directed Tregalles to a seat in one of several cushioned armchairs. 'Can I offer you some tea or coffee, perhaps?' she asked. 'It's no trouble.'

He was about to decline, then thought, *Why not?* Comfortable chair, *very* pleasant company, and he was in no particular hurry to get back to the office. 'If you're sure?' he said. 'Perhaps coffee . . .'

'I think Sammy Pollock was telling the truth about where he found the car,' Tregalles told Paget later. 'I read his statement, and he described the place where he found the car perfectly. I think Doctor Bryant was lying when she said she wasn't in town that night; I can't prove it, but I'm willing to bet she spent the night in Parkside Place. Her husband was staying in Birmingham that night, as he does every Wednesday night, and, with no one else in the house, she could be gone all night and no one would be any the wiser. I spoke to the manager there, but, as she said, people let visitors in all the time.'

'But not by the back door, surely?' said Paget.

'That's right,' Tregalles said. 'You can't buzz people in through the back door, but if you knew they were coming, you could be there to let them in. Or, because it's such a recognizable car, the doctor parked it there out of sight and walked around the block to enter by the front door. But if she is meeting someone in secret, I can't see her doing that.'

'So how did she get home in the morning?'

'The person she was with could have driven her home,' Tregalles suggested, 'or she could have called a taxi. If she did take a taxi, it shouldn't be hard to track down a fare from Parkside Place, or somewhere close by, to Falcon Ridge on Thursday morning.'

'What was your impression of Doctor Bryant?' Paget asked. 'I've only spoken to her on the phone, and she sounded pleasant enough. Upset about losing her car, of course, but quite reasonable otherwise.'

Tregalles considered the question. 'Struck me as a bit of a cold fish,' he said. 'All business. She's probably all right, but I don't think I'd like her messing with my psyche or whatever it is she does, even if it is on a couch. Now, if it was her secretary . . .'

'What did Doctor Bryant have to say when you told her that her car was stolen from Parkside Place?'

'She said either our information was wrong or it had been stolen twice.'

'Any nervousness at all? I'm thinking about the body,' said Paget.

'Not a flicker,' Tregalles told him. 'I don't know what else she was up to, but I can't see her leaving the car where she did if there was a body in the boot. Make a good book title, that would. *The Body in the Boot* . . . or maybe not,' he said quickly when he saw the look on Paget's face. He gave a little cough and cleared his throat. 'There are thirty-two apartments in Parkside Place,' he said, 'but only twenty-two of them have been sold, and I'm including the manager's in that number. Nineteen are occupied by married couples, or, in one case, an elderly woman with a live-in carer, so I think we can rule all of them out, but the rest look more promising.' He glanced down at his notebook. 'First, we have a solicitor by the name of O'Connor. He's in his late thirties, so he's a possible. There's Mr Dunsmuir, a surgeon at the hospital, fortyish and recently divorced, and then there's Larry Latham. Remember him? The manager of Woodlands Golf and Country Club? Charged with molesting a young woman a couple of years ago, but it was another case of "he said, she said", and he got off. Don't know how old he is, but he can't be more than forty-five or fifty, so he's a possible candidate.'

'How old is Doctor Bryant?'

'Hard to say under all that make-up. Forty to forty-five, maybe?'

'Why are the rest of the apartments empty?' Paget asked. 'Parkside Place must be at least two years old, so what's the problem with them?'

'The problem is the economy and timing,' Tregalles said. 'They're at the top end of the scale. To be fair, they are very nice – top quality all the way. Audrey would kill for one of their kitchens. But they misjudged the market, and the prices are just too rich for Broadminster. Most of the people who are in there got a discount when they bought off the plans three or four years ago, but by the time the place was built, people were starting to think twice before spending that kind of money. They haven't made a sale in almost six months.'

'What about CCTV?' Paget asked. 'Anything covering the back lane or the street?'

'Not directly, but there is a camera on the corner of Carlisle Street and King George Way, so anything coming out of the lane – like Pollock driving the doctor's Audi, for example – should be on that tape. That would corroborate young Pollock's story, but there is nothing covering the other end of the lane, which is where Doctor Bryant would have to drive in to park where she did. What we could do is look at the tapes on the route from Falcon Ridge into town on Wednesday night. With all those lights covering the roundabout at the bottom of Strathe Hill, we might see who's driving, and I'll bet it wasn't Sammy Pollock.'

'Good idea,' said Paget, 'but that can wait till Monday. The doctor may be lying about where her car was when it was stolen, but that may be to cover an extramarital affair rather than murder, so we don't want to stir things up needlessly. Apart from the body's proximity to the car, there is nothing to connect the two, and until that body is identified, we have virtually nothing to investigate. So enjoy the weekend while you can.'

'Well, at least we know the body isn't that of Doctor Geoffrey Bryant,' Tregalles said. 'He's been in his office since nine o'clock this morning. I checked.'

Sunday, 13 May

Ten o'clock on a Sunday morning, the whole day off, and she was still in her dressing gown. Molly poured herself another mug of coffee, then wandered lazily from the tiny kitchen to the living room. She took a slim folder from the bookshelf, then settled down on the sofa, legs tucked under her. Savouring the moment, she sipped her coffee slowly before setting the mug aside and opening the folder.

Emails from David. She'd saved every one of them, printing them off, as well as saving them to a separate flash drive. They were probably safe enough there, but she'd printed them because she liked to hold a piece of paper in her hands and read the printed words. It might not make much sense, but, to her, it brought the writer closer, and the words seemed to be more real.

Molly moistened her finger and flipped back several pages to the one dated the sixth of April. Strange how the days flew by at work, yet time slowed to a crawl when you were waiting for something really nice to happen at home. Like waiting for Christmas when she was a child. Molly slipped the page out, then closed the folder and set it aside. Another sip of coffee, adjust the cushions, wriggle around a bit to make sure she was really comfortable, because everything had to be just right before she read the email from David once again.

Dear Molly, I don't know how I can begin to apologize for . . . There it was again! That same surge of apprehension as she read the opening words. She knew there was no need to feel that way – she knew the words by heart – but it happened every time.

He was apologizing, he said, for not having written before,

then went on to explain that the malaria he had contracted in Africa, while working for Doctors Without Borders, had caught up with him again. The combination of long hours at the hospital, where he'd been working in Hong Kong, lack of sleep and ignoring the warning signs had led to his collapse. As a result, he wrote, *I've been 'completely out of it' for some time.*

He went on to say that his daughter, Lijuan, had been great, visiting him every day after school, even when he didn't know she was there, and it was she who had kept his aunt and uncle, Ellen and Reg Starkie, informed of his progress. Unfortunately, Lijuan had done all the emailing from her own Archos tablet, which, he explained, was what almost everyone was using over there, and Molly's email address wasn't programmed into Lijuan's tablet. So it wasn't until he had recovered enough to start looking at his emails that he realized what had happened.

Molly paused there as she always did. Did Lijuan even know about her? And if she did, even though her parents had been divorced for several years, and her mother was now dead, would Lijuan be resentful of her father exchanging emails with another woman? Not that Lijuan had any reason to be jealous or feel threatened. Molly and David had known each other for such a short time before he'd had to rush off to Hong Kong that they were really no more than friends keeping in touch . . . no matter how much she might wish for them to be more than friends.

Molly took another sip of coffee. It was cold. Frowning, she looked at the clock on the mantelpiece. Ten thirty? Where did that half hour go? She had things to do today; she should get on . . .

She snuggled down. She'd been saving the best part till last, and she was going to enjoy it, even if she had read it at least a dozen times before.

David and Lijuan were coming to England when Lijuan's school year finished in June. For a month! Partly, David explained, to help him get back on his feet again. The malaria had left him drained, he said, and the change would do him good. He was looking forward to seeing her again, and hoped that her new job as a detective sergeant wouldn't keep her so busy that they couldn't spend some time together!

SIXTEEN

Monday, 14 May

Dr Reginald Starkie unzipped the body bag and stood looking down at the black plastic-wrapped figure on the table. There was almost as much duct tape as plastic wound around the body from head to foot. The tightly bound and mud-caked body had been kept in the body bag to preserve the external evidence. Once the wire, duct tape and bin bags had been cut away, the body would be lifted clear, the bag zipped up, and it would be sent for further forensic examination.

After cutting off the two ten-kilogram plates to lighten the load in getting the body to the surface, the divers had left the rest of the wire in place, twisting the cut ends together to keep the wire from unravelling. It was copper wire – old, pitted with age and hard to bend – and Starkie was surprised that they'd managed to do such a neat job of it while under water. The weights themselves were sitting in an evidence bag on the floor of Starkie's office, and they, too, would be sent for examination. From what he had seen of them through the heavy plastic bag, they, like the wire, were old. Cast iron beneath a chipped gold-coloured metallic paint. Big mistake by the person or persons who had gone to all that trouble to dispose of a body, thought Starkie, because it had been the reflection from the paint that had drawn the weights to the divers' attention.

The pathologist glanced over to where Paget stood with arms folded, gowned and masked, and wondered why the DCI had decided to attend this particular autopsy personally.

With a nod to his assistant, they stripped away the body bag and began to untwist the wire.

Tregalles toyed with his coffee mug. Should he go out to the machine and refill the mug, or not? The coffee from the machine was even more bitter than usual this morning, but at least it was hot and it helped keep him awake after a restless night. Restless because, while he'd been pissed off with Paget for taking over a case that should have been his, he was experiencing an undercurrent of relief. He'd hardly dared admit it, even to himself, but it was beginning to feel like old times again, when he and Paget were a team, and he was feeling more comfortable in that role than he'd felt for some time.

He was sure that he could pass the inspector's exam, but the question was: Did he want to? Was he prepared to move out from under Paget's shadow and accept the responsibilities that went with the promotion?

His phone rang. He scooped it up as if it were a lifeline. 'DS Tregalles.'

'Got someone here who says you want to see him,' Sam Broughton said. 'Says he's a part-time cab driver for Ajax. I'm short-handed out here, so if you want him, you'll have to have someone come and get him. All right?'

Tregalles had been lucky. One phone call to the only taxi company of any consequence in town had produced a result when he'd asked if they had a record of anyone going from the Victoria Park area to Falcon Ridge, before nine o'clock last Thursday morning. There was one, the dispatcher told him, a woman who had called in at seven forty-five a.m. asking to be picked up at the Shelbourne Street entrance to Victoria Park. The name she had given was Rogers, but it had to be Lydia Bryant.

'I'll come myself,' he told Broughton, and grabbed his empty mug.

'They call me in if someone's ill or away for any reason,' Gordon Sloane explained. He was an older man, heavyset, grey hair, rheumy eyes and a breathing problem. 'Been doing it for more than a year now after I was made redundant. I used to be a manager at Draper's until they were taken over by a chain and they downsized. It meant I wasn't going to get as much pension, so I had to look round for work. Sometimes I get as much as a week's work out of it, but more often than not it's a night shift.'

Now, sitting facing the man on the other side of the table in the interview room, Tregalles sipped his coffee. He'd offered to get one for Sloane, but the man had taken one look at the machine as they passed by and said he preferred water. 'So, you were working last Thursday morning?' Tregalles prompted.

'That's right. Coming to the end of the night shift, when I got the call to pick up this woman outside Victoria Park.' Sloane pulled a folded paper from his shirt pocket and handed it to Tregalles. 'Lou, the dispatcher – he's the bloke you talked to – said you wanted to know what time she was picked up and so on, so he made a copy of the log. I got the call at twelve minutes to eight, and my log says I picked her up at four minutes to eight.' He handed Tregalles a second sheet of paper.

Tregalles looked at it and frowned. 'Destination 128 Condor Crescent?' he said with a sharp glance at Sloane. 'Are you quite sure of the address?'

'Oh, yes. Except she told me there was no need to go up the drive when I got there. She said something about it being hard to turn round up there, so she'd save me the trouble. It didn't make a lot of sense to me. I mean, a big house like that and a driveway where you can't turn round? But that's what she wanted, so I dropped her at the foot of the drive.'

'Outside 128 Condor Crescent? Not Eagle Crest Way?'

'I *do* know the difference,' Sloane said coldly. 'But she didn't go up to the house. She started walking up the drive as I drove away, but I had my sheet to fill in before going off shift, so I stopped a bit farther down the road, and I saw her in my mirror. She'd come out of the driveway and was legging it back the way we'd come to the steps.'

'The steps?'

'Steps that go all the way up the hill for dog walkers and the like,' Sloane explained. 'Saves them from having to go round all them winding roads to get down to the park at the bottom. Anyway, when I'd filled in my sheet, I carried on round the crescent to where it comes out on Eagle Crest Way, and I see her again. She was some distance away and her back was towards me, but it was her all right.'

'Did you see where she went? Which house, or at least which driveway?'

Sloane shook his head. 'I was going the other way, and I was late for my breakfast as it was.' Sloane sat back in his seat and folded his arms. 'So what's this all about, then?' he asked. 'What's this Mrs Rogers done?'

'I'm not sure she's done anything,' Tregalles said. 'Can you describe her?'

'She was tall; didn't get much of a look at her face. She was wearing a mac, all buttoned up, with the hood up . . . except it wasn't raining. Mind you, it was a bit nippy out. Oh, yeah, and high-heeled shoes. Shiny with real spikes on 'em. Not the sort for wandering about in the park, I shouldn't have thought.'

'Would you recognize her if you saw her again?'

Sloane thought about it, then shook his head. 'Like I said, I didn't get much of a look at her face, but I'd recognize the shoes, if that's any help?'

Tregalles smiled. 'It might be,' he said. 'You say you picked her up on the Shelbourne Street side of the park. What was she doing there?'

'Dunno. She was just standing there waiting for me.'

'Did she say anything when she got in?'

'Just gave me the address, then moved over to sit behind me so I couldn't see much of her in the rear-view mirror.'

'She didn't say anything else?'

'Not a peep till we got to the address, like I told you.'

When Tregalles returned to the office after assigning a DC to take Gordon Sloane's statement, he found Molly and Sophie Kajura looking pleased with themselves. 'We've been looking at the CCTV tapes from last Wednesday,' Molly told him, 'and Doctor Bryant's car came out of the lane behind Parkside Place on to Carlisle Street at nine minutes past eleven. You can't see who's driving, but there's no doubt about the car.'

'So young Pollock was telling the truth about that,' Tregalles said. 'What about earlier in the evening? Did we pick up anything from the cameras covering the roundabout at the bottom of the hill?'

Sophie turned the screen towards him. 'As you can see, we have a couple of clear shots of Doctor Bryant driving the car at nine fifty-three. They're a bit grainy, but there's no doubt about who is driving the car.'

'No doubt about it,' Tregalles agreed, attempting to match

Sophie's broad Welsh accent, and failing miserably. 'We'll need stills of both, timed and dated, and—' A short burst of musical notes interrupted whatever he'd been about to say. 'It's Paget,' he said, glancing at the screen before answering. His face became grave as he listened. 'You're quite sure?' he asked, as if not wanting to believe what he was hearing. 'Yes, yes, I see. Of course, but . . . Right. Two o'clock.' Tregalles drew in his breath and let it out again slowly as he pocketed the phone. 'They've identified the body the divers found in the river last week,' he said. 'It's Justine Delgado.'

Molly caught her breath and sat down hard. 'Oh, that poor girl!' she breathed. 'I was afraid she might be dead, but to treat her body like that . . .' She had never known Justine in life, but it felt as if she had, and she could feel the sting of tears behind her eyes.

'I know how you feel,' Tregalles said sympathetically. 'I wish we could have done more, but we had no leads. Anyway, there's to be a briefing here at two o'clock this afternoon, and Paget wants everyone who worked on the case to be here. Will you be all right, Molly?'

'I'll be fine,' she said as she got to her feet. 'It just took me by surprise, that's all. Don't worry, I'll be here.'

'And so will I,' Sophie said. She sounded as though she was looking forward to it.

A smile tugged at the corners of Tregalles's mouth as he moved away. He should be used to Sophie Kajura by now, but it still came as something of a surprise to hear the girl speak with such a strong Welsh accent. Sophie didn't talk much about herself or her family, but Tregalles had learned, mainly through Molly, that Sophie had been born in Uganda to a Ugandan father and Welsh mother, where both worked as teachers at a Christian missionary school.

Sophie was three years old when her father was killed by the LRA – the Lord's Resistance Army, as they called them-selves – during a raid on the school. By sheer chance, it was Sophie's mother's turn to drive into town for supplies that day, and she'd taken Sophie with her. A decision that saved both their lives, because, when she returned, it was to find her husband and every one of her colleagues butchered, the school and living quarters in flames, and the children gone – all thirty-three of them.

Less than a month later, mother and daughter arrived in Swansea, where they lived with Sophie's Welsh grandmother until Sophie's mother found a teaching job in Llanelli, which was where Sophie had grown up.

'Sophie may be Ugandan by birth,' he remembered Molly telling him, 'but she's as Welsh as they come.'

Tregalles had been suspicious when Sophie had first arrived from Uniforms with a scant two years in the service behind her – hardly a fair trade for Tony Brooks, who'd had close to ten years' service when he left. Was this, he wondered, a case of Uniforms getting rid of someone thought to be incompetent or who just 'didn't fit'?

But, if that had been their thinking, they'd made a bad mistake, because DC Sophie Kajura had turned out to be a gem. For a start, she'd put two years of legal training behind her before opting to join the police. She was a quick learner and a hard worker, and he appreciated the good work she had done for them. But that Welsh accent . . . He didn't think he would ever get used to it.

'Height, weight, hair and other physical features all match the information we have on Justine Delgado,' Paget said, 'and while we won't have the DNA results for a few days, she did have quite a lot of work done on her teeth by a local dentist, and those records match perfectly as well.'

'Do we know the cause of death?' asked Tregalles.

'There was a severe blow to the left temple with a rounded object,' Paget told him, 'and a second triangular-shaped blow to the back of the head, which may have been caused when her head came into contact with something sharp as she fell backwards from the first blow. However, in Dr Starkie's opinion, neither blow was fatal. Justine Delgado died of asphyxia. She was suffocated. There were signs of bruising around the mouth, cuts and bruising inside her lips, and bits of material were found between her teeth. She choked on her own vomit. Also, postmortem lividity blotches suggest that the body was moved several times following death. As a result, Sergeant Ormside will be setting up an incident room immediately following this briefing.' He gave a nod in the direction of the grizzled sergeant who sat with arms folded at the end of the table.

'The body is relatively well preserved due to the water being extremely cold,' Paget continued, 'and it was so tightly wrapped that it was waterproof, so decomposition was slowed considerably. Unfortunately, some of the worst decomposition is around the eyes, and it is not a pleasant sight, so I'm a bit reluctant to ask one of her employers to identify the body.'

'What about her friend, Maria Navarro?' Tregalles suggested. 'She works in Casualty. It won't be pleasant for anyone, but at least she's a nurse, so she should be used to that sort of thing.'

Paget hesitated. 'Very well,' he said, 'but make sure she understands what she will be looking at. If she agrees, notify the family liaison officer to arrange a time. Now, time of death. Doctor Starkie allowed himself a fairly wide margin due to the conditions under which the body was found, so he puts it at five to eight weeks ago. But we know that Justine was alive just over six weeks ago, so it's reasonable to assume that she died very close to the time she disappeared.' He paused. 'And she was approximately three months pregnant at the time.'

A quiet murmur rippled through the room. 'Do we have any idea how long she's been in the water, sir?' someone asked. 'Aren't we looking at the possibility that the body was thrown out of the boot of the car when it went into the river last week?'

'Not any more,' Paget replied. 'Doctor Starkie observed the beginning of plant growth on the duct tape, which suggests that the body has been in the water for at least two or three weeks and possibly more. Forensic may be able to tell us more about that, but we can drop that line of enquiry . . . at least as far as the body is concerned. The question still remains as to why Doctor Bryant lied about where her car was when it was stolen.'

'What about Justine's clothes?' Tregalles asked. 'Any clue there?'

Paget shook his head. 'The body was completely naked.'

Tregalles blew out his cheeks. 'Looks like somebody went to a hell of a lot of trouble to make sure she wasn't found,' he said soberly. 'Anything on what she was wrapped in, or the weights and the wire?'

'Not so far,' said Paget, 'but Forensic will be taking a good look at them, and finding out where they came from will be a priority. However, that's all I have to say for the moment. Sergeant Ormside, DS Tregalles, DS Forsythe and I will be doing a full review of the original missing person file, together with this latest information, first thing tomorrow morning, and I suggest that those of you who were involved in that investigation, even if it was only marginally, review your notes as well. I think that's all for now . . . Oh, DC Kajura, a moment, please,' he said as everyone began to leave.

'Yes, sir?" said Sophie apprehensively, wondering what she had done to be singled out.

'I seem to recall that you did some good work on the CCTV tapes and on background checks in the Delgado case,' he said, 'so I would like you to join us at the review tomorrow morning. All right?'

Sophie let her breath go. 'Absolutely, sir! And thank you, sir.'

'Good. See you in the morning, then.'

Sophie could barely stop herself from skipping as she walked away.

SEVENTEEN

Tuesday, 15 May

Sergeant Len Ormside was a tall, lean string-bean of a man with deeply chiselled features, prominent nose and a ruddy complexion. His once fine head of sandy hair was thinner now and mostly grey, but his deep-set eyes were just as bright and hawkish as ever.

Running an incident room had once been part of his regular job, and he was good at it. With twenty-odd years behind him, there were few who could match his phenomenal memory for facts, figures, names and dates, and his general knowledge of the area.

But seven years ago, his talents had been noted, and he'd been asked to set up a newly formed group called Forward Planning, based in head office in New Street. Ormside had been torn: he liked his job, but perhaps it was time to move on. The then Superintendent Alcott was reluctant to let him go, but he didn't want to stand in Ormside's way, so he worked out a deal with head office. In the event of a serious crime where a full-scale incident room had to be set up, subject to the demands of his own job, Ormside would be seconded temporarily to CID to run it.

The system had worked well, mainly because Ormside himself was left to decide whether he could spare the time away from his regular job, and so far he'd always found a way.

Now he cast an eye over the room to see if there was anything he'd missed. He'd gone to work immediately following the briefing yesterday, so now what he needed most of all was information: every scrap of information from everyone who had been involved in the Delgado disappearance. The whole purpose of an incident room was the gathering of information, examination of the evidence and orderly direction of an appropriate response. Everything would be checked and double-checked.

Statements, times, locations, all would be looked at again. Basic background checks had been done when Justine Delgado was first reported missing, but now they would need to go deeper. And HOLMES 2, the national police investigative management system, would be searched for crimes with the same or similar characteristics.

Len Ormside had been on his feet since six a.m. and his corns were beginning to hurt. He'd be glad to sit down, but there was still one very important job to do before Paget and the others arrived. He walked over to an old steel cabinet in the far corner of the room and pulled out a chipped and battered coffee pot and a jar of coffee left over from the last time he was there. And the extension cord, a bit ragged and worn, but no bare wires were visible, so it would be safe enough as long as no one spilled water or coffee on the floor. He taped the cord to the floor and plugged it in, and minutes later, when he heard the gratifying rumble from the pot beside his desk, he settled into his chair with a sigh of satisfaction. It was like coming home.

Tregalles slumped back in his chair and rubbed his eyes. He and the others had spent the morning going over everything, from the moment Justine Delgado had been reported missing until the file had been handed off to Missing Persons. Now it was back in their hands, but this time as a major crime.

'It's no good,' Paget declared as he, too, sat back in his seat. 'We have to look at this another way.'

There was a cautious stirring of interest from the others, but no one spoke.

Paget looked across the room to the whiteboards where the picture of Justine Delgado was once again displayed. Even at that distance, her dark, serious eyes seemed to be looking directly back at him. 'I don't know about the rest of you,' he said, 'but in spite of everything we have done to prove that Justine Delgado left Simla House on Easter Sunday, there isn't a shred of evidence to support it. I don't think she ever left.'

There was a moment of silence, then, 'You're saying Mrs Lorrimer and her son *lied* about Justine leaving to go to mass?' Tregalles said tentatively.

'No, I'm not saying that,' said Paget, 'although I'm not ruling it out, either. Mrs Lorrimer certainly sounded credible when she came in to report Justine missing. In fact, she appeared to be very concerned and very worried, so I'm trying to keep an open mind. I think it's just *possible* that Justine did leave the house, but made her way back inside without being seen. Once she was through the gate, all she had to do was turn to the right and use the cover of the tall hedge to make her way along to where the hedge meets the south wing of the house. If you look at the pictures, you can see there's a gap in the hedge next to the wooden stairs leading to the first floor. Once through the gap, Justine could be up those steps and into the house in a matter of seconds without being seen.'

'Why would she do that?' Ormside asked. 'Seems like a lot of trouble to go to when she could have simply stayed in her room in the first place.'

'Possibly because it would have looked suspicious, or at least raised questions, if she didn't go to mass, especially on Easter Sunday,' said Paget. 'As to why she would go to all that trouble, I have no idea.'

'Could be because she wanted to have it out with Sebastian,' Tregalles suggested. 'Justine told Maria that she couldn't stand Sebastian, but maybe that was a lie and she was actually having it off with him. She knew that Mr and Mrs Lorrimer would be going off to church around nine thirty, and Michael would be over at Mrs Tillman's, so she and Sebastian would have the house to themselves. Maybe that's when she told him she was pregnant; he didn't want any part of that, she threatened to bring it out in the open, he panicked, they fought or he hit her, and she wound up dead. Case closed.'

Ormside grunted. 'Assuming she did go back into the house,' he said, 'but we don't know that, do we? According to the autopsy report, there would have been a fair amount of blood wherever she was killed, so did you see any blood in the room when you were there, Tregalles?'

'No, but we weren't looking at it as a crime scene back then,' Tregalles said defensively. 'It was a missing person case. Besides—'

'If it's any help, sir,' Sophie Kajura said tentatively, 'we have Sebastian Mills leaving in his car at a few minutes to nine that morning, and Mrs Lorrimer was still in the house during that time.'

'Although she was out of the house briefly when she took Michael over to Tilly's around eight thirty,' Molly pointed out. 'But if Justine was killed by Sebastian, how did he get the body out of the house in broad daylight, assuming, of course, that he took her out in his car that morning?'

'Maybe he left her there in her room until the following night,' Tregalles suggested.

'We're talking theories,' Paget broke in quickly, 'and an alternative to the one I just mentioned is that Justine never did leave the house in the first place, and Mrs Lorrimer and her son lied. So let's go back to the very beginning. When do we *know* that Justine was last seen alive? Never mind what we've been told; when was the last time Justine was *seen* alive?'

Tregalles thought for a moment. 'That would have to be at lunch on Easter Saturday,' he said. 'Mr and Mrs Lorrimer were there, and so was Terry Baxter. He confirmed that they all had lunch together when Molly spoke to him on the phone, and Lorrimer was going on to Molly and me about Terry chatting up Justine during lunch.'

'I don't know when Justine was last *seen*,' said Molly, 'but Justine rang Tilly shortly before eight o'clock on Saturday evening to remind her to watch *Midsomer Murders* on television. There should be a record of the call, so I'll check on that.'

Ormside, who had been studying pictures of Simla House taken from the car park, was shaking his head. 'I suppose it's *possible* that she returned to the house that way,' he said, 'but it's a bit devious, wouldn't you say?'

'Especially when virtually everyone we've talked to about this girl praises her for her dedication to her work, her love for the boy, and how seriously she takes her religion, and, by implication, her honesty,' said Molly.

'That being said, she did get pregnant,' Tregalles pointed out. 'And she was up to something when she told Mrs Lorrimer that she was going to be spending the day with her friend, Maria.'

'*If* that is what she told Mrs Lorrimer,' Ormside growled.

Paget looked at him. 'If it's not,' he said slowly, 'it suggests that Mrs Lorrimer and her son are barefaced liars or worse. And, if that's the case, I completely misjudged Mrs Lorrimer when she reported Justine missing.' He took a deep breath and blew it out again. 'But, it would explain a number of things,' he conceded, 'so let's put it to the test.'

Grace had just arrived home and was getting out of her car when Paget pulled into the driveway behind her, and they entered the house together. 'Charlie told me we're going to be doing a search of Simla House tomorrow,' said Grace as they were hanging up their coats in the hall. They'd agreed a long time ago that they would leave work behind once they got home, but she was dying of curiosity. Grace Lovett was a crime scene investigator, a member of what was still referred to as SOCO locally, rather than CSI, which seemed to have taken hold in other areas, and Charlie Dobbs was her boss. 'Do we actually have a crime scene, or are we trying to establish one?'

'To be honest, I'm not sure myself,' he told her after they'd given each other a hug and a kiss.

Grace eyed him curiously, but remained silent as she led the way into the living room, where she kicked off her shoes and sat down. 'Considering how far away from the house the body was found, what makes you think she might have been killed there?' she prompted.

Paget settled into his favourite chair and loosened his tie. 'We're starting there,' he said, 'simply because, despite all our efforts to prove otherwise, there isn't a scrap of evidence to show that Justine ever left the house or grounds. In fact, for all we know, she could have been killed at any time after eight o'clock on the Saturday evening.'

Grace eyed him thoughtfully. 'Are you saying you believe that Mrs Lorrimer *lied* about the girl going off to church that morning?'

'If she did, she made a damned good job of it, and I bought it,' Paget said dourly. 'On the other hand, she and her son could be telling the truth as they know it.'

Grace dismissed that with a shake of her head. 'But you don't believe that, do you?' she said. 'Which is why we're going in there first thing tomorrow morning. Right? But how did you get Brock to agree, considering how sensitive he is when it comes to dealing with people like the Lorrimers?'

Paget eyed Grace for a long moment before he replied. 'I didn't,' he said quietly. 'It was getting late in the day, and he was in a meeting, so I thought it best to wait till morning to let him know.'

Grace's eyes widened in astonishment. 'But surely Pierce wouldn't . . . ? Oh, God, you didn't tell her either, did you? What on earth were you thinking, Neil?'

He shrugged. 'I knew it wouldn't fly with either of them,' he said, 'but I have to get in there to satisfy myself that we haven't overlooked the possibility that Justine was killed in the house, and Mrs Lorrimer has been lying to me from the very beginning.'

Grace looked up at the ceiling and puffed out her cheeks. 'You know what will happen if we don't find anything, don't you?' she said quietly. 'Brock will come down on you like a ton of bricks, and Pierce will be caught in the crossfire. Why take the risk? Is it because you think that you were taken in by Mrs Lorrimer . . . assuming, of course, that you *were* taken in, and Justine was actually killed in the house?'

'It's partly that, I suppose,' he admitted, 'but I think you'd understand if you had seen that poor woman's body, as I did, on the slab. I want to see someone held responsible for what they did, and if that means having to put up with some flack from the likes of Morgan Brock, then so be it.'

Paget pushed himself up out of the chair. 'And I think that's enough shop talk for one evening,' he said firmly. 'Would you like a drink? I know I could use one.'

EIGHTEEN

Wednesday, 16 May

The shock in Stephen Lorrimer's eyes was not unexpected, but the intensity of it and the way the colour drained from his face took Paget by surprise. Standing behind his desk, Lorrimer's legs began to shake, and he put a hand down on the desk to steady himself. He closed his eyes and took several deep breaths while shaking his head slowly from side to side. 'No! That can't be right,' he muttered between breaths. His voice rose. 'You've made a mistake. In the river? No.' His mouth suddenly went dry; the muscles in his throat constricted, and he was having to force the words out. 'If the body has been in the water . . .' Lorrimer turned away to grab a handful of tissues from a box on his desk, and blew his nose.

Lorrimer had made no secret about his admiration for Justine Delgado, and for what she had done for his son – indeed, for his family – but Paget found himself wondering again if there had been more to their relationship. 'I'm sorry,' he said, 'but the body has been identified by dental records, and by Justine's friend, Maria Navarro. If you wish to identify the body yourself . . . ?'

'No, no, that won't be necessary,' Lorrimer said huskily. He mopped his face and deposited the tissues in the wastepaper basket beside his desk. 'Do you know . . . how she died?'

'I'm not at liberty to give you any details,' Paget told him, 'but we now believe that, instead of continuing on to church on Easter morning, Justine Delgado may have re-entered the house by way of the outside stairs, and I have a warrant to search the house and grounds.' He took the warrant from his pocket and handed it to Lorrimer.

Lorrimer had the papers in his hands before the words registered in his brain. Frowning, he looked at the first page, then the second, and, suddenly, his manner changed. 'This is absurd,' he said. 'Based on some theory that Justine came *back* into the house after leaving here? Are you seriously suggesting that something could have happened to her here? Are you telling me that we are *suspects*?'

'No one is talking about suspects at this point,' said Paget firmly, 'but the house will be searched and, hopefully, eliminated. As you can see, the search warrant restricts us to the living quarters of the house and outbuildings, so nothing on the constituency office side will be disturbed or compromised.' He turned towards the door, then paused; when he spoke again, it was in a more moderate tone. 'I'm assuming that you are just as keen to find out what happened to Justine as we are,' he said, 'so it really would make things much easier for all concerned if I could have the keys to any locked rooms, cupboards or drawers.'

Lorrimer looked startled. 'You mean *now*?'

'Yes, Mr Lorrimer,' said Paget. 'I mean now.'

'Why the *hell* did you let them in?' Julia hissed. 'And then to just hand them the keys . . . ?' She rolled her eyes. 'What were you *thinking*, for God's sake? And where did they get the idea that Justine came back into the house after she left for church? That's nonsense.'

Lorrimer shrugged helplessly. 'No idea,' he said, 'but what I do know is that you don't get a magistrate to sign a search warrant without some sort of evidence.'

'Which magistrate?' Julia asked sharply.

'John Blair. He—'

'So call the man. Tell him to cancel the damned thing. He's a friend, for God's sake! He's on one of our committees. Tell him it's harassment, and we're not going to stand for it.'

Lorrimer shook his head. 'And how would that look?' he said. 'I don't like it any more than you do, but why not let them look all they want? They will anyway, and it will only make them think we have something to hide if we try to block them.'

'But the very fact that they are here means that they think she could have been killed here, and that makes us all suspects in their eyes,' Julia insisted.

'Not necessarily. As I told Paget, the most likely explanation for Justine returning – *if* she did return – was to pick up something she'd forgotten, and she probably left again shortly after. He said they'd considered that, but they still need to begin here in order to eliminate the house as the place where Justine was killed. So let him get on with it, because the less interference he has from us, the sooner he and these SOCO people will be out of here.'

Julia made a face. 'So what have you done with the boy?' she demanded. 'I thought you were supposed to be keeping him with you? Fine time you picked to bring him back here, I must say.'

Stephen Lorrimer sighed. 'Do you *really* begrudge me the little time I have to spend with our son, Julia? It will only be for a couple of weeks, then he'll have to go back to the farm, unless, of course, the agency can find someone who—'

'Oh, for God's sake, Stephen, grow up and face reality!' Julia cut in angrily. 'There isn't going to *be* another Justine, and even if there were, there is no place for her or Michael in this house, and the sooner you face up to that, the better! Justine is gone and we simply cannot go on like this. It's not Michael's fault that he's the way he is, and it's not yours or mine, but the fact is I can't deal with him; you're not here most of the time, and getting another nanny isn't the answer. Now, I know taking him out to the farm was supposed to be a temporary solution – a distraction to give him time to get over losing Justine – but perhaps that's what's best for him. Did Richard speak to you about that when you picked up Michael?'

The muscles around Lorrimer's mouth tightened. 'He did,' he said tonelessly, 'and it's out of the question. I told him to forget it. I know he thinks he's being helpful, but there is no way I'm going to have Michael live out there on the farm where he'll be—'

'Happy?' Julia exclaimed. 'Did you really *listen* to what Richard had to say? Did you talk to Eloise or the girls? Do you know what Eloise told me? She said that Michael and the girls get along wonderfully well, and they don't know how, exactly, but both Chelsea and Loren seem to make sense of those awful noises he makes when he tries to speak. He loves the animals, and he is fascinated by the work Eloise is doing in the animal shelter.' Julia put her hand on her husband's arm. 'As for his schooling, Eloise was a teacher before she met Richard and

became a vet herself, so the girls are being taught at home. Eloise
can't do it all, of course, because of her work, so they have a
tutor who comes in twice a week, and he's said he's willing to
work with Michael as well. Eloise thinks the life there would be
good for Michael, and they would love to have him stay. In fact,
considering what's going on in this house at the moment, it might
be best to take him back out there now.'

Stony-faced, Lorrimer stared blankly at Julia, but in his mind's
eye he was seeing the expression on Michael's face when he had
told him he was taking him home. To say that the boy's reaction
was lukewarm would be an understatement. Lorrimer had tried
to convince himself that things would be different once they were
back in familiar surroundings, but even he could see the difference
in Michael's behaviour now that they were home, compared with
the way he'd been at the farm.'

'This is his home,' he said stubbornly. 'He stays, and that's
final!'

A contemptuous smile touched Julia's lips. 'And in two weeks'
time, when you return to London?' she asked softly. 'What then,
Stephen? Are you planning to take him with you? Give up your
job? Take an extended leave of absence? Funny, but I can't quite
see that happening when you are so close to achieving your
dream of becoming a cabinet minister. Can you?'

Lorrimer shook his head slowly from side to side. 'Oh, Julia,'
he said, more in sorrow than in anger, 'you can be such a hard
and spiteful bitch!'

Julia reached out and put her hand under his chin and tilted
his head until they were looking into each other's eyes. 'That
may well be so,' she said softly, 'but I'm *your* hard and spiteful
bitch, Stephen. You need me, and you'd do well to remember
that. Anyway,' she continued briskly, 'whether you like to admit
it or not, we both know there is really only one practical solution
as far as the boy is concerned, so I suggest we stop wasting time
talking about it and get back to the matter at hand. Did Paget
say how long this search will take?'

'No, he didn't!' Lorrimer snapped. He was angry, not just
because Julia had dismissed the future of Michael so lightly, but
because he knew she was right. 'And I didn't ask,' he said,
'because, to tell the truth, I don't remember much of anything

after he told me they'd found Justine's body at the bottom of the river.' He took a deep breath and blew out his cheeks. 'God knows what we're going to tell her grandfather.'

'*We* are not going to tell her grandfather anything!' Julia said firmly. 'The police will take care of that, so I suggest that you stop worrying about things like that and concentrate on what's happening here and now. And watch what you say to any of them. I think the police are grasping at straws. I don't think they really believe Justine came back into the house. I think that was just an excuse, so they'll be looking for anything to bolster their case.'

While two other members of the team began with the classroom, Grace Lovett and Geoff Kirkpatrick, a senior colleague, made straight for Justine's room, pausing at the door to take pictures before moving inside. They had a copy of the notes and pictures taken by Tregalles and Forsythe when the two detectives had made their initial search of the room, but there had been no suggestion of foul play back then. Now it was a murder investigation, and a forensic search was a very different matter. Everything would be examined in minute detail.

First impressions on entering the room: bright, neat, clean, tidy, sparsely furnished, but some thought had gone into the placement of furniture, pictures and a couple of colourful travel posters of islands of the Philippines taken from the air. Grace wrinkled her nose, trying to identify an elusive, slightly musty smell that seemed at odds with the fresh appearance of the room. But the simple act of opening the door had been enough to stir the air, and before she could identify it, the smell had all but disappeared.

Returning to his office, Stephen Lorrimer found Jim Bradley slumped in one of the armchairs in front of the desk, while Michael sat curled up in one of the other chairs, earbuds in place, facing away from Jim.

Jim pushed himself out of the chair and stood up. Six feet tall and broad-shouldered, one's first impression of Bradley was of solid dependability. His wiry black hair was flecked with grey, but dark, wide-set eyes, crinkled at the corners, and a generous

mouth made him look younger than he was. Now, just short of
fifty, his once finely chiselled features were becoming slightly
less distinct, but Jim Bradley was still a fine-looking man. He
had the sort of face that people trust, and that alone was worth
more than gold to Stephen Lorrimer when it came to raising
funds.

'I think he's a bit out of sorts,' said Bradley quietly to Lorrimer,
with a nod towards the boy. 'I can usually get him to talk to me
through that electronic gadget of his, but not today. Is there a
problem?'

Lorrimer glanced over to make sure that Michael's earbuds
were in place before he answered. 'He's still upset about Justine,'
he said, 'and he's going to be even more unhappy when he finds
out she's dead. God knows how I'm ever going to tell him.'

'*Dead*?' Bradley stepped back to stare hard at Lorrimer.
'When? How?' Lorrimer took him by the arm and steered him
through the open doorway into the corridor and closed the door
behind him. 'Remember the body the police found when a car
went into the river last week and three kids were drowned?'
he said, almost whispering. 'Well, they're saying it's Justine,
and now we've got police crawling all over the house. They
arrived here this morning with a search warrant. No warning
– nothing.'

Bradley whistled softly. 'So those *are* police vans I saw down
there when I came in,' he said. 'And those chaps in white over-
alls – I was going to ask you about them.' He frowned. 'But why
here? What are they looking for?'

Lorrimer shrugged. 'It seems they've got it into their heads
that Justine came back into the house after she left for church
that morning, so they've got a forensic team in to search the
place for clues.' Bradley looked puzzled. 'They *say* they think
she went along behind the hedge and came up the outside steps,'
Lorrimer explained, 'but I get the feeling there's more to it than
that.' He sounded worried.

Bradley rested both hands on Lorrimer's shoulders and bent
slightly to peer into his friend's face. 'I know this is unsettling,'
he said, 'but you're not really *worried* about this, are you,
Stephen? I mean, there's nothing you're not telling me, is there?'

'No, no, of course not,' Lorrimer said testily. He ran his fingers through his hair, then dropped his hands to his sides. 'It's just that . . . Oh, I don't know!' he ended irritably.

Jim Bradley sighed in sympathy. 'I'm afraid you do look a bit . . . well, stressed out, if you don't mind my saying so, Stephen, but the police aren't going to find anything, are they? So there's really nothing to worry about on that score.'

Lorrimer sighed. 'I suppose you're right, Jim,' he said, trying to sound as if he meant it. 'I haven't been sleeping well lately, and now with the police in the house, and trying to decide what to do about Michael before I have to go back to London in a couple of weeks . . . It's all a bit much.'

'Yes, yes, of course it is,' Bradley said soothingly. 'Speaking of which, I'm assuming that no one in the media is aware of this as yet? The police searching your house, I mean?'

Lorrimer glanced at his watch and grimaced. 'They're going to announce the identity of the body at a press conference this afternoon,' he said glumly, 'so we can expect the media to be all over this place once they do.'

Bradley glanced at his own watch. 'That gives us a couple of hours to get something out before this breaks,' he said. 'You said they had a search warrant? Tell me, Stephen, how did you react when it was served?'

'For Christ's sake, Jim, how do you think I reacted?' Lorrimer flared. 'I was stunned!'

'Yes, well, you would be, of course,' Bradley said hastily, 'but do you remember what was actually *said*? Did you put up any kind of a fight? Resist them in any way?'

Lorrimer shook his head. 'Actually, the chap who served the warrant was quite decent about it,' he said, 'so there wasn't much I *could* do. He had a legal warrant, so I told him to go ahead and search if he thought it would help.'

'Excellent!' Bradley rubbed his hands together. 'You did the right thing, Stephen, because now we can say that you were devastated when you were told of Justine's death, and if there is anything you can do to help, the police will have your full co-operation. Other than that, say nothing to the media. Anyway, I'll see what I can do to smooth the way; I won't waste any more of your time, but I will keep in touch. Meanwhile, I suggest that you spruce yourself up a bit and get yourself prepared for the media. Now, I don't know if you think it would be a good idea to have Michael by your side when they come to the door, or . . . well, no, I suppose not,' he amended quickly when he saw the expression on Lorrimer's face. 'Sad but in control. You know the sort of thing.'

Bradley patted Lorrimer on the shoulder. 'It's unfortunate that this had to happen right now, because the press is going to try to make a meal out of it, but you have a solid reputation, and I'm sure we can ride this out. Believe me, Stephen, everything will be fine.'

With a final encouraging pat on the shoulder, Jim Bradley was turning to leave when Lorrimer stopped him. 'I'm sorry, Jim,' he said, 'but with everything that's going on, I forgot to ask: what did you want to talk to me about?'

Bradley brushed it aside with a wave of the hand. 'Nothing that can't be left till later,' he said. 'This is much more important, so the sooner we get ahead of it, the better. But call me if anything significant happens. OK?' He set off down the corridor, then paused, 'How's Julia taking all this?' he asked. 'I mean, it must be terribly upsetting, having these people tramping about the house.'

'Oh, you know Julia,' Lorrimer said with a toss of the head. 'She wanted me to call John Blair and have him rescind the search warrant, but I told her—'

'Jesus Christ! Don't even *think* of doing that!' Bradley burst out. 'That would *really* make it look as if you had something to hide, and Blair wouldn't do it anyway.'

'That's exactly what I told her,' Lorrimer said, 'and I think she realizes how it would look.'

'I should hope so,' Bradley said with feeling. 'Anyway, I can't stop. Rumours will be flying soon enough, so I'd better get going on damage control. And, as I said, call me if anything else happens. Oh, yes, and tell everyone in the office they're to say nothing to the media. Tell them to refer anyone asking questions to me.'

The two white-clad figures moved into the room and closed the door behind them. Grace Lovett set her case down on the wooden floor to one side of the door, while Geoff Kirkpatrick did the same on the other side. They moved slowly, mentally photo-graphing everything before setting to work. Normally, they would be working in an area where it had been established that a crime had taken place, but their job today was to try to determine *if* a crime had taken place. They would be looking for signs of a struggle, blood, hair, fibres, and anything that looked out of place. The room would be dusted for prints from top to bottom as if it were an established crime scene, but Grace was all too conscious of the fact that they were on a fishing trip. She drew in a breath and let it out slowly, then mentally crossed her fingers as she set to work.

A few minutes later, Grace paused beside the bed. There was that smell again, faint but persistent. She stood still and closed her eyes. Two smells, faint but fighting one another, one sweet and just a bit cloying, while the other . . .

'Something wrong, Grace?' asked Kirkpatrick.

She opened her eyes. 'I'm trying to place that smell,' she said. 'It's—' She stopped abruptly, put a finger to her lips and pointed to the door. The knob was turning. The door opened and a small boy carrying a folded white cane poked his head inside. He stood there, motionless for several seconds, head tilted to one side, listening. Grace and Kirkpatrick stayed silent, curious to see what the boy was up to. They watched as he started forward, only to catch his sandal against the edge of the rug and drop to one knee. Head down, the boy remained in that position, fingers spread as he swept his small hands back and forth, stroking the pile.

Keeping her voice low as she moved forward to help the boy up, Grace said, 'Hello. You must be Michael. My name is Grace. Are you looking for someone?'

A strangled cry burst from the boy's throat as he scrambled to his feet. The white cane flicked open and he thrust it in front of him like a rapier, jabbing wildly at the air as he backed through the doorway, then turned and literally ran down the corridor, cane swinging from side to side ahead of him.

'It's all right, Michael,' Grace called out as she ran after him, but by the time she reached the top of the stairs, he had reached the bottom and was gone.

Returning to the room, Grace bent to straighten the large rug where the boy had tripped on it. The edge was bound and curled just enough to catch the toe of a sandal. The colours, deep burgundy and beige, were faded now, and, like the boy, Grace ran her hands lightly across its surface, reminding herself that Michael Lorrimer's world was defined by sound and smell and touch, and she wondered what it was that had caught his attention.

She stood up and looked around the room. 'I think it's the smell,' she said to Kirkpatrick. 'Especially the bedspread; it doesn't smell as if it's been properly aired for some time. And there's a bit of that same smell about this rug as well; it's not as strong, but it's there. And the bedspread doesn't really go with the rest of the room, does it?' she continued. 'Justine Delgado had an eye for colour, and she's gone to some trouble to make the room look cheerful, but that bedspread is a big blob of . . . well, *nothing* as far as colour goes. It's dull; it doesn't go with the rest of the room.'

They walked side by side from Chief Superintendent Brock's office to the lift in silence, but once they stepped into the lift and the doors closed, Amanda Pierce let loose. 'Why?' she demanded. 'What the hell were you *thinking*? You made me look an absolute fool in there! I rarely agree with Chief Superintendent Brock, but he's right in this case, and now we're both on notice. God knows what you told Blair to get him to sign that search warrant. And telling Brock that you *think* that Mrs Lorrimer may have lied to you, without producing a shred of evidence, was hardly helpful. You went behind my back, Neil, and I want to know why.'

Paget held up his hands in a gesture of appeasement. 'I'll admit I was wrong,' he said, 'and I know it doesn't really help, but I apologize. But, after looking at this case from every angle, I'm convinced that Justine Delgado was killed in that house, and I allowed myself to be taken in by Mrs Lorrimer. I knew you would have to turn me down if I asked your permission to get a search warrant, which was why I didn't ask. I didn't see it as going behind your back; I looked upon it as giving you deniability, but obviously I was wrong, and I'm sorry.'

Still fuming as they left the building, Amanda stopped at the top of the steps and turned to face him. 'Not good enough, Chief Inspector!' she declared tightly. 'I really don't know what you were thinking. But right now I want you to get over there to Simla House, and get SOCO out of there. And I want you to apologize *sincerely* to Mr and Mrs Lorrimer for the intrusion. As for—'

A burst of sound from Paget's phone stopped her in mid-sentence. He was about to switch it off when he saw the text. Wordlessly, he held it out for Amanda to see the screen. It was from Grace, short and to the point.

We have a crime scene.

NINETEEN

'**M**ind the rug,' Grace warned as she guided Paget and Tregalles around the rolled-up rug to a spot in front of the fireplace. Both men were wearing disposable paper suits, headgear and footwear. 'We still have much more work to do, but it looks as if you were right, Neil, and Justine did come back here, if she ever left. I believe this is where she died, so we thought it best that you see for yourself.' She nodded to Kirkpatrick. 'Window's still covered, so I'll get the lights if you'd like to spray the area again,' she said.

'Right,' he said. 'Mantelpiece first, then the tiles and floor.'

'As you can see,' said Grace a few minutes later when the lights were back on, 'someone has gone to a lot of trouble to clean up the bloodstains on the mantelpiece, the hearth tiles and the floor, but the luminol spray makes the patterns quite clear. So, when we put what we've found here, together with the description of the wound in the back of Justine's head, we think the blow to the front of her head caused her to fall back and hit her head on the corner of the marble mantelpiece. She then fell forward on to the rug. But certainly not *this* rug, because we think the original rug was soaked in blood to the degree that it bled through to leave a stain on the floor. Bleach has been used to try to get rid of the bloodstains, but it takes a lot more than that to get rid of blood completely, so the original rug was replaced with this one. They did quite a good cleaning job on the hearth tiles because they're glazed, but they couldn't get rid of the blood absorbed into the grout between the tiles. And I suspect the bedspread has been changed for the same reason. We haven't found any blood on the bedclothes, but they will be going in for further examination, and we'll be looking at all the other sheets in the house as well. Of course, we don't *know* that it is Justine Delgado's blood until we have the lab report,' Grace continued, 'but it's certainly a reasonable assumption. We've also taken material from the U-bend under the basin in the bathroom.

There wasn't much, just a few hairs and a bit of sludge stuck to the bottom of the U, but if someone washed their hands there, the lab will probably find enough to work with. We'll be making a mould of the corner of the mantelpiece, and once we have that, we can make a plaster cast, and see if it matches the shape of the wound in the back of Justine's head.'

Tregalles was looking puzzled. 'Bleach has a strong smell,' he said, 'but I don't remember smelling it when we were in here the day Mrs Lorrimer reported Justine missing.' He closed his eyes, trying to recall the scene. 'I'm sure I didn't,' he said. 'I mean, it would have been a dead giveaway, wouldn't it? And Molly never said anything, either. As I remember, it smelled pretty much like it does now; maybe a bit stronger. A perfume of some sort.'

'It's lavender,' Grace told him. 'It's quite faint now, but if it was introduced into the room just before you arrived, it would have been strong enough to cover the smell of two-day-old bleach followed by soap and water. There's a bottle of lavender-scented spray in the bathroom. It's been opened and partly used, but there are no prints on the bottle. Justine could have wiped it clean herself, of course, but I thought it worth mentioning, especially as I couldn't detect any smell of lavender in her clothing in the wardrobe or in her underclothes in the drawers.'

'We can ask her friend, Maria, if Justine liked lavender,' Tregalles said.

Even Chief Superintendent Brock would find it hard to argue that this was the work of some stranger who had wandered in off the street, thought Paget as he looked around the room. 'How long do you think it would take to clean up after Justine was killed?' he asked.

Grace looked at Kirkpatrick. 'Two, three hours, perhaps?'

'More,' Kirkpatrick said, 'unless they had a clean-up squad. This whole area between the bed and the fireplace has been scrubbed down. The girl's prints are all over the rest of the room, together with a few as yet unidentified ones, which is pretty much what we would expect to find. But up at this end of the room, around the bed, we have no prints. Absolutely none. Everything has been wiped clean. This wasn't done in haste; this was carried out methodically and carefully. They took their time.'

'They?' said Paget.

Kirkpatrick and Grace both nodded. 'Apart from everything that had to be dealt with here,' Kirkpatrick said, 'there's the matter of getting rid of the original rug and bedspread, and getting the body out of the house, and then down to the river, so I can't see one person doing all that by him or herself.'

'Have they found anything of interest in the classroom at the end of the corridor?' asked Paget as he and Tregalles made their way to the door.

'The only personal things they've found so far belong to Michael,' said Grace. 'Books, toys, Braille computer, that sort of thing, but just about everything belonging to Justine has to do with her work – records of what she has done with Michael. Absolutely nothing about her personal life.'

'If she actually had one,' Kirkpatrick put in.

'Oh, she had one,' Tregalles assured him. 'There's nothing much more personal than getting pregnant.'

Before leaving the room, Paget used his phone to take several pictures of the rug and the bedspread. Then, with one last look round, he and Tregalles left the room. Divesting themselves, in the corridor, of the disposable suits, they stuffed them into the bin bag provided by SOCO.

'Gloomy old place, this,' Tregalles observed as they made their way to the head of the stairs. 'I wouldn't fancy spending my days up here with no one to talk to except a boy who can't speak. It can't have been much of a life.'

They reached the top of the stairs and were about to descend when Paget motioned for Tregalles to stop and be quiet. In the entrance hall below them, Julia Lorrimer and a dark-haired man were standing with their heads almost touching as they talked. He was a big, solid-looking man, and he was speaking quietly, but Paget sensed an intensity in the words that made him curious. But what intrigued him even more was when the man slipped his hand around Julia's back and drew her to him for a brief moment before she pushed him gently but firmly away. The man walked to the door, then paused before opening it. 'You will let me know if anything changes, won't you?' he said.

'Of course I will, Jim,' she said briskly. 'And *do* stop worrying.

I'll talk to Stephen when he gets back. Promise. Now, for heaven's sake, go!'

'Try to catch him and find out who he is and what he's doing here,' Paget said to Tregalles as they started down the stairs, 'but don't let on that we saw him with Mrs Lorrimer.' He raised his voice. 'Ah, there you are, Mrs Lorrimer,' he called as she was about to leave the hall. 'I wonder if I might have a word.'

Julia Lorrimer started to shake her head even before Paget had finished telling her that Justine Delgado had been killed in her own room.

'That can't be,' she stated flatly. 'I was in the kitchen, so I didn't actually *see* her leave the house, but she spoke to me before she left, and I heard her go out. And Sebastian saw her leave as well.'

'Nevertheless, there is more than sufficient physical evidence to suggest that Justine died in her room,' said Paget, 'and since you and your son, Sebastian, were, as far as we know, the only two adults in the house at the time, I need to ask you some questions.' He glanced around the hall. 'Perhaps somewhere more private?'

Julia Lorrimer eyed him coldly for a long moment, then looked down the corridor leading to the kitchen at the far end. The door was open, and they could hear the sound of someone moving around. 'I think the veranda might be best,' she said, moving towards the door, 'but I don't know what I can tell you.'

There were rattan chairs with colourful cushions on the veranda, but Julia chose to stand at the rail. Although the sky was clear, the veranda was in shadow, and there was a chill in the air, but Julia didn't seem to mind. She turned to rest her back against one of the pillars and said, 'Well, Chief Inspector?'

'When you first reported Justine missing, you said that you and Mr Lorrimer had been into Justine's room on Easter Monday to see if you could find anything that might tell you where she'd gone. Do you recall what time that was, and whether this rug was on the floor then?' He brought up a picture of the rug on the screen of his phone and showed it to her.

Julia peered at it, then shot him a quizzical look. 'Yes, it was,' she said, 'and it's funny you should mention it, because it's not the original rug, and I was surprised to see that Justine had changed it. Not that she didn't have every right to do so, of course. I told her at the very beginning that, if she needed anything in the way of furniture for her room, she was welcome to take what she wanted from the storage room up there, so I suppose she must have swapped it with the one she had. As for the time I went into her room, I thought Justine had overslept – she was usually up by six thirty – so when she hadn't appeared by eight, I went up and knocked on her door. When she didn't answer, I poked my head inside. When I saw that her bed hadn't been slept in, I called Stephen, and we looked around to see if there was anything that might tell us where she had gone. We were worried about her, because she's always been so good in letting us know if she was going to be late, or if plans had changed, and she'd never stayed out overnight before.'

'You say Justine must have swapped rugs,' said Paget. 'Do you have any idea what happened to the original rug? We will be searching the house and grounds, of course, but I thought you might know? According to what we've been told, Justine was a very responsible person, so it seems unlikely that she would have thrown it away without talking to you first.'

Julia shook her head emphatically. 'It's not as if that old rug was worth anything,' she said, 'but you're quite right: Justine wouldn't do that without asking me . . . unless, of course, she spoke to Stephen about it and he forgot to mention it. That's probably it. I can ask him if you think it's important, although, to be honest, I don't see what it is you're driving at.'

Ignoring the implied question, Paget said, 'Apart from Easter Monday, when was the last time you were in Justine's room?'

Frowning, Julia shook her head slowly. 'I really can't remember,' she said. 'Sometime last year, I suppose. It wasn't long after she came to us.'

'Really?' said Paget. 'Surely there must have been other times?'

Julia smiled and shook her head. 'I don't think you quite understand the arrangement, Chief Inspector,' she said. 'Once we had satisfied ourselves that Justine was the right nanny and teacher for Michael, we quite literally gave her the run of the south wing up there. The other bedrooms are never used, so she was free to treat everything on that floor as her own. Which she did, and I was grateful for it, because it relieved me from having to bother with it. Betty – that's Betty Jacobs, our daily – can't climb stairs, so I look after our bedrooms and everything in the north wing, and I was quite happy to leave the rest to Justine. In addition to looking after Michael's needs, she did whatever housekeeping was necessary, including the usual dusting, hoovering, the washing and ironing of her own and Michael's clothes, sheets, pillowcases and things like that. She was well paid, but we felt it was money well spent, and she was grateful because she was sending money back to Manila to help pay for her grandfather's care there. We had access to the classroom and Michael's room, of course, and we could go up there whenever we wished to discuss Michael's progress and see how he was getting along. But Justine's room was her own, so we had no reason to be in there.'

'So you have no idea when that rug was changed, or what happened to the original one, Mrs Lorrimer?'

'I thought I had made that clear,' she said, clearly annoyed by the question. 'And I don't understand what is so important about an old rug?'

'It's just that I'm having a problem matching what you are telling me with the evidence in Justine's room,' said Paget. 'You see, bloodstains were found in various parts of the room, including an area on the floor *under* the rug. Yet there were no stains on the rug itself, which suggests that the rug and, quite possibly, the bedspread were changed *after* Justine was killed. And if that's the case, then Justine must have been in her room when you went up to wake Michael on Sunday morning. Are you quite sure you didn't see or hear anything that may not have meant anything at the time, but might be of significance now?'

Julia shook her head. 'It's simply not possible,' she declared. 'I don't care what your evidence says, it has to be wrong. And if you are suggesting that I had something to do with Justine's death, you are also wrong.'

Julia Lorrimer pulled the cardigan draped around her shoulders closer to her as if suddenly cold. Shaking her head as if confused or bewildered, she moved away from the veranda rail and sat down in one of the chairs. Paget moved another chair into position and sat down to face her.

'Now look, Chief Inspector,' she said carefully, 'I am as keen to find out who did this to Justine as you are, but I find the implication that she was killed in her room, while I was in the house, not only ridiculous but impossible. As I told you when I reported her missing, Justine left the house around twenty minutes to eight. I went up to get Michael a few minutes after that – maybe ten minutes to eight. I was up there for about ten minutes or so helping Michael get washed and dressed, then we went downstairs. Sebastian can verify that, because he was coming up from the gym when we were going down. I gave Michael his breakfast, then took him over to Tilly's about eight thirty or quarter to nine – I'm not sure exactly, but Tilly will probably remember. I came back to change and get ready for church before Stephen arrived. Sebastian came downstairs just as I got back, so I told him he'd have to get his own breakfast, but he said he was going to meet Jim Bradley for breakfast before going off into the country somewhere. He left and I did a quick tidy-up in the kitchen before going up to get changed. Stephen arrived, and we left shortly afterwards for church. So, if you're looking at me as a suspect, I'm afraid you'll have to think again, Chief Inspector, because there simply wasn't time.'

Julia placed both hands on the arm of the chair as if about to rise.

'Just one question before you go,' said Paget. 'How long were you out of the house that morning?'

Julia thought for a moment. 'We left here about ten minutes to ten, and it must have been close to twelve thirty by the time we got back here.' Julia glanced at her watch and got to her feet. 'And that, I'm afraid, is all the time I can spare,' she concluded. 'With Stephen away trying to get Michael settled, and all that's going on in the house, Sebastian has been doing his best to cope with things in the office, but much of what we do here is new to him, so I need to be there.'

'In that case, I'll come with you,' Paget said, falling in step beside her, 'because I need to talk to your son as well. And since both you and Mr Lorrimer were in Justine's room on Easter Monday, I'll need you both to come down to Charter Lane to give statements, and we can take your fingerprints and DNA swabs for elimination purposes at the same time. Tomorrow will be soon enough.'

'We can use Jim's office,' Sebastian Mills said as he led the way into a vacant office and closed the door. 'He just left and I don't expect he'll be back today.'

'Jim . . . ?' Paget queried. 'Was that the man I saw leaving a few minutes ago. Tall, sturdy-looking chap, dark hair, middle-aged?'

'Jim Bradley,' Sebastian said. 'I think he started out as Stephen's campaign manager, originally, but he can turn his hand to anything – fundraising, programme arranger, speech writer, you name it.'

Sebastian stood to one side and waved Paget towards the desk. 'I suppose, if I'm to be interrogated,' he said flippantly, 'then you should have the chair behind the desk and I should take the suspect's chair on this side. Isn't that how it works, Chief Inspector?'

'Do you consider yourself a suspect?' asked Paget as he sat down behind the desk.

Sebastian settled comfortably into one of the chairs and stretched his long legs out in front of him. 'According to my mother, we both are, although I think you could be making a mistake if you've dismissed Michael as a suspect. He can be pretty violent at times, you know.'

Paget eyed Sebastian dispassionately for a long moment. 'Suspect or not,' he said coldly, 'the last thing I need when investigating the brutal murder of a young woman is snide and flippant remarks. Any more of them and we will continue this conversation in Charter Lane under caution. Is that clear, Mr Mills?'

Sebastian made a face. 'I didn't mean . . .' he began truculently, then changed his tone when he saw the expression on Paget's face. 'Sorry. It's just that I'm a bit nervous about all this. Not that I've got anything to hide,' he added quickly. 'It's just the idea of being interviewed about what I was doing when Justine was, well . . .' He took a deep breath and straightened himself up. 'What do you want to know?'

In fact, Sebastian didn't have much to tell. He stuck to his

story of seeing Justine from his bedroom window as she went
through the gate, but could add no details beyond those he had
given to Molly Forsythe. He said he'd spent about half an hour
in the gym, then corrected himself, saying it was probably more
like twenty minutes because he had a bit of a hangover from
drinking in the pub the night before. After showering, he said he
got dressed, then left the house a few minutes before nine. 'And
that's it,' he concluded. 'I was out all day and didn't get back
till late Sunday evening.'

Paget nodded. He knew that part at least was true, because
they had Sebastian on CCTV as he'd come out of Lorrimer Drive
and turned south on Edge Hill Road. 'Tell me, where did you
go and who were you with?'

'I was with Jim Bradley,' Sebastian replied. 'I happened to
mention something to him the other day about not being too keen
on the family plans for Easter Sunday, so he asked me if I'd like
to come along with him and a mate of his to do a tour of the
car boot sales in the area. It wasn't really my thing, but it was
better than hanging around here, so I went along. We met at
Woodlands Golf and Country Club for breakfast, then set off
about ten and drove to a little place near Ludlow, where we
picked up Danny Speers. He's Jim's cousin or nephew, or something like that, and the three of us spent the rest of the day going
from one car boot sale to another, ending up in Ross-on-Wye.
We had dinner in a pub, then came home. As a matter of fact, I
paid for dinner, so I can dig out the receipt if you like, but Jim
and Danny will confirm that I was with them.'

'Did you buy anything at the boot sales?'

'Got a portable radio for six quid,' he said proudly. 'Talked
the bloke down from ten, so I did all right.' He sat back, looking
pleased with himself.

'What was the purpose of the trip?' asked Paget. 'Were the
others looking for anything in particular?'

'Jim picked up a pretty good power drill, but I don't think he
was actually looking for one when we set out. I think he just
likes meeting people. Danny's a bit different; he was looking for
bargains that he could sell on. He bought a couple of lamps, and
a few other bits and pieces, but that was about it. It was just a
day out, really, and quite enjoyable as it turned out.'

'What was your relationship with Justine Delgado?'

Sebastian blinked at the sudden turn in the questions. 'There wasn't one,' he said after a moment's hesitation. 'In fact, I hardly knew the girl. I've been away at uni, so I only see her briefly when I'm home during the holidays. Anyway, she spent most of her time with the kid in the south wing, so the only time I would see her was at the odd meal or in passing.'

Paget looked sceptical. 'She was an attractive young woman living under the same roof. I'm surprised that some sort of relationship didn't develop. Did you ever ask her out?'

Sebastian shook his head. 'It wasn't like that,' he said. 'Justine was really all work and no play. That was all she ever talked about. She wasn't interested in a social life, and she made that clear from the beginning. Besides, I have a girlfriend. We're not officially engaged, but we've been together now for several months, so it's pretty serious. She's taking a summer course in Leeds at the moment; otherwise, she would be down here with me now.'

'Did you know that Justine was between three and four months pregnant when she died?'

'Aahh . . . was she?' Sebastian looked more startled than surprised. 'No, I mean, good God no! It's news to me, if it's true. And if it is, I hope you're not suggesting that I'm the father?'

'Oh, it's true,' said Paget. '*Are* you the father?'

'No, I'm bloody well not!' Sebastian snapped. 'So you can forget that, and I'm tired of all these questions. Are we finished here?'

'Not quite. Tell me how you spent your time on the Saturday evening before Justine disappeared.'

Sebastian eyed Paget suspiciously. 'I don't see what that has got to do with anything,' he said.

'Tell me anyway. I'd like to know where everyone was before as well as after Justine disappeared.'

Sebastian shrugged. 'There's not much to tell,' he said. 'A chap I shared digs with for a while, when I was in Bristol, rang me, said he was in town, and suggested we get together for a drink and a chat. He suggested the White Hart, though God knows why. Anyway, we met, had a few drinks, and that was it.

I got home around eleven, maybe eleven thirty – I don't remember exactly – and went to bed.'

'The name of your friend?' queried Paget.

'Oh, for God's sake! Is that really necessary? You don't trust my word?'

'It's not a matter of trust,' Paget replied blandly. 'It's a matter of verification. I can check at the White Hart, but I'd prefer that you tell me now.'

'Simon Lerner,' Sebastian said sullenly. 'But you're out of luck if you want to talk to him, because he's a volunteer on a dig somewhere in Israel. He's an archaeologist – at least that's his field. He's from here originally, but I first met him in Bristol when I was at uni a couple of years ago. He was in town for a few days before heading off to Israel, and he gave me a ring. As I said, we had a few drinks and a chat.' Sebastian wrinkled his nose and shrugged. 'All he wanted to talk about was this dig in Israel. Boring as hell. Finally, he said he had things to do and pushed off. I stayed on for a while, then came home.'

'So where was he staying?' asked Paget. 'You say he was from here originally. Is he married? Do his parents live here?'

'I know he's not married, but as for the rest . . .' Sebastian shook his head. 'I've no idea. Can I go now?'

Paget nodded. 'But I would like you to come down to Charter Lane to make a formal statement; while you're there, we'll take your fingerprints and a DNA swab for the purposes of elimination. Your mother will be coming in sometime tomorrow; perhaps you can come in at the same time.'

'His name is Jim Bradley,' Tregalles told Paget as they got into the car. 'He started off as Lorrimer's campaign manager, but he does a bit of everything. He says they've become very close friends over the years.'

'As a matter of fact, Sebastian told me who he was and what he does,' said Paget. 'But friend of the Lorrimers? Or Mrs Lorrimer in particular?'

'I didn't ask, but I did ask how well he knew Justine, and he said he'd never actually met her. He said all he really knew about her was that Stephen Lorrimer spoke highly of her and was impressed with what she was doing for the boy. He said he'd seen her with Michael the odd time or two, but that was all.'

'Did you believe him?'

Tregalles shrugged. 'Didn't seem to be any reason not to,' he said.

'He is certainly on familiar terms with Mrs Lorrimer,' Paget said, 'so give Ormside a ring and tell him we need a background check on Bradley, and his relationship with Mrs Lorrimer in particular. It may have nothing to do with the murder of Justine Delgado, but let's check it out anyway. And while you're at it, tell him I want the footage from the cameras on River Road checked for sightings of any of the cars belonging to the Lorrimers and Mills on the nights of Easter Sunday and Monday, because that body didn't get to the river by itself.'

TWENTY

Thursday, 17 May

'I think Mrs Lorrimer has boxed herself into a corner,' said Paget as he studied the timetable on the whiteboards. 'There is no way Justine could have been killed and the room completely sanitized *after* eight o'clock on Sunday morning.'

'And considering the time it must have taken to clean that room and get the body away, there had to be at least two people involved,' Tregalles said. 'Which reminds me. I rang Maria Navarro to ask if she knew whether Justine liked lavender, and she said no. She said Justine didn't like any strong-smelling perfumes or sprays.'

DC Sophie Kajura approached the group and caught Molly's eye. 'Got it!' she said in a stage whisper, grinning as she handed the clipboard to Molly. She paused just long enough to give Molly a brief explanation before returning to her desk.

'Something we've being working on, sir,' said Molly in response to Paget's enquiring glance. 'Kajura spotted the discrepancy when she was doing a background check on Stephen Lorrimer. He used his parliamentary credit card at the all-night petrol station on the corner of King George Way and Worcester Road on Easter Sunday. It was dated and time-stamped at thirty-seven minutes past midnight, which is at odds with his original statement, when he said he spent the night in Worcester. So we put in a request for an ANPR check on the roads between Broadminster and Worcester for that night, and these are sightings of Mr Lorrimer's car. Beginning late Saturday evening, we have Mr Lorrimer's car leaving Worcester at seven minutes past ten. It appears again on King George Way here in Broadminster at ten fifty-five. And again at the same intersection at twenty-eight minutes past midnight, going the other way. Nine minutes later he's at the all-night petrol station, where we have a picture of the man himself when he uses his credit card. And the last sighting we have is when he comes off Broadminster Road in Worcester at one twenty-seven on Sunday morning.'

'Well done,' said Paget. 'Do we have anything from the camera covering the entrance to Lorrimer Drive?'

'Haven't had time to get to that yet,' Molly told him, 'but now that we have the times narrowed down, it shouldn't take too long to check.'

So, Stephen Lorrimer had lied about where he was that night, thought Paget. Lorrimer wasn't the first person to have an alibi blown by the watchful eyes of the automatic number plate recognition cameras on the major roads and thoroughfares. This could prove to be the break they needed.

'He didn't mention *that* when we questioned him,' Tregalles muttered darkly. 'Must have slipped his mind. Looks like he has some explaining to do. Shall I bring him in?'

'I'm beginning to think that the whole family has some explaining to do,' Paget said grimly. 'Do we have anything more from Forensic?' he asked Ormside.

'They've examined the weights in the gym in Simla House,' Ormside told him, 'but they're nothing like the ones used to hold the body down. Nor does the wire they found in the garden shed match the wire on the body.' The sergeant looked at his notes. 'You asked if there had been any unusual reports of happenings on River Road over the Easter weekend,' he continued. 'There was one that might mean something. On the Tuesday following Easter, a Mr Lance Eagleton reported the theft of a skiff from its mooring under the old boathouse below River Road, which just happens to be close to where the body was found. He said he used it on the Sunday, and it was properly secured when he left it, but it was gone on the Tuesday. It was found by a couple of boys a week later in the reeds about three miles downstream.'

'Sounds as if the skiff might have been used to get the body out into the deepest part of the river, then abandoned when the killer or killers had finished with it,' said Paget. 'Thanks, Len. I think things might be coming together at last.' He turned to Tregalles, but the sharp sound of his phone cut him off before he had chance to speak.

Tregalles, anxious to be off, started edging away.

Paget answered, then motioned for Tregalles to stay where he was. 'Right,' he said tersely. 'Put them in room number one, and tell them we'll be there in a few minutes.' Frowning, he slid the phone into his pocket. 'Speak of the devil,' he said. 'It seems that Mr Lorrimer is here and is asking to see me. Apparently, he wishes to make a voluntary statement, and he's accompanied by his solicitor.'

Once the dual tapes were running and the date, time and names of those present had been properly entered, it was the solicitor who spoke first. His name, he said, was Howard Melrose, and he was a partner in a law firm based in Worcester. He was a small, middle-aged man, quite unremarkable in appearance, except for a pair of heavy horn-rimmed glasses that looked almost too big for his narrow face. But the eyes behind the glasses were sharp enough, Paget noted.

'For the record,' Melrose said in a thin, precise voice, 'my client is here of his own free will to make a statement regarding his relationship with Justine Delgado. But I want it clearly understood that this has nothing whatsoever to do with the untimely death of that young woman.' He sat back in his chair and stared owlishly at Paget.

'Understood, Mr Melrose,' Paget said. 'Mr Lorrimer?'

Stephen Lorrimer sat a little bit straighter in his chair and clasped his hands together in front of him on the table. 'I have a question first,' he said. 'Is it true that Justine was pregnant?'

Paget nodded. 'Yes, it's true, Mr Lorrimer. Why do you ask?'

Lorrimer avoided the question by asking, 'How far along was she?'

'According to the autopsy report, roughly fourteen weeks.'

'And I imagine you will be doing DNA testing to try to determine who the father was?'

Paget frowned. 'I was given to understand that you were here to make a statement,' he said, 'but you seem to be here in search of information. So which is it, Mr Lorrimer?'

'Sorry. It's just that . . . well, I had to be sure,' Lorrimer said with a glance at his solicitor. 'You see, I didn't know – at least not until last night, when Sebastian told me – that Justine was pregnant. He said you accused him of being the father, and—'

'For the record, Mr Lorrimer, I did not *accuse* Mr Mills of being the father, but I did *ask* him if he was. And, again for the record, he said he was not the father. However, once we have the DNA results, I think we can settle the matter.'

Lorrimer was shaking his head. 'There's no need to wait for them,' he said quietly. 'That is what I came here to tell you – for the record, as you say. I am the father of the child. It wasn't meant to happen, but it did, and I take full responsibility.' He leaned forward, fingers spread on the surface of the table. 'You see,' he continued, speaking earnestly now, 'you have to understand—'

'There is no need for elaboration, Stephen,' Melrose broke in quickly. He placed a restraining hand on Lorrimer's arm. 'You've given them your statement; there's no need to say more.' He moved his hand to Lorrimer's shoulder and started to get up, but Lorrimer shook it off and remained stubbornly seated.

'No, Howard,' he said tightly, 'that is *not* all I have to say. I knew that if the police found out that I was the father, and thought Justine had told me back then at Easter, they might think that I had a motive for . . .' His voice faded into the back of his throat, and he had to cough several times to clear it. 'For getting rid of her,' he ended huskily. 'And I really *didn't* know until Sebastian told me last night.'

'Stephen, there is no need to elaborate,' Melrose cautioned once again, only to have Lorrimer round on him. 'I need to give them the whole picture,' he insisted,' so thank you for your advice, Howard, but I know what I'm doing. I'm not proud of what happened, but I have to make them understand how it was.'

Paget and Tregalles exchanged glances. It was not uncommon for clients to argue with their solicitors while being questioned, but it was seldom a good idea.

Lorrimer turned back to face Paget. 'We were both so focussed on Michael's progress,' he said earnestly. 'We spent so much time together whenever I was home. Justine worked so hard with Michael, and she came to love him as if she were his real mother. But much as she loved her work and Michael, it was no life for someone like Justine to be stuck up there, day in, day out, with only Michael for company, and Julia, well . . .' Whatever he'd started out to say was dismissed with a wave of the hand. Frowning as if at some past memory, Lorrimer focussed his attention on his hands. 'Last Christmas was the worst time for

Justine,' he said. 'She was homesick and worried about her grandfather. I offered to pay her way there and back to visit him, but she wouldn't hear of it. I tried my best to comfort her and suddenly . . . it just happened.' He shrugged guiltily. 'I know it shouldn't have happened, but it did.'

Melrose lifted his head and closed his eyes as if trying to pretend he hadn't heard what his client had said, and a soft sigh escaped his lips.

'We only had a few days before I had to return to London,' Lorrimer continued, 'and even then there were so many last-minute things to do with my work that we barely saw each other. It wasn't until I returned at Easter that I realized that something was troubling Justine. I was going to talk to her the first chance I got, but with young Terry following her about like a puppy, and so many other things that needed my attention, I didn't get the chance before she disappeared.'

Tregalles remembered the crucifix wrapped and hidden away in the drawer of the bedside table. Justine had been wrestling with her conscience, unable to reconcile her religious beliefs with what she had done. It made sense now, and it explained why Justine's friend, Maria Navarro, and Tilly and Father Leonard had noticed a change in her.

Lorrimer sat back in his chair and closed his eyes. 'I'm sorry,' he said, 'I should have told you this before, but I just couldn't bring myself to do it.'

'Does your wife know about you and Justine?' asked Paget.

Lorrimer nodded slowly. 'She does now,' he said. 'I told her last night; we talked it out, and that's partly why I'm here. Julia thought it best to get everything out in the open.'

'That's very understanding of her,' Paget observed drily.

Lorrimer nodded in a vague sort of way as if thinking of something else. 'So, that's it, then,' he said, preparing to rise. 'Do I have to sign something . . . ?'

'We can do that later,' Paget told him, 'but I have a few questions before you go.' He opened a slim folder in front of him. 'For example, you told DS Tregalles and DS Forsythe that you spent the night of Saturday, March thirty-first, in Worcester, and didn't return to Broadminster until shortly after nine o'clock on Sunday morning. Is that correct?'

Lorrimer looked puzzled by the question. 'That's right,' he said, 'I got back just in time to change before Julia and I went off to church. Why?'

'And you stayed at the Raebourne Hotel in Worcester?'

'Yes.'

'And you were there all night, were you, sir?' The question came from Tregalles, who had opened a similar folder and appeared to be studying it intently.

'Of course I was there all night,' Lorrimer said impatiently. 'It had been a long and tiring day.'

'Then, can you explain to me,' Tregalles said as he slid several pictures out of the folder, 'how your car came to be caught on camera, leaving Worcester at seven minutes past ten on the night of Saturday, March thirty-first, and was seen again on King George Way here in Broadminster at five minutes to eleven that same night? And,' he continued before Lorrimer had a chance to reply, 'we see your car again on King George Way as it is leaving Broadminster at twenty-eight minutes past midnight on Sunday, April first . . . and here you are again at thirty-seven minutes past midnight at the all-night petrol station at the turn-off to Worcester, where you used your government-issue credit card.' He slid the still pictures across the table one by one. 'Can you explain that, Mr Lorrimer?'

The colour had drained from Stephen Lorrimer's face. He looked to Melrose for help, but the solicitor merely spread his hands and shook his head in a way that said Lorrimer was on his own on this one.

'Mr Lorrimer?' Paget prompted.

Stephen Lorrimer puffed out his cheeks and made a vague gesture of apology. 'All right,' he said, 'I lied, and I apologize. I know it was wrong, but it had nothing to do with the disappearance of Justine, and I didn't see what good it would do to have my . . . association with Justine brought out into the light of day for no good reason.'

'Apart from concealing your affair from your wife,' Tregalles said bluntly.

'It wasn't an *affair*, Sergeant,' Lorrimer said testily. 'It was . . .' Seeing the expression on Tregalles's face, he decided it was pointless to try to explain. 'Anyway, it had nothing to do with your investigation, because Justine didn't disappear until the following day.'

'I think we will have to be the judge of that,' said Paget, 'after we've heard your version of events – under caution, of course, Mr Lorrimer. Sergeant?'

When the caution had been given, Melrose laid a hand on Lorrimer's arm. 'You're not obliged to say *anything*, Stephen,' he warned. 'I think we should talk about this before we continue.'

But Lorrimer pulled his arm away and shook his head impatiently. 'It's all right, Howard,' he said brusquely. 'I really didn't think it was anybody else's business, but now that my relationship with Justine is out in the open, I'm quite prepared to explain what happened. It's not as if I'm trying to hide anything.'

Even Howard Melrose had trouble masking his reaction to that statement by his client, as did the two detectives.

Lorrimer closed his eyes for a moment to collect his thoughts. Or to try to work out what he could get away with, thought Paget cynically.

'Yes, well,' Lorrimer began nervously, 'I suppose it really began when I received a message from Justine before I left London at the beginning of the Easter break. It was very short. All it said was "Must talk as soon as you get home. Urgent!" I replied right away – in fact, I sent several messages, but Justine didn't reply to any of them.'

'This was a text message from Justine?' asked Paget.

'That's right.'

'On your BlackBerry? Is it still there?'

Lorrimer shook his head. 'I deleted it on the train before I got home.'

'But the original message to you might still be on Justine's phone, if we can find it,' said Paget, but Lorrimer was shaking his head again. 'She sent it from a disposable phone. I bought it for her so we could keep things more . . . well, more private.'

'A disposable phone that is also missing,' Paget observed drily. 'Go on, Mr Lorrimer.'

'As I said earlier, I could see something was troubling Justine, and we tried to talk several times, but we just didn't get a chance, so I told her I would come back from Worcester on Saturday night. Justine was to leave the door to the outside stairs on the latch, and we could talk in her room without anyone else in the house knowing I was there.' Lorrimer grimaced again. 'But it all went wrong,' he said. 'I didn't want anyone to hear me drive in, so I parked the car a couple of streets away and walked in. But nothing worked out as planned.'

'So what went wrong, exactly?'

'For one thing, the light was on in Justine's room, and I'd told her to turn it off so it would look as if she'd gone to bed. As well, the door at the top of the outside stairs was locked and I didn't have a key. I thought that perhaps Michael was having trouble sleeping – he does sometimes – and Justine was looking after him. But the door stayed locked and the light stayed on. I sat there on the top step, expecting Justine to come to the door at any moment, but after about an hour, or maybe a bit more, I decided we would have to find another opportunity to talk, so I left.'

'You didn't attempt to phone or text her?'

'I didn't know what was going on in there, or who might be around, so I didn't dare try to contact her. Besides, I'd waited this long to find out what was troubling Justine, so I didn't think another few hours would hurt. At least Terry would be out of the way.'

'And in all this time,' said Paget, 'that is, from the time you got home on the Wednesday of that week, till Saturday, you are saying there was no opportunity for Justine to tell you that she was pregnant? Is that correct, Mr Lorrimer? I find that very hard to believe.'

Lorrimer shrugged. 'Believe what you want, Chief Inspector, but it's true.'

An audible snort of disbelief came from Tregalles.

'Does your wife know all this?' asked Paget. 'About your coming back from Worcester to see Justine, then sitting outside for an hour or so before going back without seeing her?'

Stephen Lorrimer blinked as if taken by surprise by the question. 'I . . . well, no, actually, she doesn't,' he said. 'I mean, I didn't think it necessary to mention it. I didn't want to hurt her any more than I had.'

TWENTY-ONE

Ormside set his coffee aside. 'I'll buy the first part about Lorrimer being the father of the child, because he knows that DNA will prove it,' he said, 'but driving back to Broadminster from Worcester in the middle of the night to have a serious talk with his girlfriend, then turning round and going back to Worcester without making more of an effort to see her? That doesn't make sense to me.'

'Nor me,' Tregalles said. 'The boss let him go, but I still think he's lying.'

'So do I, if we're talking about Stephen Lorrimer,' said Paget, who had caught the last few words as he entered the room. 'But until we can prove it, he goes free. Which means we will have to work just that much harder to get at the truth.'

'Speaking of lying,' said Ormside, 'Lorrimer isn't the only one who's been lying to you.' He walked over to his desk to pick up a sheet of paper, and put his glasses on. 'I got a very cool reaction from the university in Leeds when I mentioned Sebastian Mills's name,' he said. 'The person who finally agreed to speak to me about him, would only say, "Mr Mills is no longer enrolled in any course or programme here; in fact, he left before the end of the spring term and is not expected to return."' Ormside took off his glasses. 'Which made me curious, so I contacted the university security service. Even they were pretty closed-mouthed, but they finally told me that Mills was asked to leave after several female students complained of "persistent and aggressive sexual harassment".'

'What about this girlfriend he is "almost" engaged to?' asked Paget.

'He isn't,' Ormside said. 'Apparently, he was pretty serious about one of the foreign students, but when she heard that he was telling people that they were about to become engaged, she dumped him. A few days later, rumours that she was having an affair with one of the profs began to circulate on line. It escalated into hate mail – hideous, suggestive stuff. Everybody knew that Sebastian was behind it, but it was coming from all directions, and they couldn't prove it. The result was the girl abandoned her studies in the middle of the semester and went home. The person I spoke to wouldn't give me her name or where she came from, and they said if we needed more information, we would have to go through official channels. However, that seems to have been the trigger for other young women to come forward to complain of sexual harassment and rough treatment from Mills, and he was asked to leave. Which,' Ormside concluded, 'is when he came down here in March.'

'I told you,' Tregalles said smugly. 'So, what's the betting he tried it on with Justine and it all went wrong? He hit her and the next thing you know, she's dead. Well?' he said, looking for some reaction from the others.

'It's *one* possibility,' Ormside conceded neutrally. He picked out a couple of pictures from several on his desk. 'Once we learned that Lorrimer was here in town on Saturday night, I had Kajura look at the tapes covering the earlier part of Saturday evening, and these are some of the stills she took from it.' He handed Paget a picture showing the back of an SUV as it was turning off Edge Hill Road into Lorrimer Drive. The picture was time-stamped 21:40. It wasn't as clear as it might have been, but the number plate was readable. 'It belongs to James Bradley,' Ormside said, 'and he doesn't leave again until well into Sunday morning.' He handed Paget another picture time-stamped 04:21.

'Maybe Mrs Lorrimer invited Bradley over for the night after her husband rang to say he'd be staying on in Worcester,' Tregalles suggested. 'Come to think of it, Lorrimer must have seen Bradley's SUV in the car park when he came in, but he never mentioned that, did he?'

'Perhaps he did notice it, but wasn't surprised,' said Paget. 'Do we know if Sebastian was in the house?'

Ormside looked at his notes. 'He went out at nine minutes past eight and came back at eleven nineteen.'

'Stephen Lorrimer made no mention of that, either,' said Paget, 'and yet he must have seen Sebastian drive in *if* he was sitting at the top of those stairs. And Sebastian must have seen Bradley's SUV when he came home, and wondered what he was doing there at that hour. It sounds as if there was a lot going on in Simla House that night. We have Mrs Lorrimer, Bradley, Sebastian, and Justine and Michael inside the house, and Stephen Lorrimer outside . . . assuming he's telling the truth.'

'So what are you thinking, boss?' Tregalles asked.

'I'm thinking we've been lied to by practically everyone in that house from the moment Mrs Lorrimer walked in here to file a missing person's report,' Paget said grimly. 'And I swallowed her story hook, line and sinker. There was no reason *not* to believe her at the time, but still . . .'

He pointed to the whiteboards. 'Now,' he said, 'we know that Justine was alive at eight o'clock on Saturday evening when she phoned Mrs Tillman. We also know that the rug had been changed and the room sanitized by eight o'clock on Monday morning. Mrs Lorrimer herself was forced to confirm that when I asked her about it, because to say anything else would have been inconsistent with what she'd been telling us. She and the others have gone to great pains to give themselves alibis that can be confirmed from roughly eight o'clock on Sunday morning right through till Monday, including a session at the hospital on Sunday night and the early hours of Monday morning with Michael.'

Paget tapped the whiteboard. 'Put all that together, and that tells me that Justine Delgado never left the house to go to mass on Easter Sunday, because she was already dead. And since we know it had to have taken at least two people several hours to sanitize the room, and we can account for everyone's movements for the rest of the time that weekend, the only time Justine could have been killed is late Saturday night or early Sunday morning. I think Stephen Lorrimer *did* get into the house, and *did* meet with Justine in her room on Saturday night, and that is when she was killed. Whether he killed her or someone else did, I don't know, but he certainly didn't hang around to do any of the cleaning up. He took off back to Worcester and left someone else to do that, and I see Mrs Lorrimer's hand in that part of the cover-up. And if she was directly involved, Jim Bradley must have been involved as well, since he didn't leave till sometime after four on Sunday morning.'

'Perhaps we've been looking for the wrong cars on River Road,' Ormside suggested. 'We've been looking for cars belonging to the Lorrimers and Sebastian, but perhaps we should have been looking for Bradley's SUV. If he was involved, he could have taken Justine's body out when he left. I'll have Kajura look at the tapes again, and have her check from the time Bradley left the house.'

'I suspect you might have better luck if you check the River Road tapes from, say, midnight to three o'clock on *Monday* morning,' Paget told him, 'because Bradley didn't leave Simla House until after four on Sunday morning, which wouldn't leave him much time to get rid of the body before daybreak. Now all we have to do is prove which one – if it was only one – actually killed Justine.'

There weren't many people in the White Hart pub when Tregalles popped in late that afternoon. 'Easter Saturday? Sorry, can't help you,' the man behind the bar said when shown a picture of Sebastian Mills. 'I wasn't working that night, but Kelly was. Kelly Goodman – she's the manager. You'll find her in the office in the back. You can go through if you like. Down the passage, second door on the right. Just knock and go in.'

The woman seated behind a cluttered desk when Tregalles opened the door looked vaguely familiar. Blonde, trim figure, a little plump in the face and under the chin, but still a good-looking woman, he thought appreciatively.

She looked surprised, then suspicious. 'I know you,' she said warily. 'Used to be a regular in the Hart a few years back. You're the copper, right?'

'DS Tregalles,' he said. He remembered her now; she'd been the barmaid back then – and one of the reasons he used to drop into the White Hart after work. 'You've got a good memory,' he said. 'That was before I was married.'

A sly smile touched her eyes. 'So you told me several times, if I remember,' she said. 'So, what brings you back now?'

'I'm not here to give you any trouble,' he assured her. 'It's one of your customers I want to ask you about. He says he was in the White Hart with a friend on Easter Saturday. I wondered if you would remember him.' He took a picture of Sebastian from his pocket and showed it to her.

Kelly Goodman looked at it and nodded. 'Easter weekend,'

she said slowly. 'Oh, yes, I remember him. Made a right nuisance of himself. I refused to serve him in the end and sent him packing.' She handed the picture back. 'Why? Someone complained, have they?'

Friday, 18 May

Stephen Lorrimer had just stepped out of the shower when he heard the sound of his mobile phone ringing insistently in the bedroom. He ignored it. Six forty-five in the morning? It had to be a wrong number. And if it wasn't, they could ring again if it was really all that important. He towelled himself dry and padded naked into the bedroom. His BlackBerry was on the bedside table, but he didn't pick it up until he was completely dressed and ready to go downstairs. Even then, he was tempted to put it in his pocket without looking to see who had called, but curiosity wouldn't allow him to do that. He looked at the screen and caught his breath.

'Two eggs?' Julia asked when her husband appeared in the doorway. She stood by the Aga, frying pan in hand. 'There's a nice bit of ham left from yesterday's lunch if you'd like it?' She frowned. 'Stephen? What's wrong?'

Lorrimer took a deep breath as he moved into the kitchen and sat down. 'Jason Cutter rang while I was in the shower,' he said. 'I called him back. He wanted to know if it was true that the body recovered from the river "down our way", as he put it, was that of our missing *au pair* girl. When I said yes, he expressed his sympathy and that of the prime minister, then asked if there were any "implications" that he should know about.'

Julia set the frying pan down. 'What did you tell him?'

He shrugged. 'What could I say? I just told him that we were all very shocked and quite devastated, and the police were investigating.'

Julia's eyes narrowed as they searched his face. 'And . . . ?' she prompted.

Lorrimer furrowed his brow and pursed his lips as if thinking deeply. 'Let's see, now,' he said. 'How did he phrase it? Ah, yes. He said that, while he was quite sure there was nothing to worry about in my case, he just wanted to remind me that there were those in the media who might try to make something of the fact that Justine had been employed by a sitting MP. He suggested that we keep responses to a minimum, and focus their attention on how devastating this has been for our son. Oh, yes, and by the way, he'd liked to be kept "in the loop, so to speak", regarding any progress in the investigation into Miss Delgado's untimely death.' Lorrimer pushed his chair back and got to his feet. 'I think that about covers it,' he said tightly. 'And don't bother about breakfast; I'm really not hungry. I think I need some fresh air.'

It was mid-morning when Paget arrived in the incident room after attending a meeting in New Street. He was greeted by Ormside, who eyed him critically. 'Can't see any scars,' he said. 'How are things in New Street these days?'

Paget smiled. 'A lot quieter than they were,' he said, but didn't go into details. 'What's happening here? And where's Tregalles?'

'He's gone to pick up a fax,' Ormside told him. 'He should be back any minute now. As for anything new, we're not doing very well. I was hoping we'd have some results on how they got that body to the river, but there is no sign of Bradley's SUV on any of the tapes. Forensic thought they might be able to trace the ten-kilo weights that were wired to the body, but it turns out they were made by a Belgian firm that went out of business in the 1970s, so that came to a dead end.'

Tregalles appeared with a sheet of paper in his hand. 'Just got this in from Simon Lerner,' he said. 'He's in Tel Aviv. Got his number from his parents here in town, so I spoke to him early this morning, and he faxed me a brief statement confirming what he told me on the phone.' He saw the quizzical expression on Paget's face, and grinned. 'But, then, you don't know, do you? I dropped into the White Hart on my way home, yesterday, checking up on Sebastian's movements on Easter Saturday, and I spoke to Kelly Goodman – she's the manager, but she was behind the bar that night. She remembers Mills and Lerner coming in – Sebastian in particular because he wasn't a regular, and secondly because of his good looks.

'She said the two of them went off to sit in a corner, but later on she saw two young women, both locals, were sitting with

Mills and Lerner and they all seemed to be enjoying themselves. It was a busy night, so she didn't see what happened, but suddenly there were raised voices and some sort of commotion at their table, and the two women were pushing their way through the crowd and heading for the door. A few seconds later, Lerner hurried out after them. Then, a few minutes after that, Sebastian came up to the bar, all serious and apologetic, telling Kelly that he's afraid his friend had a bit too much to drink and made unwanted advances to one of the girls.

'Kelly says she thought it was decent of him to apologize on behalf of his friend, and thought no more about it. But he stayed there at the bar and started coming on to her. She said she usually takes that sort of thing in her stride, but he was getting quite persistent and suggestive, and he was drinking heavily, so she finally told him she couldn't serve him anymore, and if it was female company he was looking for, he should look elsewhere, or better still go home.'

Tregalles paused for effect. 'Which is when Sebastian said, "Now, why didn't I think of that? I can do both at the same time." He laughed and asked Kelly for a bottle of wine to take out. She said by that time she was only too happy to be rid of him, so she sold him a bottle of Sauvignon Blanc, and that was the last she saw of him.

'But that's not the end of it,' Tregalles said. 'The following week, one of the women came in and told Kelly what really happened. She said the place was crowded when they came in, so Sebastian offered them a seat and bought them each a white wine. She said he was very nice and quite funny. The drinks kept coming, and they were having a good time, until, suddenly, Sebastian started groping her under the table and whispering in her ear. She said she tried to get him to stop, but he wouldn't, so she kicked him as hard as she could, grabbed her friend by the arm and took off out of there. She said that Lerner, who had been quiet all evening, followed them out and called to them, but they just kept running.'

'So you contacted Lerner in Israel.' Paget pointed to the fax in Tregalles's hand. 'What did he have to say?'

'He confirmed the girl's story. He said he hadn't seen Sebastian for a couple of years, and he realized soon after they sat down that they didn't have much to talk about, so he was quite relieved when Sebastian offered the two young women a seat. He said Sebastian bought them drinks, and, for the first little while at least, they were having a good time. Sebastian kept them all entertained with stories, and the drinks kept coming. But then, Lerner said, the stories began to get a bit more raunchy, and he was already beginning to feel uncomfortable, when, suddenly, Sebastian gasped, grabbed his leg and started swearing. He said the woman next to Sebastian jumped up so fast that she knocked the drinks over, as well as her chair, and it was only then that he realized what had been going on. He said both women ran out and he tried to follow them to apologize for Sebastian's behaviour, but he couldn't catch them.'

'Do you believe him?' Paget asked.

'I do,' Tregalles said. 'Lerner is quite a bit older than Sebastian, and I think he was quite shocked by Sebastian's behaviour. He said he's never been so embarrassed in his life, and the only thing he wanted to do was get out of there.'

He walked over and drew a line under Sebastian's name on the whiteboard. 'I think that, after an evening of drinking and two failed attempts to pick up a woman, Sebastian went off home with his bottle of wine and tried it on with Justine. There was a struggle, he hit her, she fell back and hit her head on the mantel, and went down. I think we should have him in.'

'I agree,' said Paget, 'so go out there and pick him up. Take Forsythe with you, and make sure she is a witness when you caution him. Arrest him on suspicion of conspiring to conceal a suspicious death, perverting the course of justice, wasting police time, etcetera, etcetera, but *not* murder. Allow him one phone call, then take his phone away from him. Bag it and turn it over to the custody officer when you bring him in. I want the Lorrimers to see that they are no longer protected and it will only be a matter of time before it's their turn.'

TWENTY-TWO

It was stuffy in interview room number three. It was the smallest of the interview rooms – properly ventilated, but windowless – and some people found it claustrophobic . . . which was why Paget chose it. Sitting beside Sebastian Mills was Arthur Williams, the solicitor sent in by Sebastian's mother when Sebastian had scoffed at the need for one.

'So, Mr Mills,' Paget said, 'as I've explained, in the light of what we now know about your movements that Saturday evening, I'm sure you can see how a judge or jury might look at it. You'd been drinking heavily; you'd been rejected by one young woman at your table, for good reason according to her and your friend, Mr Lerner. And your attempt to chat up the woman behind the bar didn't go too well, either, did it? But suddenly you buy a bottle of wine, saying you might do better at home. And, since Justine Delgado was the only one there, apart from your mother, it isn't hard to see the connection.'

'That's bullshit!' Sebastian said. 'The woman was drunk, so her word means nothing. Her word against mine. And Simon's somewhere at a dig in Israel, so I know you haven't been talking to him.'

'Believe it or not, Mr Mills, they do have phones in Israel,' Tregalles told him. 'And fax machines.' He slid a paper across the table. 'Mr Mills is being shown a copy of a fax received this morning from Simon Lerner,' he said for the tape.

Sebastian read it, then tossed it aside. 'That's bullshit as well,' he said scornfully. 'In fact, he was the one who was almost slavering over Jane something or other. I don't think the poor bugger has had a woman in years, if ever. Now he's trying to put the blame on me. Some friend!' He slouched back in his chair. 'And as for the barmaid, chance would be a fine thing if she thought I was chatting her up. God! Give me some credit for taste!'

'Nevertheless,' said Paget, 'she remembers clearly what you

said about going home to find a girl, and buying the bottle of wine. Add to that your track record with young women at Leeds, it's not hard to see a pattern forming here, is it, Mr Mills?'

Sebastian flinched at the mention of Leeds.

'You don't take rejection well, do you?' Paget continued. It was a statement rather than a question. 'So, when you arrived home in your inebriated state, and Justine turned you down, I can see how one more rejection might be the last straw and cause you to lash out. You may not have *intended* to kill her, but, unfortunately for you, that blow caused her to hit her head on the corner of the mantel, and that was it. Suddenly, you had a body on your hands, and the only other person in the house was your mother. So, either you ran to her for help or she heard the commotion and came to see what was going on. Which was it, Mr Mills? Because you certainly didn't do all that cleaning up yourself.'

'Are you quite finished?' Arthur Williams asked in a pained voice. 'Because, from where I sit, you have nothing. As for the barmaid's testimony, it was a busy Saturday night, and it simply isn't credible that she would recall *exactly* what was said when my client asked for a bottle of wine before leaving.'

'And the wine was for . . . ?'

'His mother, who is partial to that particular wine,' Williams replied blandly. 'Once home, Mr Mills went straight to bed, and his mother will testify to that. As for the rest, you can't even prove when Miss Delgado was killed.'

'Oh, I think we can, Mr Williams. Mr Mills and the Lorrimers spent so much time establishing alibis for their whereabouts *after* Justine supposedly left the house on Sunday morning that the only time she could have been killed in her room was late Saturday night or very early Sunday morning. They've boxed themselves in with alibis for the wrong period of time. I put the case to the CPS and they agree with me that we certainly have enough to charge Mr Mills with conspiring to conceal a suspicious death, and I'm confident that there will be more serious charges to follow. As I said before, apart from his mother, Mr Mills was the only person in the house when Justine Delgado was killed.'

'Then go ahead if you really think you have a chance,' said Williams airily.

'Now, just wait a bloody minute!' Suddenly alert, Sebastian

glared at Williams. 'I'm not having this. You're supposed to be defending me, and I wasn't the only one in the house that night. I went straight up to bed. My mother met me at the door and helped me up to my room and dumped me on my bed. She'll tell you.'

'Really?' said Paget softly. 'So, who else was in the house?' He knew, of course, that Bradley was in the house because they had the evidence on the CCTV tapes, but he wanted to hear what Sebastian had to say.

'Jim,' Sebastian said sullenly. 'Jim Bradley was there.'

Paget shook his head. 'Now, why would Mr Bradley be there at that time of night, Mr Mills?'

Sebastian snorted. 'You're not much of a detective if you can't work that out,' he said disdainfully. 'He's often there when Stephen's away, and he was there that night.'

'You saw him? Spoke to him?'

Sebastian shook his head. 'I saw his car when I drove in,' he said. 'My mother met me at the front door and steered me upstairs to bed. I think Jim must have been in her bedroom, but I heard him and my mother talking in the hall afterwards.'

'Did you hear what they were saying?'

'It was muffled. It sounded as if Jim was upset about something, and I wondered if it was because I'd come home and caught them together. Not that I was bothered. I like Jim, and I've had an idea for some time that he and my mother were . . . well, you know. But then I must have fallen asleep, because next thing I knew, daylight was coming in the window.'

'Who told you to lie about seeing Justine leaving the house on Sunday morning?' asked Paget.

'No one,' Sebastian said stubbornly. 'I saw her.'

'Justine was dead long before that, Mr Mills. You lied and so did your mother. Are you protecting her or is she protecting you?'

Arthur Williams stirred in his seat. 'I don't think you have a case against my client,' he said, 'so I suggest you let him go.'

'And I suggest he remain exactly where he is,' Paget replied, 'because I don't believe him, and he is still under arrest.'

Julia Lorrimer was arrested on suspicion of conspiring to conceal the death of Justine Delgado, perverting the course of justice and wasting police time. The arrest was carried out by DCI Paget and a uniformed WPC, and she was taken down to Charter Lane in a patrol car. She'd protested that she couldn't leave the office because her husband had gone out to the farm to spend the day with Michael, but Sylvia Lamb had piped up to say, 'No problem, Mrs Lorrimer. I'll call Mr Lorrimer and tell him what's happened, and I can manage till he gets back. It's quite quiet here today.'

Julia Lorrimer's solicitor, a woman by the name of Rita Thurlow, who was clearly a friend as well as Mrs Lorrimer's solicitor, was amazingly quick to respond to Julia's call. She arrived at Charter Lane while her client was being processed by the custody officer, and Paget wondered if she'd been alerted earlier to the possibility of Julia Lorrimer being arrested.

Dressed all in black, except for a dove-grey neck scarf tucked into the top of the jacket of her two-piece suit, Rita Thurlow couldn't have been much more than a couple of inches over five feet tall, including her three-inch heels. Long, dark hair framed a rather pleasant face, but there was a stubborn set to her mouth, and the eyes gave no secrets away.

Now, she and Julia Lorrimer were sitting in the same two chairs that had been occupied by Stephen Lorrimer and his solicitor the day before. Julia had been cautioned, both at the time of arrest and a second time for the record in the interview room, so Paget wasted no time in getting down to business.

'Mrs Lorrimer, according to what you told me on the third of April this year, and confirmed in the missing person report you signed on that same day, the last time you saw Justine Delgado was when she spoke to you in the kitchen at approximately twenty minutes to eight on Easter Sunday morning, before going off to mass. Is that correct?'

'Yes, it is.'

'And yet you knew that to be a lie,' said Paget. 'Because we now know that Justine was killed either late Saturday night or early Sunday morning. We know this because, having verified your movements and those of your family over the Easter weekend, that is the only possible time it could have happened.'

'Except for the time we were all away from the house on Sunday morning,' Julia pointed out.

'You're suggesting that Justine was killed by someone who came in from outside?'

'Of course. We were gone for almost three hours.'

'Someone who knew where to find another rug to replace the blood-soaked one?' Paget suggested. 'Someone who also knew where to find a bedspread, bleach, cleaning materials and lavender spray? The same kind of spray that you use, Mrs Lorrimer. And someone who was not only able to do all that, but managed to spirit the body away from the house in broad daylight without detection? I don't think so, Mrs Lorrimer. Tell me, what time did your son Sebastian come home the previous evening. Do you remember?'

'Of course I remember,' Julia said tightly. 'It was about eleven thirty. I was on my way to bed when he came in. I was annoyed with him because he'd obviously had too much to drink, and I had to help him up the stairs to bed.'

Tregalles looked up. 'Did you actually *see* him go to bed, Mrs Lorrimer?' he asked.

'As I said, I was annoyed with him, so I left him *on* his bed, fully clothed, then I went to bed myself.'

'Where was Jim Bradley while this was happening?' asked Paget.

Julia Lorrimer's mouth opened and closed, but she recovered quickly. 'What on earth does Jim have to do with this?' she asked, as if genuinely puzzled.

'Well, for a start, he was in the house, and I suspect he was in your bedroom,' said Paget. Tregalles slid a sheet of paper across the table. 'The CCTV camera on Edge Hill Road shows him arriving at Simla House at twenty minutes to ten that night,' he said. 'Could you tell us the reason for his visit, Mrs Lorrimer?'

Julia sighed. 'He dropped in because he thought Stephen would be back from Worcester by then, and he was curious to know how things had gone. He didn't stay long; he left about . . .' Belatedly, she remembered the CCTV camera.

'Twenty-one minutes past four on Sunday morning, to be precise,' Paget told her with a nod to Tregalles. The sergeant slid a second piece of paper across the table. 'And Jim Bradley didn't just "drop in" expecting to find Stephen there,' he said. You rang Bradley yourself only minutes after your husband telephoned to say that he would be staying in Worcester overnight.' Tregalles produced another sheet of paper. 'This shows the time and length of both telephone calls,' he explained. 'And we believe that Justine Delgado's body was in Mr Bradley's SUV when he left Simla House that morning,' he added deliberately.

Julia Lorrimer ran the tip of her tongue around her lips as she stared at the papers in front of her. The silence between them lengthened. Lips compressed, she closed her eyes tightly and hung her head. She remained in that position for several seconds, then lifted her head to look at Rita Thurlow.

'I can't do this,' she said simply. 'I thought I could for Stephen's sake, but—'

'*Don't* say any more!' The first word came out like the crack of a whip, startling Tregalles, who had been rather taken with the diminutive solicitor facing him across the table. But it had the desired effect. Julia Lorrimer stopped speaking, and Rita Thurlow turned to Paget. 'I'm advising my client to say no more until we've had a chance to talk about this in private.'

'Thirty minutes?' Paget suggested.

The solicitor nodded. 'I'll let you know if I need more.'

'Fair enough,' said Paget, with a nod to Tregalles.

'Interview suspended for thirty minutes at solicitor's request. DCI Paget and DS Tregalles leaving the room. The time is fifteen fourteen.' He turned the recorder off.

'We've had a break,' Ormside greeted him when Paget walked into the incident room. 'As I told you earlier, Kajura has scanned every inch of the CCTV footage from midnight to daybreak on Easter Monday, and there's no sign of Bradley's SUV. But that girl just doesn't give up, so she started to look for any car that had gone up River Road after midnight, and had come back down again within an hour or so, and she found one.' He tapped the notebook in his hand. 'She identified a Kia Picanto going up the hill at twenty minutes to two, and coming back down again at two thirty. The Picanto is registered in the name of the late Theresa Bradley, Jim Bradley's mother. She died last November, and there's no record of the car or her house being sold.'

Bless the girl! Paget felt as if a weight had been lifted from his shoulders. Finally, something they could get their teeth into.

'Thank you, Len,' he said, 'that is good news. I want that car found; I want Bradley brought in, his house searched, and, depending on where we find the car, I want a door-to-door around the neighbourhood asking if anyone saw or heard the car leaving or coming back that Monday morning. You shouldn't have any trouble getting a warrant, so—'

'All in hand,' Ormside assured him when he could finally get a word in. 'DS Forsythe and DC Falkner are on their way to Bradley's house as we speak; a second team is on its way to Bradley's mother's house, and SOCO is on standby.'

'Excellent! And please thank DC Kajura for her good work. This could be the turning point in the investigation.'

'I think she might appreciate it more if you told her yourself,' Ormside suggested. 'She spent a lot of her own time staring at that screen, so I think a word from you wouldn't come amiss.'

It wasn't *quite* an admonition, but it served to remind Paget that things had changed with the arrival of Superintendent Amanda Pierce. He'd been spending more time in the office upstairs and less time down here and in the field.

'Which is the way it is supposed to be,' Pierce had argued. 'As DCI, you should spend more time in the office and let your people do what they do best. You have a good team; let them get on with the job.'

She was right, of course. The late Superintendent Alcott had allowed him far too much freedom in the field, and he'd taken advantage of it, because it was what he liked to do. But there was a price to pay. He hadn't thought about it before, but, prompted by Ormside's not so subtle reminder, he realized he was losing touch with the men and women with whom he'd worked so closely in the past.

'Point taken, Len,' he said. 'I'll have a word with her.'

TWENTY-THREE

'Interview resumed at fifteen forty-three,' Tregalles said, having set the tape recorder in motion and recited the names of those present once again.

'I'd like to begin by asking about your relationship with Mr Bradley,' Paget began, only to be interrupted by Rita Thurlow.

'With regard to Mr Bradley,' she cut in sharply, 'Mrs Lorrimer wishes to make a voluntary statement. Against my advice, I might add, but it is her choice. As I said, it is voluntary, and I trust it will be taken into consideration when this matter is resolved.'

'That may not be up to me, Ms Thurlow, as I'm sure you know,' said Paget, 'but it is now on record. Mrs Lorrimer?'

But again, before Julia Lorrimer could reply, the solicitor cut in ahead of her. 'I feel compelled to warn you that this could have serious consequences, Julia, including a prison term, although I would hope it won't come to that.'

Julia nodded. 'You've made that very clear, Rita, and I'm grateful for your advice, but I'm tired of lying, and I just want this whole thing to be over.' She raised her eyes to meet those of Paget. 'I'm afraid I've been very foolish, Chief Inspector. We all have, for that matter, but once we started down that path, we couldn't stop. But that's not what you want to hear, is it?' she said in a firmer voice, 'so I'll go back to the beginning.

'It really began when Justine came downstairs that Saturday evening to tell me that she was pregnant, and Stephen was the father. She said she was sorry that it had happened because she was genuinely very fond of Stephen, but she knew that if it ever became public knowledge, it could damage his career, and it would almost certainly lower his chances of becoming a cabinet minister. Oh, yes,' Julia said, seeing the question in Paget's eyes, 'I'm not supposed to say anything, but he's been told he's being considered for a cabinet post, and I'm afraid it was that as much as anything that clouded my own judgement in trying to protect him.'

Paget frowned. 'You accepted Justine's word without question that your husband was the father of her child?'

'Oh, yes.' The little shrug of resignation said more than words. 'I knew they were having an affair. They were both passionately fond of Michael – I only wish to God I could feel the same, but I can't – and it was almost inevitable that the two of them would . . .' She spread her hands and left the rest unsaid.

'You didn't mind?'

Julia seemed to think about that for a moment or two. 'In a strange way, I think I was relieved,' she said. 'It made me feel less guilty about my own affair with Jim. And before you ask, Stephen knew about that as well, so he probably felt less guilty when he was with Justine. However,' she hurried on, 'that's all by way of history. Stephen and I do love each other, and we make a great team. It's just that with him being away so much, we made . . . adjustments.'

'But it wasn't until that Saturday evening that you knew Justine was pregnant?' said Paget in an attempt to get back to the matter at hand.

Julia pursed her lips. 'Let's just say I had begun to wonder, but I didn't *know* until Justine told me. Anyway, Justine was very practical in everything she did, and she had it all worked out. She said she would make no claim on Stephen as the father. She said she was prepared to return to Manila and have the child, but it would mean giving up a well-paying job, and without it she would not be able to keep her grandfather in the home he was in. She said he was ailing and was not expected to live long, but until that time she wanted Stephen to promise to continue paying her present salary into her account in Manila. She said once her grandfather died, she would let Stephen know, and she would expect no more payments from him, and we would never hear from her again.'

'Did you believe her?' asked Paget.

Julia hesitated. 'I did,' she said slowly. 'Justine was very honest, but there were no guarantees. I mean, what if her grandfather carried on living for another ten years or more? What if Justine decided not to tell us if he died? Or if she just became used to the money and continued to demand it as the price of her silence? I mean, I did trust her, and it wasn't an unreasonable request under the circumstances, but still . . .'

'But it was still blackmail,' Paget said. 'You say this was Saturday evening; was this before or after your husband phoned to say he would be staying the night in Worcester?'

'Before.'

'What did he have to say about it?'

Julia shook her head. 'I didn't tell him,' she said. 'I wanted to think about it. To be honest, I was afraid his emotions would impair his judgement. Which is why I rang Jim and asked him to come over. Jim is a pragmatist, and he has Stephen's best interests at heart, so I wanted to talk it over with him before I said anything to Stephen.' Julia paused, brow furrowed as she looked past Paget into the distance. 'Jim is such a dear man,' she said softly, 'always so dependable, always willing to help, but I wish I'd never called him that night.'

'Why was that, Mrs Lorrimer?'

'Because none of this would have happened,' she said sadly, 'and it's all my fault!'

'That may be the way my client is *feeling*,' Rita Thurlow cut in quickly. 'So let it be clearly understood that this is in no way an admission of guilt or responsibility for anything that happened that evening.'

Julia sighed. 'Unfortunately, Rita, it *is* the way I feel,' she said, reaching out to pat the solicitor's hand before turning back to Paget. 'I told Jim what Justine had said, and he agreed with me that we should try to sort something out before telling Stephen. I could understand where Justine was coming from, and if she stuck to her word, I could live with that. But I really wasn't sure how Stephen would take it if he knew that Justine was carrying his child. He can be very emotional about such things, and we had no idea how he might react to the news. He might even want to become involved in the child's welfare, and I couldn't risk that. He's worked so hard to get where he is – we all have – and we want him to receive the recognition he deserves, but one wrong move on his part, and all those years of work would mean nothing.

'You see,' Julia continued, 'Justine said she hadn't told Stephen that she was pregnant. In fact, she said he was driving back from Worcester later that night to see her, and she was going to tell him then. So Jim and I began to wonder if there was any way we could persuade her to simply leave without Stephen ever knowing about the child, but the problem was the money. How could we continue to pay her without Stephen knowing? I have some money of my own, but not enough to handle a steady drain like that over a number of years. Jim said there might be a way to draw money from the business accounts – fake some expenses or something like that – but Stephen keeps a pretty sharp eye on the bank accounts, and we couldn't hide that sort of thing for very long.'

Julia Lorrimer spread her hands in a gesture of helplessness. 'We weren't getting anywhere until, finally, Jim suggested that he go up and talk to Justine, and I agreed. To be honest, I didn't know if it would help or not, but Jim has a way with people, and I suppose I was hoping that he would work something out with Justine.' She took a deep breath. 'Unfortunately, it didn't work out that way. In fact, it was a total disaster. Jim was only gone a few minutes when he came running downstairs, looking as if he'd seen a ghost. He could barely get his breath, but when he did he said, "I think Justine's dead! Honest to God, it was an accident, but she's not breathing."' Julia shut her eyes. 'I can still see his face,' she said. 'It was chalk white, and I knew that something was dreadfully wrong because there was blood on his hands and the sleeves of his jacket. Even then, I couldn't bring myself to believe it until I went upstairs to see for myself. Justine was lying on the floor in a pool of blood, and I knew at once that Jim was right and she was dead. I didn't know what to do; I couldn't think, and Jim was there beside me, saying over and over again that it was an accident.'

Julia paused, eyes fixed on some distant scene. 'I don't know how long I stood there,' she said quietly, 'but when I finally managed to pull myself together and got Jim to calm down, I asked him to tell me exactly what had happened. He said that he had knocked on Justine's door; she opened it, and he explained why he was there. He said she told him to come in, and said something like "I'll just turn the gas off", then bent down quickly to do that and hit her head on the mantelpiece. Jim said he'd followed her in and was right behind her when she staggered back and bumped into him. He put out his hands to stop her from falling, but she spun away from him, and fell backwards and struck her head on the corner of the mantel. Jim said she just crumpled, and suddenly there was a pool of blood around her head. He said he got down on his knees and tried to stop the blood, but he couldn't, and he realized that she was dead.'

Julia Lorrimer shook her head sadly. 'There was nothing either of us could do,' she said. I remember saying we should call an ambulance, but Jim kept saying, "No, we can't do that; they'll never believe it was an accident. There'll be an autopsy. They'll find out she's pregnant. There'll be questions, and that's the last thing Stephen needs right now. It could ruin his career."' Julia lifted her head to look straight at Paget. 'I knew he was right,' she said. 'I mean, I knew that it would be wrong to cover up what had happened, but I also knew that he was right about Stephen's career. Justine may have died exactly as Jim said she did, but who would believe it? Even a whiff of scandal could destroy a lifetime of work. Stephen wasn't even in the house, but that wouldn't matter to the press.'

Julia looked away. 'So we set to and spent the rest of the night setting the room to rights. Jim went down to the basement and gathered up some plastic bags, then took the rug and bedspread and various other things down the outside stairs to his car, along with Justine's body. We cleaned and scrubbed until we were satisfied that it would pass inspection, then brought in the other rug and bedspread.'

'You said, "Justine *may* have died exactly as Jim said she did,"' said Paget. 'Did you doubt his story, Mrs Lorrimer?'

Julia gave a flick of her head as if dismissing a disturbing thought. 'It was so bizarre,' she said. 'It *was* hard to believe. But knowing Jim as I do, there was no way that he could make up a story like that on the spur of the moment. He'd only gone up to talk to her. He barely knew Justine, and it's not as if he's a violent man. But I could see what the media would do with a story like that, which was why I finally concluded that there was nothing we could do for Justine, and agreed to help Jim cover it up.' She shot a guilty look at her solicitor. 'And I might as well tell you the rest and have done with it,' she said. 'It was my idea to report Justine as a missing person, and I'm truly sorry for all the trouble I've caused.'

'What time did this take place?' asked Paget. 'When Jim went up to talk to Justine?'

Julia thought for a moment. 'Ten thirty, quarter to eleven, perhaps,' she said tentatively.

'Where was Sebastian while all this was going on?'

'He came in around eleven thirty,' Julia said. 'I saw the headlights of his car hit the window as he came down the drive, so I went downstairs to meet him. He had no reason to go into the south wing upstairs, but I wanted to make sure that he didn't. As it turned out, he was drunk, so I got him up to his room and on to his bed. I knew that once he was asleep, he'd be dead to the world until morning. Then I went back to help Jim.'

'Do you remember if Sebastian was carrying anything?'

'He was waving a bottle of wine about,' she said. 'I took it away from him.'

'What happened to it?'

'I'm not sure,' Julia said slowly. 'I remember telling Sebastian that he'd had more than enough to drink for one night, and I took it away from him. It's probably in the kitchen somewhere. Why? Is it important?'

'It could be, but we've not been able to find it anywhere in the house.'

'Then I don't know what happened to it,' Julia said. 'I know I didn't drink it.'

'Did you know your husband was sitting outside on the steps while you and Bradley were in Justine's room?'

'Good heavens, no! At least not until he told me after he'd been to see you. Fortunately for Jim and me, Stephen had given up and gone back to Worcester by the time Jim started taking things down to the car.'

'What did Mr Lorrimer say when you told him what had happened?' asked Paget.

'I didn't tell him until last night. Jim and I both thought it best to leave him out of it for his own sake, so he really believed that Justine had gone missing.'

A questioning glance from Tregalles caught Paget's eye. He responded with an almost imperceptible nod, then sat back in his chair to focus his attention on Julia Lorrimer as the sergeant took over. 'I know you said that Mr Bradley barely knew Justine,' Tregalles said, 'but are you quite sure about that, Mrs Lorrimer?'

'I don't know what you're suggesting,' Julia said cautiously. 'To the best of my knowledge, they barely knew each other.'

'Yet he was the one who went upstairs to talk to her,' Tregalles countered. 'I would have thought she might be more receptive to what you might have to say.'

Julia Lorrimer shrugged. 'I had nothing to offer her,' she said. 'But Mr Bradley did?'

'As I said before, Sergeant,' Julia said patiently, 'Jim just said he'd go and talk to her to see if something could be worked out, and I was grateful for anything he might be able to do. I'm not sure that even he had anything specific in mind when he went up. He was just trying to help.'

Tregalles glanced at his notes. 'When you went upstairs to see for yourself if Justine was really dead, you said, and I quote, "I knew she was dead." Did you examine the body closely, Mrs Lorrimer?'

Julia swallowed. Her hands fluttered. 'I . . . well, close enough to know she wasn't breathing,' she said. 'There was so much blood.'

'Did you have any doubts about the cause of Justine Delgado's death?'

Julia frowned. 'I don't know what you mean,' she said. 'It looked pretty obvious to me. There was blood coming from a gash in the back of her head.'

'I think what the sergeant is asking you *again*,' Paget said quietly, 'is whether or not you were satisfied with Mr Bradley's explanation about *how* Justine died.'

'I . . .' Julia spread her hands and shrugged. 'I know it sounds . . . well, almost too incredible to be true, but things like that do happen, don't they? I mean, it's not the sort of story one would make up and expect to be believed, is it?'

'The point is, Mrs Lorrimer, did *you* believe it?' said Paget.

'I . . .' Julia moistened her lips and raised her head defiantly. 'Yes, I did,' she said firmly. 'I've known Jim a long time; he's a good friend and very loyal to Stephen, so yes, of course I believed him.'

Tregalles didn't say anything, but the look he gave Paget said much more than words.

TWENTY-FOUR

When Paget and Tregalles left the room, Rita Thurlow followed them out to ask if her client could be released. 'Mrs Lorrimer has given you a voluntary statement, so there's nothing to be gained by holding her. I mean, it's not as if she's liable to disappear. She knows she's in trouble, and she's resigned herself to facing the consequences. You haven't charged her, so there's no reason to hold her.'

'I haven't charged her *yet*,' said Paget. 'But there will be charges, so Mrs Lorrimer will be held until I've had time to decide exactly what those charges will be.'

'Ah, good!' said Ormside when they entered the incident room. 'I was just trying to decide whether to interrupt your interview with Mrs Lorrimer or just send in a note. Bradley is with the custody officer. Forsythe and SOCO are searching Bradley's house and garage, and the second team is at Bradley's late mother's house. They found the Kia Picanto in the garage, and they're arranging for it to be brought in.'

'Good work, Len. It looks as if—'

'There's more,' Ormside broke in. For a man who rarely smiled, he was looking particularly pleased with himself. 'Stephen Lorrimer is here,' he continued. 'He was out of town when Mrs Lorrimer was arrested, but when the girl in the office phoned him, apparently she told him that his wife had been arrested for the *murder* of Justine Delgado, so he came charging in here, demanding to have his wife released. He says it was Bradley who was responsible for Justine's death and persuaded Julia to help him cover it up.'

'Did he now?' said Paget. 'That is very interesting. Was Lorrimer under caution when he said that?'

'Unfortunately not,' Ormside said. 'Apparently, he said that to the man on the front desk before I got to him. I arrested him on suspicion of conspiring to conceal a suspicious death, and cautioned him. He said he only found out about Bradley yesterday when his wife broke down and told him. I tried to question him further, but he refused to say anything more. He's in room number two if you want to talk to him.'

'Later,' Paget said. 'Let him stew for a while. It sounds as if he and his wife have their stories straight at least, but he's going to have to wait his turn. I want to hear what Bradley has to say for himself before I talk to Lorrimer.'

'It's about time!' Jim Bradley said truculently when Paget and Tregalles entered the room. 'My house is being torn apart, my car has been taken away, and I'm told I'm suspected of disposing of a body in an unlawful manner, whatever that means.'

'It means exactly what it says,' Paget replied. He held up his hand for silence while Tregalles proceeded to put new tapes into the recorder and enter the requisite information. 'I'm told you have been cautioned; your rights have been explained to you, and you have been given the opportunity to call a solicitor, which you refused to do, Mr Bradley. Is that correct?'

'You know it is, so just get on with it,' Bradley growled. 'And I don't know what you are talking about.'

'Oh, I think you do,' said Paget, and proceeded to lay out the pictures of Bradley's SUV entering and leaving Lorrimer Drive on Easter Saturday and Sunday, together with pictures of his mother's car on River Road on the following Monday.

'Doesn't mean anything,' Bradley said, but his tone was more subdued. 'I mean, how do you connect that with a body? They're just pictures of cars. There's nothing to show what's in them, or even who's driving.' He folded his arms as if that ended the matter.

'Then perhaps you should hear this,' Paget said, producing a cassette recorder and setting it on the table between them. He turned it on.

Bradley couldn't hide his surprise as the sound of Julia Lorrimer's voice filled the room. Grim-faced at first, his expression slowly changed. He bent his head to listen more closely. Colour began to rise in his neck, and the muscles around his jaw stood out like cords beneath the skin by the time the tape came to the end. Paget switched it off. Head bowed, elbows on the table, Bradley ran his fingers through his hair.

They waited for him to say something, but Bradley remained silent. Tregalles, impatient to get on, said, 'So how do you respond to that, Mr Bradley?'

Bradley raised his head. His face had undergone a complete change. He looked older, almost haggard. 'She makes it sound so *bloody* plausible, doesn't she?' he said in a voice barely above a whisper. 'And she leaves you thinking that all that stuff about blackmail really happened, and I killed Justine to keep her quiet. Oh, yes,' he breathed, 'Julia's very good with stories. God knows she's had a lot of practice over the years, believe me. But it's still a load of bollocks from beginning to end. In fact, I never even met the girl while she was alive. I've seen her around a few times, but never close enough to be introduced or to even say hello.'

Bradley picked up the pictures on the table and studied them closely. Considering his options, thought Paget. The silence lengthened.

'Mr Bradley is looking at the pictures of his late mother's car on River Road,' Tregalles said for the benefit of the tape.

Bradley roused himself and tossed the pictures on the table. 'I've always known that Julia would do anything to help Stephen get ahead,' he said, 'but I never thought it would include murder, and that she would try to pin it on me. I loved her; even knowing that she would never feel the same about me, I was prepared to do as she asked as long as no one was hurt. We were doing it for Stephen, she said, and I'll admit I went along willingly, because I didn't think that Stephen should suffer because of an unfortunate accident.' Bradley tilted his head back, closed his eyes and shook his head slowly from side to side. 'I *really* thought I meant more to her than that,' he said. He was silent for a few moments, and when he opened his eyes again, the contours of his face had undergone a subtle change. His tone of voice was almost light as he said, 'I suppose this is a foolish question, Chief Inspector, but do I get any credit if I tell you what *really* happened the night Justine died?'

'All I can tell you is that your cooperation will be noted,' Paget told him. 'No promises, I'm afraid.'

Bradley nodded as if to say he'd thought as much, and had resigned himself to the inevitable. 'So, where to begin?' he said pensively, looking at Paget as if seeking direction.

'You might start with the phone call Mrs Lorrimer made to you shortly after learning that her husband would be staying overnight in Worcester,' Paget suggested.

'Ah, yes, you know about that, don't you?' said Bradley. His voice was perceptibly stronger. 'Very well, then, Julia rang me to say that Stephen wouldn't be home that night, and asked me to come over. As she says on the tape, we've been sleeping together fairly regularly when Stephen's away. He knows, but as long as we don't actually talk about it openly, he lives with it, and we're still friends. In fact, he has a similar arrangement when he's in London. Tania, I believe her name is. One of the opposition members' wives.'

'Lorrimer claims he didn't know until his wife told him yesterday,' said Paget.

Bradley snorted. 'Of course he knew. In fact, he as good as told me he was glad Julia was sleeping with someone he knew. But then that's Stephen for you. He would say that. Always conscious of the image, is Stephen.'

Paget wasn't surprised. 'So you went over . . .' he prompted.

'That's right. Julia and I had a drink, We talked for a while, then went up to Julia's bedroom about quarter past eleven. We were just starting to get undressed when we heard shouting coming from down the corridor. Julia stuck her head out the door and said something like, "That sounds like Sebastian. He's drunk and he's brought someone home with him." Then she told me to stay there while she went to see what was going on.

'But I didn't stay there,' he said, 'because I was sure that it was *Stephen's* voice I'd heard, as well as Sebastian's. I was curious, so I slipped out and followed Julia at a distance down the corridor.'

'Weren't you afraid of being seen?' Tregalles asked.

Bradley shook his head. 'Not really,' he said. 'Julia was well ahead of me, and that corridor is very poorly lit at night, and with those deep alcoves every few feet, I wasn't worried. Even if they did see me, I'd just say I was downstairs, heard the noise and thought someone might be in trouble. That wouldn't have been too hard to believe, because there was one hell of a shouting match going on, and one of those voices was definitely Stephen's, and it was coming from Justine's room.'

'How did you know it was Justine's room?' Tregalles cut in. 'You said you had never really met the girl, so how did you know it was her room?'

'I didn't until then,' Bradley shot back, 'but it became pretty obvious once I could see inside. The door was wide open and Stephen and Sebastian were yelling at each other, and Justine was in the middle trying to break things up.'

'And you saw all this without anyone realizing you were there?' Tregalles shook his head in disbelief.

'As I said, there are alcoves,' Bradley said patiently, 'deep alcoves in the corridor between the rooms; you must have seen them. They go back the depth of the rooms on either side, and if you stand well back in any of them at night, no one would know you were there unless they *really* stopped to look. But, yes, I was afraid I might be seen, so when Julia went into the room, I crossed the corridor to the alcove on the other side and stayed there out of sight. I didn't know it at the time, but it turned out to be next to Michael's room. And from there I had a clear view through the open door across the corridor into Justine's room. Go and take a look for yourself if you don't believe me.'

Tregalles gave a non-committal grunt. 'So what happened then?'

Bradley thought for a moment. 'Julia just stood there for a moment in the doorway. I don't think she could believe what she was seeing, and neither could I. Stephen was supposed to be in Worcester, but there he was, wearing nothing but boxer shorts; Justine was wearing some sort of short negligee with nothing underneath, and Sebastian was fully clothed and screaming obscenities at his stepfather while trying to brain him with a bottle. In any other setting, it would have been a farce. But not in this case,' he ended soberly. 'They were deadly serious.' Bradley blew out his cheeks as if he'd been running. 'As I said, Sebastian was trying to hit Stephen with the bottle, and Stephen was trying to get it away from him, while Justine was trying to get in between to part them. I don't think they knew Julia was there until she screamed for them to stop. And I mean *screamed*!' Bradley said. 'And that's when it happened. Sebastian let go of the bottle just as Stephen was trying to wrench it away. Stephen's arm flew back and the bottle hit Justine square in the face. She staggered back, whacked her head on the mantel, then fell forward and collapsed on the floor.'

Bradley paused to slow his breathing. There was sweat on his brow. 'It was as if time had stopped,' he said. 'Everyone just stood there for two or three seconds, then Stephen dropped to his knees and started screaming for someone to call an ambulance, while he was dabbing at Justine's head, trying to stop the bleeding. Sebastian just stood there like an idiot, saying things like, "I didn't do it. You saw it, Mother. He hit her. I didn't do it; it was him, not me," until Julia slapped him so hard that he almost fell over.

'But it shut him up, and, from that point on, Julia took charge. She pushed Stephen out of the way and got down on her knees to feel for a pulse, then shook her head. I couldn't hear what she said, but I think she said that Justine was dead. Stephen was panicking about getting an ambulance, and I think he was about to call one when, suddenly, there was this godawful noise bouncing off the walls of the corridor. I didn't know what the hell it was until I saw young Michael standing in the middle of the corridor, bawling his head off, and he was heading straight for Justine's room. He couldn't see, of course, but he could hear, and I suppose he woke up to hear the shouting, and he was scared. Scared the hell out of me, too, because his door was only a few feet away from where I was standing, and I hadn't seen him come out.'

Bradley took another deep breath and let it out again. 'The boy was almost at the door before anyone reacted, but Stephen got there just in time to scoop him up and try to calm him. The boy was crying and I think Stephen was, too. He stood there rocking the boy and sort of crooning to him. Then Julia called to him from inside the room. She said, "Take him back and stay with him until he goes to sleep, Stephen. There's nothing you can do here."'

Tregalles snorted. 'And you just stood there and did nothing?' he said.

'What *could* I do?' Bradley turned to Paget. 'You have to realize that everything I've told you took place within the space of two or three minutes.'

'Go on,' said Paget.

Bradley didn't respond immediately, and Paget had the feeling that the man was thinking carefully before he carried on.

Bradley put a hand to his head and ran his fingers through his hair. 'Yes, well, sorry,' he said vaguely as if finding it hard to concentrate. 'Stephen took the boy back to his room and closed the door. I was afraid I might be caught if I stayed there any longer, so I went back to Julia's room to wait and think about what I'd seen.'

Tregalles flicked a questioning glance at Paget, but the DCI shook his head.

'I don't know how long it was before Julia came in,' Bradley said dully. 'Fifteen minutes, half an hour perhaps – I really don't know. I remember how upset she looked as she sat down on the bed beside me and told me there had been a terrible accident, and Justine was dead. She said Sebastian had come home after an evening of drinking, with some silly idea of going to Justine's room with a bottle of wine and asking her to have a drink with him. She said Justine told him to leave, he wouldn't, they argued and it turned into a pushing match. Sebastian pushed her back, she tripped and fell back and hit her head on the corner of the mantel, and, suddenly, she was on the floor and bleeding. Julia said it happened just as she got there; she'd tried to revive her, but Justine was dead.'

Tregalles groaned. 'So now we have three versions of what happened,' he said, 'and I don't believe any one of them. And you're saying she expected you to buy a story like that? What about her husband? How did she explain his presence there?'

'She didn't,' Bradley said. 'There was no mention of him being there.' Bradley looked directly at Tregalles and said, 'Look, I knew she was lying. She didn't know that I'd followed her down the corridor and had seen what really happened, but I was still trying to work out what to do to avoid a scandal that could destroy Stephen's career. I mean, I knew Justine's death was an accident; Stephen wasn't at fault, but I also knew what the media could do with such a story, so I was looking for a way out. The girl was dead; we couldn't bring her back, so, as Julia said, it would be in the best interests of everyone if Justine simply disappeared. And if Julia was prepared to let me think that her son had killed the girl, *accidentally or not*, then she was, indeed, desperate. Which is why I agreed to go along when she asked me for my help.'

'You must love that woman very much to take a risk like that,' said Paget.

Bradley turned to meet his gaze. 'I've loved her from the first day she came to work for Stephen,' he said softly. 'I even asked her to marry me, but she married Stephen instead. Even so, I always hoped that one day . . . .'

'You knew she didn't love you, but by agreeing to help her, it gave you a hold over her,' Paget said. 'Right, Mr Bradley?'

Bradley chewed on his lip, but he didn't answer.

'Whose idea was it to make up the story of Justine going missing?'

'Julia's,' Bradley said promptly. 'As she said, it would focus attention outside the house if it was believed that Justine had been seen going off to mass on the Sunday morning.'

At least Julia had told the truth about that, thought Paget. As for the rest . . .

Bradley went on to say that when they left the bedroom to go to Justine's room, there was no sign of Stephen Lorrimer, nor was there any mention of him as they set to work to clean things up. Michael was fussing, so Julia went into the classroom and warmed some milk, then gave him half of one of her sleeping pills, and that soon put him to sleep. Sebastian was sent to bring up as many bin bags as he could find, together with duct tape, and it was he and Bradley who had wrapped the body and secured it with tape. Once that was done, he said they spent most of the rest of the night cleaning and scrubbing and changing the rug and bedspread.

'You took the body with you when you left that morning,' Paget said.

'That's right, and I took the old rug and bedspread and all the cleaning stuff as well – in fact, I took everything remotely associated with what had happened. But it was too late to get rid of it all that night, so I chucked a bunch of things out of the freezer I have in my garage, and put the body in there.'

'What did you do with the rug and the other things?' asked Paget.

'Cut them up and dropped them off in individual bags in waste bins in different places while we were doing the boot sale tour on Easter Sunday,' Bradley said. 'They'll all be gone by now, of course.'

'You couldn't have had much sleep?' Paget observed. 'How did you and Sebastian manage to stay awake all day?'

'We didn't. When we picked up Danny – my cousin, Danny Speers – I told him we were both a bit hung-over, and asked him to drive while we nodded off.'

'And you moved the body on Monday morning,' Paget said. 'Still the long weekend, still quiet, very little traffic about, but why your mother's car?'

'I used to belong to the boat club years ago,' said Bradley, 'and I knew the track leading down there wasn't all that safe even then, so I didn't want to chance it with the Lexus. Too heavy, whereas the Picanto is about a third of the weight.'

'How did you get the body out into deep water?'

'Borrowed a skiff,' Bradley said. 'Unfortunately, I lost control of it when I went to tie it up again, and it drifted away.'

'And you still maintain that Justine's death was an accident? That no one struck her intentionally?'

'That's right. It was sheer bad luck that Justine was in the way when Stephen pulled the bottle out of Sebastian's hand.'

'Have you talked to Stephen Lorrimer about it since that time?'

Jim Bradley frowned. 'I thought I told you,' he said. 'Stephen has no idea that I know he was there that night. And neither does Julia know that I saw the whole thing from the very beginning. And Stephen is still acting as though he believes Justine went missing after she left the house on Sunday.'

'Unless his wife told him about your part in all this,' Tregalles suggested.

'Why would she?' Bradley countered. 'As far as Julia was concerned, the less he knew, the better. Which was why it came as such a shock to him when her body turned up in the river, because I told no one what I'd done with it, not even Julia, and she was just as happy not to know.'

'Where did the weights come from?' Tregalles asked.

'From an old set that I've had for years,' Bradley told him. 'I dropped the rest of the set at different points along the river in case someone came looking around my place.' Bradley rubbed his face with his hands. 'I hated doing it,' he said. 'But Stephen wasn't responsible for Justine's death; it was just one of those weird accidents. No one was to blame, and I didn't see what good it would do to drag his name through the mud. He's a good friend, for God's sake!'

Who had just told someone at the front desk that it was Bradley who had killed Justine. Clearly, Julia and Stephen Lorrimer had decided that Bradley was to be the sacrificial lamb. Some friend, thought Paget.

He gathered up the papers in front of him and nodded to Tregalles. 'We'll take a break,' he said, 'but we'll be back after we've had a word with Mr Lorrimer.'

TWENTY-FIVE

Before going on to talk to Stephen Lorrimer, Paget and Tregalles returned to the incident room for a word with Ormside, where they found him talking to Molly Forsythe. 'Has anyone mentioned to Stephen Lorrimer that we have Jim Bradley in custody?' Paget asked.

Molly shook her head. 'I haven't seen Mr Lorrimer today,' she said, 'so no.'

'I didn't mention it,' Ormside said. 'Lorrimer knows his wife and stepson are here, of course, which was why he came down in the first place.'

'Good,' said Paget. 'That is all I need to know. Come on, Tregalles. Let's go and see if we can wrap this up once and for all.'

But instead of leading the way to interview room number two, he went instead to room number three, explaining to Tregalles what he was about to do. 'It's a bit of a gamble, I know,' he said, 'but with all of them lying their heads off, we just need one of them to crack.'

'I really must protest,' said Arthur Williams as soon as they entered the room. 'My client has told you everything he knows, and I want him out of here now.'

'I'm afraid that's not going to happen, Mr Williams,' Paget said as he took his seat at the table, while Tregalles began entering the pertinent information into the recorder. 'Sorry it took so long, but we do like to get it right.' Paget opened a slim folder. 'We've been talking to Mr Mills's mother, and it seems she's had a change of heart, and she had quite a lot to say in the end.'

He looked across the table at Sebastian and held his gaze for some fifteen seconds. 'And you,' he said deliberately, 'have been telling us a pack of lies, haven't you, Mr Mills?'

Sebastian's only response was a cautious narrowing of the eyes.

'Do you know very much about duct tape, Mr Mills?' Paget

continued. 'No? I thought not. Amazing stuff, duct tape, especially the adhesive, because it holds impressions and the DNA of anyone touching it. And being waterproof, it preserves the DNA from things like sweaty fingers, especially when it's stuck to something like a plastic bin bag.'

Paget continued to eye Sebastian thoughtfully. 'We have your mother in custody, and she's finally acknowledged that Justine did die on the Saturday night, and she lied about seeing her go off to mass on Sunday. We've heard several versions of how Justine died, but the one I favour is where you barged into her room with your bottle of wine; she took exception to that, and she ended up dead on the floor. Does that sound familiar, Mr Mills?'

'She wouldn't say that!' Sebastian burst out. 'It was an accident, for Christ's sake. She *knows* that! She was there when it happened. It was him. He pulled the bottle out of my hand and that silly bitch got in the way and it hit her. It was him, not me. I'm not taking the blame for that.'

'By him, you mean . . . ?'

'Stephen! Serves him bloody well right, sleeping with that woman. She was half his age. And he gets to go back to Worcester, leaving us to clean up after him.'

'Hardly seems fair,' Paget agreed. 'Tell me about that.'

'Now let's see what Stephen Lorrimer has to say for himself,' said Paget as they walked down the hall.

'You were taking a bit of a chance in there, boss,' Tregalles observed. 'I mean, that story didn't come from his mum; that came from Bradley, and he could have made it all up.'

'Sebastian may have *thought* it came from his mother,' Paget said, 'but if you listen to the tape, that's not what I said. I knew at least one of them had to be lying, and, good as Mrs Lorrimer is, I still felt that Bradley was telling the truth, although I have the feeling he's still holding something back.'

'Mr Lorrimer,' said Paget as he and Tregalles entered the room. 'Your solicitor not with you? Are we waiting for him?'

'I don't need a solicitor,' Lorrimer grated. 'What I need are some answers. I came down here to tell you my wife is innocent, and I've been arrested on some trumped-up charge. Julia had nothing to do with Justine's death. She only did what she did out of loyalty and concern for me. I couldn't believe it when she told me yesterday that it was Jim who . . . well, was there when Justine had that accident. And I demand—'

'You are in no position to demand anything!' Paget snapped. 'You and your family have lied to us, you've wasted hundreds of hours of police time, and you have done your best to cover up a brutal murder. So sit down and we will begin this interview properly. Sergeant, are we ready?'

'Tape's running, sir.'

'Right,' said Paget, and he proceeded to caution Lorrimer again for the record.

'Now, let's forget about this ridiculous story made up by you and your wife about Jim Bradley and Justine. And just to make matters clear, your stepson, Sebastian Mills, tells us that it was you who struck Justine with a bottle of wine, and it was your wife who told you to get back to Worcester without being seen, and orchestrated the clean-up after you left. He claims it was an accident during a scuffle between the two of you after he found you in Justine's room when you were supposed to be in Worcester. And he's prepared to sign a statement to that effect.'

Paget leaned forward across the table. 'And I am prepared to accept that the blow to Justine Delgado's head might well have been an accident, but her death was no accident, was it, Mr Lorrimer? That was deliberate, cold-blooded murder. And for what? Your precious career?'

Lorrimer reared back in his seat. 'Deliberate?' he spluttered. 'You just said it was an accident, so what the hell are you talking about? Cold-blooded murder? That's crazy. It *was* an accident. Justine had just told me she was pregnant when that drunken idiot, Sebastian, came bursting in and came at me. He tried to hit me with a bottle. I tried to get it away from him, but, even drunk, he's strong. We struggled. He was shouting obscene, disgusting things and Justine was trying to get us parted . . .' The words died in his throat. His face crumpled and he sank back in his chair, half gasping, half sobbing. 'It *was* an accident,' he whispered. 'I would never harm her. You have to believe that.'

'Oh, I do,' said Paget. 'But that's not why she died, is it, Mr

Lorrimer? I think once that happened, you realized how it would look if she were taken to hospital and the story came out, so you had to make sure it didn't. Which is why you finished the job by suffocating her. The autopsy report made the cause of death very clear. It showed that Justine Delgado choked on her own vomit as a result of pressure on her nose and mouth.'

Slack-jawed, Lorrimer stared at Paget. Colour drained from his face; he tried to speak, but no sound came. He pushed his chair back and tried to stand, but suddenly his eyes rolled up, his legs gave way and he slid sideways on to the floor.

Saturday, 19 May

'I take it you've seen this?' Superintendent Amanda Pierce was standing by the window, holding a copy of the morning paper in her hand when Paget walked through the door of her office at eight o'clock the following morning. 'How is Mr Lorrimer doing? Have you heard?'

'He's fine, according to the doctors,' Paget replied. 'As far as they can tell, he simply fainted, but they kept him in overnight just to be sure. He'll probably be released today, but he's still under arrest, of course, so he'll be brought back here.'

'But you haven't charged him yet?'

'Not with the murder, no. He and the others will be charged with conspiring to conceal a murder, lying to the police, wasting police time and so on, but at least one of them is a killer, and some, if not all, are accessories to murder and guilty of aiding and abetting.'

'But you don't think it was Stephen Lorrimer?' said Pierce. 'Why not? He had the most to lose.'

'What I saw last night, when Lorrimer collapsed,' said Paget, 'was not the reaction of someone who's been caught out. What I saw was genuine shock. He didn't know that was how Justine died. I'm sure he thought she died as a result of the blow to the head and hitting her head on the mantel. I think his wife actually suffocated Justine while he was taking Michael back to bed, and I think Sebastian helped her. Then she got her husband out of there and on his way back to Worcester as quickly as she could in case he became suspicious.'

Pierce threw the newspaper on the desk and waved Paget to a seat. 'What about Bradley?' she asked as she sat down herself. 'Are you sure he's telling the truth? I mean, is it possible that he could remain hidden in an alcove while all this was going on?'

'Actually, it is,' Paget told her. I went back there last night to take a look for myself, and it checks out. The lighting up there is extremely poor: high ceiling, the old forty-watt bulbs that look as if they haven't been cleaned in God knows how many years, and alcoves that go back ten to twelve feet between the rooms as Bradley described. And you do have direct line of sight from the alcove next to Michael's room into Justine's room if the door is open. And Lorrimer's account of events matches Bradley's.

'I think once Julia realized that we'd narrowed the time of death down to Saturday night and Sunday morning, she knew she would be in the frame because she'd lied about Justine being missing, so she decided to confess to being an unwilling accomplice who had been persuaded that it was the only way to protect her husband, and hoped the court would be sympathetic. The woman is a consummate actress, and, as things stand, she might even pull it off.'

Pierce looked thoughtful. 'Does Bradley know that Stephen Lorrimer has confirmed his story?' she asked.

'No. It's on tape, but I haven't spoken to Bradley this morning.'

'So, without physical evidence, it really comes down to which story is most likely to be believed,' Pierce said. 'And I must say I thought Mrs Lorrimer's story was quite believable. It's the sort of thing that a young woman in those circumstances might feel forced to do, whereas this story of skulking around in dimly lit corridors is a bit harder to believe, and I'm not sure a jury would buy it. I think Mr Bradley should be made aware of that.'

'I agree,' said Paget, 'so I think I'll go down and have another word with him, because I still think he's holding something back. Perhaps a night in the cells will have improved his memory."

'Sleep well, did you, Mr Bradley?' asked Paget as the cell door closed behind him. 'No, don't get up; you're not going anywhere just yet.' Bradley had been stretched out on the bunk with his hands behind his head, but now he swung his feet over and sat up. He looked drawn and hollow-eyed, and he didn't bother to answer the question. Paget remained standing, arms folded as he looked down on the man.

'You have a problem,' he said gravely. 'In deciding on the charges, it was felt that your story about hiding in an alcove and watching a struggle between Sebastian Mills and Stephen Lorrimer just isn't credible without some sort of physical evidence to back it up. On the other hand, Mrs Lorrimer's story of calling on you for help in dealing with Justine is much more straightforward and believable. You knew that once blackmail begins, there's no end to it, so better to take decisive action now. Remove the threat of scandal that could destroy Stephen Lorrimer's career, and your own to some degree, and Julia would be indebted to you for ever. Isn't that what you were thinking, Mr Bradley?'

Bradley stared up at him for a long moment, then shook his head as if he couldn't believe what he was hearing. 'You can't be serious?' he said as he got to his feet. 'Have you talked to Stephen? And Sebastian?' His jaw became set. 'Just give me five minutes with that kid and he'll be more than glad to tell you.'

'Stephen Lorrimer is in hospital,' said Paget. 'He collapsed when I told him how Justine *really* died.'

Bradley's face became a mask. 'How she *really* died?' he repeated.

'That's right. Justine was suffocated.' Paget's eyes held those of Bradley. 'But then you knew that, didn't you, Mr Bradley? You knew that because it was you who killed her. You who held something over her face until she died, choking on her own vomit! Julia Lorrimer is right, isn't she? She didn't make that up, did she?'

Colour began to rise in Bradley's face, but before he had a chance to speak, Paget pressed on. 'I don't know if you two planned it together, or if you did it on your own, but what I do know, Mr Bradley, is that Julia Lorrimer will do everything she can to put the blame on you alone. She will say that she was so frightened and intimidated by you that she felt her own life could be in danger if she didn't go along.' A rueful smile creased Paget's face. 'And you know how convincing Julia can be when she really puts her mind to it, don't you, Mr Bradley?'

Jim Bradley was shaking his head. 'You don't believe that,'

he said. 'You *can't* believe that! You know Julia made it all up.
I mean, that story about the girl and blackmail? It's ludicrous!'

'Ludicrous or not, my superintendent found it believable, and
I suspect others will as well.' Bradley drew a deep breath and
put both hands to his head as if he thought it might explode.
'What I told you yesterday was the truth,' he said through gritted
teeth, 'and I really thought you believed me.'

'What I believe doesn't matter. What does matter is evidence,
and you have absolutely nothing to back up your story.'

The silence between them stretched to more than half a minute
before Bradley turned away and sat down. 'There is evidence,'
he said hollowly. 'I lied about when I left the alcove to go downstairs. I was about to go, but then I saw Justine's legs move, and
she was trying to lift her head. I couldn't believe what I was
seeing. Julia was kneeling beside her, next to the bed, and when
she saw Justine move, she didn't even have to think about it. She
snatched a pillow off the bed and thrust it down on Justine's
face, and leaned on it. But Justine was struggling, kicking and
squirming until Sebastian suddenly came to life and grabbed her
ankles and held them down. Julia was on her knees, face buried
in the pillow, pressing down for all she was worth until Justine
stopped moving.' Bradley paused to gulp down air as if he himself
had been pushing hard. 'And then it was over,' he said, 'and I
knew Justine was really dead. When Stephen came back after
getting Michael settled down, Julia didn't even give him time to
think. She made it very clear that if anything leaked out, he could
kiss his career goodbye. She literally ordered him to get dressed
and get back to Worcester as fast as he could, and leave the rest
to her. And he did. Just like that! I didn't actually see him leave,
because I got out of there while he was getting dressed.'

'And you did nothing to stop her?' Paget said. 'And even
knowing what she'd done, you agreed to help her cover up her
crime. Why?'

Bradley looked down at the floor. 'I thought . . .' He sucked
in his breath and let out a long, shuddering sigh. 'I don't know
. . . I suppose I thought it would bring us closer together, that
she would be grateful . . .' He buried his head in his hands.

'You said there was evidence?' said Paget.

Bradley nodded without looking up. 'I have a lock-up in Birch

Lane. It's where I keep placards and signs and things like that. Stuff we bring out at election time or rallies and special occasions. I kept the pillow,' he said tonelessly. 'Her saliva's on it. She'd shoved it out of sight under the bed, but when I was gathering everything together, I retrieved it and put it into a separate bin bag. Don't ask me why; I just did. Perhaps I thought . . .' He looked up at Paget. 'It was insurance,' he said, and shook his head. 'Insurance because, deep down, I knew I couldn't trust her. I loved her but I couldn't trust her. Work that one out for me if you can, Chief Inspector, because I can't.'

TWENTY-SIX

Monday, 21 May

Lunchtime had come and gone. They were all busy, but their thoughts were elsewhere. Their eyes kept flicking to the clock, and every time a phone rang, no matter whose it was, they paused to see if this was the one they'd been waiting for.

'Still nothing on Twitter, and nothing on Facebook,' Sophie told Molly when she asked, 'and you'd think there would be by now.'

'I don't get it,' Tregalles fumed. 'What do they think they're doing over there? I know they have long lunch breaks, but this is ridiculous!'

When Paget opened the door to the incident room at twenty past three, all eyes were on him as he closed it behind him.

'They all pleaded "Not guilty",' he said. 'Can't say I expected anything else; they've all got good lawyers.'

'Did any of them get bail?' Ormside asked.

Paget nodded. 'All of them, subject to some very strict conditions, of course. As I said, they have good lawyers, so now it's up to us to make sure that we give the CPS every scrap of evidence we have to make sure the charges stick.'

Tregalles groaned. 'They let that woman out on bail?' he said. 'I don't believe it. I mean, we've got her bang to rights for murder. The pillow alone . . .'

'Is the only piece of physical evidence against her,' Paget pointed out, 'and until we have the DNA results proving that the saliva on the pillow that was used to smother Justine is that of Julia Lorrimer, we have nothing but circumstantial evidence and Bradley's word. However, Forensic should have the results by Friday, so keep your fingers crossed.

'Now, beginning next week, someone from the CPS will be taking statements from each of you, so be prepared. Facts are what they'll want, not opinions, and keep in mind that whatever you say will be remembered when this lot comes to trial. Understood?'

A murmur of assent went around the room.

He turned to Ormside. 'That's about it, for now, then, Len,' he said. 'You know what the CPS will want, so once that is done, we can close up shop until the next time . . . and I'm sure there will be a next time.'

Sunday, 27 May

Stephen Lorrimer sat alone in the kitchen. He looked at the clock on the wall. The hands had hardly moved since the last time he'd looked. Six twenty-five. Too early to call Richard. He lifted the coffee pot and topped up his mug. The coffee was lukewarm, but he couldn't be bothered to make a fresh pot. He supposed he should have something to eat, but he wasn't particularly hungry.

He forced himself to get out of the chair and walk over to the window. The sun was well up, and a few strands of mist above the river were fading. Listlessly, he wandered back to his chair and sat down.

He was all by himself. He'd had the locks changed to keep Julia out. She and Sebastian were staying in a motel on the far side of town until they could sort something out, but there was no way he was going to let either of them back into the house. Betty Jacobs was still coming in through the week, but otherwise he was on his own. He couldn't even work. He'd been locked out, too. His office had been taken over by 'temporary staff' sent in from Westminster while he was on 'gardening leave', the euphemism used when a government member was being sidelined for one reason or another.

He looked at the clock again. Twenty to seven. Still a bit early . . . 'Oh, to hell with the time,' he muttered as he took out his phone. Sunday or not, Richard should be up by now. He scrolled to the number and jabbed with his thumb. Ringing . . .

'Richard! Ha! Sorry to call so early, but I'd like to come out . . . No, I mean now. I can be there in an hour. I want to talk to you and Eloise . . . about Michael.'

Tregalles looked up at the sky. It had been a nice weekend, busy running around in the car on Saturday, but the cool winds they'd had earlier in the week had died, and Sunday had been warm and spring-like.

He gathered up his tools and put them away in the garage, then came back to admire his handiwork once again. He'd been doing a bit of weeding – well, quite a lot, actually – and the garden was looking the better for it. Audrey would be pleased.

He stood there in the sun, letting his mind drift, and, as always, it drifted to work and the news from Forensic on Friday, confirming that the saliva on the pillow used to suffocate Justine Delgado was indeed that of Julia Lorrimer. It had been a good way to end the week, and, good lawyers or not, they would have a hard time getting around that.

He chuckled softly to himself as another memory surfaced. Funny how things happened, he thought. His daughter Olivia needed new shoes. 'They don't have the kind I *really* like anywhere here in town, Dad,' she'd explained earnestly, 'but they do in Tenborough, so can we go, Dad? Please?'

'Why not, love?' Audrey said. 'She does need them. It would make a nice run out, and we could stop and have lunch in the garden at that restaurant by the river.'

They'd driven to Tenborough yesterday. He and Brian stayed in the car while Audrey and Olivia went into the shoe store. Brian was nattering on about a friend of his at school, when Tregalles saw two women come out of a shop called Gabrielle's. Arms linked, they were both carrying bags bearing the shop's name, and they were giggling over their purchases like a couple of schoolgirls as they crossed the street and got into a cream-coloured Mercedes.

'Well, well, who'd have guessed it?' he'd muttered softly to himself. He could hardly believe it, but there it was: a very different Lydia Bryant . . . and Loretta Hythe. So, another little mystery solved. Not that it was any of his business, but he was glad he'd seen them together, because he'd found himself wondering from time to time which *man* in Parkside Place was Lydia Bryant's lover. Now he knew, but he felt no obligation to mention it at work. None of their business anyway. Well . . . not really, but the insurance company might be curious.

He mentally changed gear as he made his way into the garage and took off his gardening shoes. It had felt good to be partnered with Paget again. He'd been annoyed at first, when Paget had taken over; resented him butting in, until he realized he actually felt more comfortable in that role than he'd felt for months. Like an old horse putting on a familiar harness, as Audrey was fond of saying in similar situations.

And then there was the problem of Molly, he thought soberly. He liked Molly; she was good to work with, but he wished she'd move on. Since passing her sergeant's exams, he'd felt as if she were breathing down his neck, and the thought suddenly occurred to him, that, if he became an inspector and Molly was still there, would the powers that be decide it would be more economical to keep Molly and force him to look for another posting? Audrey certainly wouldn't like that, and nor would he. Maybe going for promotion this year wasn't such a good idea after all.

Tregalles looked at his watch. Time to go in, he decided. And time to have a serious think about his future.

Molly Forsythe turned the TV off. Ten o'clock. It would be five o'clock the next morning in Hong Kong. David would still be in bed, so there was no chance of an email tonight. Only ten days to go and he would be here. Well, here in Broadminster, but he and his daughter Lijuan would be staying with his aunt and uncle, Ellen and Reg Starkie. He'd said in his emails that he was hoping to spend some time with her, but Molly couldn't help wondering how that would work. David would probably have an itinerary mapped out for Lijuan, and the Starkies were sure to have plans as well. And maybe there were relatives in other parts of the country they would have to visit. That could take time, and with her uncertain work schedule . . .

Molly squeezed her eyes shut. What will be will be, she told herself firmly. Time to go to bed. She was to be first up with the CPS team the next morning, so she needed to be sharp. She would be facing lawyers, and you could never be too careful with lawyers.

Ten days . . .

It was almost midnight before she went to sleep.

Lightning Source UK Ltd.
Milton Keynes UK
UKHW01f010203071 8
325137UK00001B/12/P